The Wind Passes

To Nick & Ann
Our good friends &
my #1 Doctor
Bobby

By Bob E. Johnson

ISBN: 1461024374
ISBN-13: 9781461024378
LCCN: 2011904792

COVER COURTESY

DANNY GAMBLE
- ARTIST

This is fiction! This is fiction! This is fiction!!!

If anyone in this novel reminds you of someone…
That's your problem and not mine.

This book is dedicated to all those in agriculture
that have lost their "place".

Many thanks to Marty Davenport,
Bill Hawker& Bobbi Bates for their editorial expertise.

PROLOGUE

Two flowering Salt Cedars sky-lighted the thick chested dog as he watched the pickup creep its way up the sandy road. At 200 yards, in the last light of the day, his pale white eyes failed to make out the muzzle of a rifle slowly protruding from the driver's window.

As his mind recorded the flash of a scoped rifle, his body was struck with a searing pain. The bullet had sliced through the fleshy part of his chest. Seconds later, still stunned, and unmoving, he was aware of the truck winding its way out of the sandhills. He could tell by the sound that it was Stoney's pickup.

"I got that son-of-a-bitch this time," the passenger said.

"Little Stoney is going to be mad as hell at you for shooting his dog," replied his driver, a little sadly "That's two of his dogs you've shot."

"Screw the little bastard. I had a grudge against that dog for a long time. Besides that, Fat Bud told me he would buy me a fifth of Wild Turkey if I would shoot that mutt, and Eddie said he would double it."

It had been a long afternoon and it was a twenty-mile drive back to Clovis. The driver was sleepy and wished Pete hadn't made him pick him up at the bar and drive back out to Stoney's old ranch. He slouched down behind the steering wheel and said, "Remind me not to borrow money from that greedy banker. Why in the hell is he so pissed off at Stoney and his dog; I always got along with Stoney. In fact he has done me a couple favors."

The passenger didn't respond. He took another large swallow of beer, opened the window and threw the can out. .

The driver rambled on, "Pete," he said. "You know…, Bud made lots of money when he sold Stoney's ranch, and everything else, plus breaking up his family. My God, what more does he want? And besides I kinda miss seeing this pickup sitting out in front of the City Limits Bar, or driving down the road with that crazy looking dog of his in the back. That dog would sit out in the pickup and wait for him for hours. Did you ever look at that dog up close Pete? He had the damnedest eyes I ever saw."

"Emmett, why in the hell don't you just shut the hell up." Pete was trying to open another beer with fat, dirty, fingers that had the nails bitten so close he could hardly lift the tab.

"For your information, Bud kept a bunch of shares in the ranch. He's going to be rich one of these days. And if it wasn't for him, you wouldn't have a job or be drivin' around in Stone's old pickup.

"From what I been hearing; he better have a lot of money." Those were the last words Pete heard from Emmett until they pulled up in front of the City Limits Bar. They slammed the doors of the pickup with the Taylor Farms logo on them, and went in.

That was to be Pete's second mistake of the day. Two hours later Jim Bob, Travis and Stoney entered the same bar.

Gradually the dog focused his eyes and lay there in pain, making sure that the pickup was not coming back. He could now smell his own blood flowing out of him, and seeping into the sand. He thought about his small, hungry pup that was waiting for him a hundred yards off in a cedar thicket. He thought about the rabbit he had been carrying. Rabbits were getting scarce, and he had been especially proud to bring it back to his pup instead of the unsavory carrion that they had lived on for the past week. And he thought about Stoney.

When he had first heard the pickup his heart gave a tug, it has to be Stoney, and he was returning to pick him up. He lost his usual, vigilant caution, and bounded up the sandhill between the cedars. He knew what had hit him; he watched many animals in the past year die from that ominous sound. But why Stoney? The pup came up and laid down beside him and began to lick the wound.

CHAPTER 1

Pecos was born on the sundeck of Stoney and Betsy's ranch house, and the ugliest of the litter. Even as a pup Pecos was sensitive and intense. It was a trait common in his mother's Australian Shepherd ancestry. His father's bloodline was a mystery to everyone, except his mother.

Not in any way did Pecos resemble his brothers and sisters, in personality or looks. Instead of the heavier, blocky body, and short curly hair, he was tall and thin, legs almost as long as a Greyhound. A body, tail, and texture of hair more resembling a German Shepherd. While the rest of his littermates varied in color from white to dark grey, with white or black spots, Pecos was predominately black, except for four white stocking feet, a white chest, and a white tip on the end of his tail. His muzzle, from his nose to below his eyes was white with brown freckles.

Pecos had one alarming and unreal feature: large deathly white eyes, with small blue pupils. His eyes startled everyone that looked into them, they were disquieting and never displayed any emotions; just staring and penetrating, as if they possessed some secret terrifying knowledge of you that made strangers turn their heads and quickly look elsewhere.

When Stoney finally decided to wean them it wasn't hard to figure out why no one chose him. Besides his appearance, he was so shy he always ran under the sundeck when any prospective masters would show up. Betsy, Stoney's wife, once said, "He runs under there because he knows he's ugly and is ashamed to be seen."

For whatever reason, Pecos was the one left after the rest of the litter was chosen. Stoney wasn't disappointed that this strange, ungainly pup was to stay on the ranch. The pup had shown that he was a cut above the others in intelligence and courage.

Other than noticing his eyes and different features, Stoney had not been impressed with Pecos. Although he wanted to keep one of the litter, Pecos was certainly not his first choice. Then, early one morning, after all but three of the pups had been taken, an incident took place that made Stoney sure which of them would stay on the ranch.

At that time Betsy and Stoney had only one grandchild: a two-year-old, blond, blue-eyed little girl named Bobbi. They adored their granddaughter.

Betsy, after a year of teaching school, then raising their daughter, had entered the real estate profession and was very successful. She worked long hours, but she and Stoney were so captivated by Bobbi that every chance she got she would stop by their daughter's house in town and bring her to the ranch to spend the night.

They purchased the small ranch some years before and had gradually, through drought, hail, sweat and tears, built it into a viable operation, thou not a large ranch by New Mexico standards. The ranch was located in the Blackwater Draw which is an extinct riverbed some six or seven miles wide and over 100 miles long that drains Eastern New Mexico and West Texas before reaching the Brazos River. Many years ago the flowing water receded into the ground leaving rolling sandhills and a large acquifer beneath them. The area was first inhabited some 11,000 years ago by the Clovis Man, mammoth elephants, buffalo, dire wolves and other extinct species that took advantage of the small ponds and marshes left by the diminishing water.

Over time a procession of other dwellers used the sandhills and its shallow water; including the plains Indians, ranchers, and homesteaders who tried to, but were unable to hold the sandy soil with their inadequate farming tools during the recurring droughts. When circular sprinklers were placed on the market, modern day farmers moved into the area breaking out large parcels of the sandhills. Further stressing the acquifer, it became the main source of water for Lubbock, and other adjacent smaller towns. The Stones were just one of the many before them to claim a part of this land as their own.

The one improvement on the ranch, at the time they purchased it, was an old, vacant house. The house was not fit to live in but the homesteader that built it loved trees. It faced north and on all four sides he had planted elm trees, intermingled with some old species of plums. The elms had grown vigorously, some of their trunks were three feet across and when leafed out in the summer these massive old trees could be seen for many miles across the flat plains and rolling sandhills of eastern New Mexico.

Facing the formidable competition of the elms, the plums had not done as well. They were much smaller but what they lacked in size, they made up for in springtime blossoms. Their fragrance during that time of the year enveloped the whole ranch house compound.

The house was L- shaped with the open side facing south where Stoney and Betsy built a large sun deck. They spent many months and lots of hard labor renovating the old homestead; it was well worth it. There they raised their daughter, Mickie.

It was almost a ritual, on late afternoons when Betsy would bring Bobbi home, that after supper Stoney would wrap his little granddaughter in a blanket, carry her to the sundeck and they would sit in the swing so they could watch the evening slip into night.

Bobbi loved to watch the brood mares going back to their pasture after their evening drink at the water lot behind the house. The colts would lag behind with their tails and heads down, tired after a day full of playing and investigating every bush, lizard, snake, porcupine, or anything else whether it moved or not. The wind would go to it's resting-place for the night and a quiet peacefulness would settle in. It was a feeling that one can only experience in the country, far removed from other human habitation. The few sounds that could be heard were greatly enhanced: the lamentable call of a morning dove pleading for a mate, the nicker of a colt that fell too far behind its mother, the sound of Pinta laying underneath the swing with her half grown pups vying for the most comfortable and closest place to her.

Then the first evening stars would venture from their place of hiding, dimly at first, and after gaining more courage, brightly. Bobbi would be fast asleep by then.

Coyotes fascinated Bobbi; she had seen plenty of them on the ranch and during the rides to and from Clovis with her grandmother. Bobbi also heard them on many an evening while cuddled in her grandfather's lap.

Stoney found out what Pecos was made of early one morning. Bobbi had spent the night at the ranch and the two of them slipped out of bed so as not to awaken Betsy. Stoney had made them each a cup of hot chocolate topped with whipped cream, which they drank on the back deck watching the sunrise.

It was a beautiful morning on the Llano Estacado in Eastern New Mexico. They watched as the long shadows cast by the Yuccas, with their creamy blossoms, shortened by the minute. Bobbi was delighted when the mares, with their frolicking colts playing chase and herded by the impatient stud, made their way out of the cedar thickets and trailed their way back to the house for water.

A daddy blue quail hopped up on the back fence, straightened up his top-notch, carefully checked the area and gave the all clear whistle to his mate. Soon the mother quail emerged from the brush pile that Stoney had gathered for them. She was followed by seven little puffs of feathers no bigger than golf balls and running on tiny legs.

Stoney hadn't slept well that night and had lain awake a good part of the time. The mid-1980's was a tough time for cattle ranchers. A three-year drought had forced him to sell most of the cows on a down market, however he had grown some grass with the previous late summer rains. The new year looked promising due to heavy winter snows and early spring moisture. He and his new banker were not hitting it off so well and it was time to restock. He was not looking forward to asking him for money to buy more cows. But the beautiful morning and ceaseless questions from his granddaughter soon raised his spirits.

Kissing her on the forehead and taking their cups he left her outside to play with the pups while he stirred quietly around the kitchen fixing breakfast. He had just taken the eggs out of the skillet when it occurred to him that it was too quiet on the porch and he could not hear her usual constant chatter. Sliding open the screen door and stepping outside he could hear her tiny voice talking to someone around the corner of the house. He knew instantly something was wrong because Pinta and two of her pups were cowering by the porch steps. Stepping around to the side of the house he heard, "Get out of here coyote, get out of here."

It was a sight he wasn't to forget. There stood his diminutive granddaughter. Standing right in front of her was Pecos, facing, not 15 yards away, three large coyotes. The coyotes were returning to the thickets after their early morning hunt, and as they did two or three times a week, they had stopped by the house just in case the dogs were gone and had left any edibles around. Instead of something to eat there stood this petite little girl enfolded from toe to chin in bright cotton sleepers with a white cream mustache scolding them. In addition, if that was not enough, there was a small, but courageous pup with a tail almost as long as his body, raised in defiance, growling at them.

Two of the coyotes were standing, and between them, sitting on his haunches in amazement, was the third. Stoney burst out laughing and the standing coyotes left in a trot, tuning their heads to watch the proceedings. The third stood, scratched the ground to release his scent from the glands between his toes, and haughtily walked off.

Stoney reached down and picked both Bobbi and Pecos up, gave them a hug and returned to the house, absolutely assured which one of the pups he would keep.

The other two pups were given away shortly after that. Pecos and Pinta followed the last pup as it left in the car with its new owner to the county road in front of the house. They watched as car sped down the road shrouded in dust. Pinta returned to the house, wagging her tail and happy to be relieved of the responsibility. Pecos watched the car until it was out of sight, then turned, ran fast as he could to catch his mother and jumped square on her back sending them both sprawling into the dirt.

The Ranch House

CHAPTER 2

That afternoon Pinta, tired of being Pecos's playmate, slipped off from her remaining pup and followed Stoney toward town. This was an unusual for her. Stoney's ranch was a haven for lost, strayed or orphaned dogs. Sometimes there would be as many as five or six, at other times and through natural attrition, maybe down to two or three. All of them soon learned the rules of the ranch. You do not chase cattle, horses, chickens, or other ranch animals unless ordered to. If you barked at night you made sure there was something to bark about. You could bark at strangers, but not bite. You could ride in the bed of the pickup, or follow it if the pickup turned left after it reached the county road in front of the house. If it turned right, that meant that Stoney was going to town and you had to stay at home. If the dogs did try to follow him after he turned toward town, Stoney would stop, scold, and throw rocks at them until they returned to the house, tails between their legs and trying to look as dejected as they possibly could.

Pinta watched Stoney turn right but decided to take the chance. Too many weeks of being fat and awkward, and raising the pups overcame good reasoning. Stoney, preoccupied with his problems, was unaware she had followed him. He never saw her again.

She had followed the pickup the two miles to the highway and saw it turn north toward Clovis. By the time she reached the highway it was long gone. She decided since she had come that far she might as well keep going for a while, just in case he might have decided to stop at one of neighbors. She trotted up the highway for another two miles, finally gave up and started her return trip home, cutting across the range land in order to save time.

Since her pregnancy, her familiar country had changed. A corporation had purchased the grassland that lay between their ranch and the highway. Large corporate farms were lured to the area by the cheap land and the strong shallow water beneath it. They purchased peanut and other crop allotments from farmers who had pumped the water out from under their land and then started breaking out the virgin soil. The dairies quickly followed. Selling their land in California and Arizona for exorbitant prices they could buy one hundred acres of this sandy land with good water for what a developer would pay them for a single acre in their home state.

The land that Pinta was now crossing had been burned off. The small rolling sandhills had been leveled and were being turned under by large four-wheel drive tractors pulling 12 bottom plows. These monstrous rigs were guaranteed by their maker to turn under 80 acres a day of the pristine sandhills. It would then change the rolling grass land into a flat plowed field good enough to grow subsidized crops, courtesy of the U.S. taxpayer.

The large spacious cabs were designed to keep the drivers comfortable and supposedly alert for long hours behind the wheel. They featured state of the art air conditioning, heating, AM/ FM radios and tape decks, and two-way radios. The drivers of these behemoths were the most trusted and loyal employees a corporation could hire. They had to be as these machines cost their employers well over $175,000.

Pete Benson was a top hand, in addition to all the other amenities the tractor afforded the driver, he had permission to build a gun rack for his rifle, his most prized possession. It was a Sako, .243 caliber with a 20 power Bausch and Lomb variable scope. The stock was made of the finest wood available, polished with loving care and sheathed in a leather and sheepskin case, which wasn't really necessary in the dust proof, filtered air, cab.

Pinta was half way across the field when she heard the tractor stop. She glanced up nervously and saw it belch a stream of black diesel smoke. She felt uneasy and hurried her gait.

This was just what Pete had been waiting for, something challenging to shoot at. At 300 yards this was perfect. Climbing out of the tractor and carefully laying the soft gun case on the plow, so as not to mar the beautiful stock, he set the crosshairs on Pinta's neck. Then he moved it to the tip of her nose to adjust for her pace and distance.

The dog never heard the explosion of the firing cap igniting 220 grams of hand loaded powder. Nor did she feel the lead tipped, copper projectile, travelling at 2800 feet per second enter her body.

An hour later the tractor and plow came to the point where Pinta fell. From his comfortable seat behind the wheel Pete watched, unconcerned, as the plow turned her body over and under two feet of sandy soil.

When Stoney returned to the ranch later that afternoon he immediately missed Pinta when she did not come bounding down the road to greet him. Unless the wind was out of the wrong direction, the dogs always knew the sound of his pickup and would come running from behind the house and down the road. He walked to the backyard and gave his familiar whistle. Only Pecos appeared from beneath the porch. Picking him up and tossing him in the front seat of the truck he started his search.

They went first to the pens, which were located a mile from the house and a favorite place for the dogs when they grew bored waiting for Stoney at the house. Stoney fed the saddle horses and yearlings, did the rest of the chores all the time hoping Pinta would show up. When she didn't he started looking for her in earnest. By then Pecos was getting over the initial fright of his first truck ride and began to get interested in what was going on. In fact he was beginning to thoroughly enjoy himself.

It was getting dark when they drove down to the highway and saw the big tractor pull up to the pickup with the fancy Taylor Farms logo on the side. Stoney stopped next to the pickup and approached the tractor as Pete was climbing out of the cab carrying his rifle.

"What's going on Pete?" Stoney asked.

He didn't know Pete well, just had seen him a few times at the City Limits and knew he had moved down in this area from someplace in Kansas. Stoney did not like his overbearing attitude.

"Hello Stone...What the hell you doing out here?"

Stoney had left his window down and Pecos was standing on hind feet, just able to stick his head out and growling at Pete.

"I just live a couple miles down the road." Stoney replied, nodding his head in the general direction of his house.

Stoney wasn't a big man and although he stood five foot ten he had a slight build and fine features. This and the fact he had a quiet, unassuming personality, gave most people the impression that he was smaller than he really was. Some people referred to him as 'Little Stoney".

Pete enjoyed looking' down on people. He stood close to six foot four and weighed over two hundred and fifty pounds. A large part of that he carried around his waistline, courtesy of "Adolph Coors and Company".

"I am looking for my dog, and wondering if you might have seen her. She's an Aussie, you know, black and white and about this big." Stoney motioned an imaginary line. He was not too sure of Pete's intelligence and wanted to make sure he understood what the dog looked like.

"I know what the hell a Aussie looks like and I ain't seen no dogs today and ain't got time to be lookin' for 'em". He grinned and a dark stream of tobacco ran out the corner of his mouth. "You happen to have a cold beer with you, do you?" And wiped his mouth with the back of his sleeve.

"Sure don't," Stoney said. "I didn't know you worked for Taylor Farms."

"Been with 'em for a year now, damn good outfit, big too. Let's me do my own thing." He walked to the plow and got a five-gallon bucket that was hanging on one of its many levers.

"Look at these rascals," he said placing the can on the ground so Stoney could see.

"I 've got eight of the babies now, and I'm not half-way through plowing this section yet".

Inside were two fair sized rattlesnakes and a big bull snake, each one had their heads neatly shot off.

"I got a fella that gives me five bucks a piece for these. Makes belts, hatbands, and stuff outa their hides, and I get to keep the rattles."

Stoney gave the bucket a slight kick that almost tipped it over toward Pete. It made Pete jump.

"I don't know how to tell you this Pete, but that big one is a bull snake".

Pete jerked up the bucket and started toward his pickup. "You think I don't know the difference ass-hole. I killed a hell of lot more of 'em than you have."

"I am sure you're right," Stoney said, "I never killed a bull snake and really don't much enjoy killing a rattlesnake."

Pete laughed, "What'sa matter little fella, you scared of them?"

Stoney grinned back at him. Pete was beginning to get to him and he didn't like it.

Pete continued on. "I hate any of those bastards; it don't make me any difference what kind they are. These sandhills will be a hell of lot better off without them."

"That's your opinion, and maybe they would be a hell of lot better off without that prairie killer," Stoney said, pointing to the plow. He knew he was pushing the man a little hard and decided to change the subject. "Nice rig you're driving. If you like tractors."

"That son-of-bitch will plow a hundred acres a day if I get with it." Pete replied proudly.

"Well, I would be careful I didn't plow myself out of a job."

"What do you mean by that?"

"Simple arithmetic. This and maybe two or three more of these section are all that's left of the good water and it won't last long the way your boss and some other idiots are pumping it out."

"Oh, I don't know about that. They tell me the water still goes west of here for another five or six miles."

"That's what they say, but most of that is my place and it will be a cold day in hell before one of these prairie killers ever touch it."

Pete grunted and spat his wad of tobacco on the ground. "I got a hunch I'm gonna' be plowing a whole lot longer than you might think."

Stoney disliked any kind of confrontations and he knew where this talk was taking them.

"See you around Pete," he said, and started to his pickup. "I'd watch myself if I were you. One of those mean old snakes is liable to slip up on you."

"You're the one that might oughta' be careful, little fella." Then he laughed.

Pecos was curled up, fast asleep in the driver's seat when Stoney opened the door.

CHAPTER 3

Travis called Stoney at six the next morning.

"Are you going to be ready for some cows? I found some middle age, nice ones over near Reserve. About a hundred fifty of 'em. I hadn't seen the cows but I bought their calves through a sale last year. They were sure good enough."

Travis was a cattle buyer and one of Stoney's best friends. He was ten years younger than Stoney's mid-fifties. a big muscular man and former professional rodeo cowboy. There were some people that didn't like Travis because of his challenging attitude but they all respected his physical prowess and knowledge of horses and cattle. Stoney had a lot of confidence as well complete trust in Travis.

"Well..." Stoney hesitated; he hated the thought of going back to the bank and asking for more money. "I don't know Travis. I would like to buy them and it sure looks like I am going to have plenty of grass. How much are they going to cost; delivered to my place and pregnancy tested?"

"I think I can get 'em for seven hundred, guaranteed to calve in ninety days. He will have them pregnancy tested at his place but you will have to pay for it. So, let's see here."

Stoney could hear Travis's old-fashioned calculator running up the numbers.

"Looks like seven fifty, plus or minus per head, unloaded, tested and sound at your place".

Stoney punched out the numbers on his pocket calculator.

"That's a little over a hundred and twelve thousand dollars. My banker will have a fit but I need 'em. Let me go see him this morning and I'll call you tonight."

"Well hell," Travis said, "Your bank won't give you any trouble will they? You damn sure can't run a cow-calf operation without cows. You been with that bank ever since you started and they know what a long drought will do to a cow man."

"I know that and you know that," Stoney replied, "but they gave my file to Bud Thurman when Joe retired a couple months ago. And that, my friend, is a different horse to ride. Especially when things are a little tough like they are now. If Joe was still there I'd tell you to go buy them and then pick up the phone and tell him what I did."

"Bud Thurman!" Travis exclaimed. "He don't know sick'em about cows. Besides, I hear stories. They tell me he is a greedy son-of-bitch and I am telling you now; you had better damn sure watch him."

Travis was the kind that would give you the shirt off back, then tell you how to wear it.. Stoney always got a kick out of it but it didn't sit too well with some others.

"That's what I hear," Stoney said. "I'll call you tonight and tell you how I got along."

It was ten o'clock by the time he finished the chores and quit looking for Pinta. He had lost enough dogs to know that if they did not show up overnight, chances were good that you would never see them again. But that did not make it any easier for him. To lose not only a good dog but a good friend too, no matter how many, always hurt Stoney more than he would let on.

He showered, changed clothes and started toward the pickup. Walking across the porch he saw Pecos sitting out in the yard watching him with those strange eyes and just as forlorn as a pup could get.

"Come on ugly, you just as well go with me so I can practice what I am going to say to the banker." He picked him up and tossed him in the seat of the pickup.

"Every human's mission in life is the preservation and enhancement of his concept of himself." Stoney had read that somewhere and he thought that sure had to be Bud Thurman's theme in life. It was not too difficult for Stoney to figure out what Bud's concept of himself was.

Bud was in his late thirties and up until a couple years ago was a nondescript person. He had gone to work for the bank out of high school and been there ever since, except for a short sabbatical in Dallas for a banker's school. He came back wearing a big, heavy, gold and ruby ring with something inscribed on it. He made sure everybody noticed it by tapping it on his desk when he wanted to impress someone in his office.

"Wonder how he does that," Stoney thought. His hands are so pudgy he couldn't use the underside of it to make that sound. He must turn it over halfway or something. Stoney made a mental note to watch the next time.

"To each his own," he told Pecos... still thinking about that ring. Stoney had never been impressed with class rings. He hadn't ordered a high school ring or a ring from New Mexico State University where he had received a bachelor degree in animal husbandry.

The one piece of jewelry he wore was a small silver and turquoise wedding band made by the Zunis that Betsy had given him on their twenty-fifth wedding anniversary.

He began to think in earnest about his meeting. There had to be a way to get on Bud's good side.

Bud Thurman was not what you could call fat; he was thick and muscular. Even his face and neck were so thick that Stoney wondered how he ever got his collar buttoned, it always seemed to be pinching him. Maybe that was why his complexion was beet red Stoney thought. His chest, hips, legs, and even his feet were thick. His shoes must have been a triple E.

He wasn't a good banker. His only experience in the loan department, before taking over Joe's position, was making installment loans. Destined to always be a vice-president and never a president he was too quick to make a loan and too quick to call one in.

Bud thought himself to be a sharp businessman and an up and coming young entrepreneur around town.

He envisioned himself as a shrewd cattleman and farmer even though he had done neither, and he only admired those that were large operators in those fields.

Pecos grew tired of the conversation and with the motion of the truck he began to get sleepy and had a hard time holding his head up. Finally he laid down placing his head on Stoney's lap as he fell asleep. Stoney put his hand on the pup's neck and said," The man is greedy Pecos; we are going to have to watch him."

Unbeknownst to Stoney, Bud both envied and resented him. Stoney's easy attitude, his pretty wife, many friends, and respect in the community. Bud couldn't figure it out. Stoney at one time was active in the community serving as a Director in the Chamber of Commerce, President of the local Livestock Association, Fair Board and even two terms as a County Commissioner, the youngest ever to do be elected in Curry county. He grew tired of being in the public and as the ranch grew it demanded more and more of his time. By the time he and Betsy finished renovating the house and moved to the ranch he had resigned from any civic offices he held, and devoted all his time to their cattle, horses and the ranch. He had not made that much money and any he had made was turned right back into his small ranch.

Bud had watched Stoney for a long time while an underling in the bank. Now things had changed; no longer was he a nobody. He could hardly wait to get Stoney sitting in front of his desk.

Stoney drove into the bank's parking lot, patted Pecos and rolled down a window for him.

"Wish me luck partner," he said.

Entering the bank he began to feel the pit in his stomach that always came when he anticipated some sort of confrontation.

"Hello Doris. Is Bud around?"

"Hi Stoney. You just missed him. He'll be back around two if you want to come back."

Doris had been Joe's secretary ever since Stoney had been coming to the bank and was about ready for retirement herself. She and Stoney had always got along well and she kept him out of trouble with the examiners by letting him know when they were coming. He could then come in and sign the notes that Joe had forgotten about after giving Stoney the okay over the telephone. Stoney admired and respected her and would buy her some silly gifts for Christmas or her birthday.

"Nice hours you bankers have Doris. Tell him I will be in about two to see him."

Doris smiled at him sadly.

"Stoney" she paused. "Take care." Her eyes dropped immediately to the papers on her desk.

It startled Stoney, this was not a good sign, and he started to say something but Alex Maynard, the president of the bank, walked up and began to talk to Doris, not even looking at him.

Stoney returned to the pickup and decided to drop by Betsy's office to see if she had time for lunch. Driving down the main street he noticed with interest all the stores that had posted "Going out of business signs," and the ones that were already gone. It had been a long time since he driven down Main Street and was surprised how much it had changed.

"Damn, the small retail business must be as tough as the cow business," he said to Pecos who was standing up taking in the sights and enjoying himself immensely.

It was not that Clovis had quit growing and was losing population. The new 1980 census estimated a population of 30,000. This was an increase of five thousand over the 1970 census, but things were changing.

The large chain stores had built on the outskirts of town and were selling their wares for less than most mom and pop stores could buy them. He could remember when there was a little grocery store on almost every ten block section of town. Now there were just two in the entire city, both were big ones, supermarkets.

If the local merchants were hurting, the merchants in the smaller outlying communities were being devastated. Clovis was the largest town within a fifty miles in any direction. Larger neighbors and corporations were buying out the small farmers and ranchers and as a result, these smaller rural communities were losing their schools and small business people. In addition to becoming the trade center for the area, a large Air Force base was located ten miles west of town.

"Son of a buck, Pecos," Stoney said, "I guess I am growing old. Maybe I am behind times and old fashioned but I hate to see all these little stores and towns close down. But hell, I guess I am just as greedy as anybody else. It's good for Betsy's business and that's what's been keeping us fed for the past couple years."

They pulled into Betsy's office and Pecos jumped out, peed on the nearest tire and followed Stoney into the plush reception room. Betsy worked for the area's largest real estate firm. Phillip Downey, the owner and qualifying broker, employed over twenty sales people and several secretaries. Betsy was one of the best sales people: not only the leading producer for the firm, but also the number one realtor in the town. Her office, second in size to Downey's, was full of trophies and plaques attesting to her proficiency as a realtor.

Phillip did not like dogs, and might have liked Stoney even less. He especially did not like Stoney coming in and disrupting Betsy and the employees. Stoney knew that and couldn't have cared less. The receptionist and secretaries liked him and got a kick out of him and his dogs whenever he would drop by.

Pecos stayed right at Stoney's heels, peeping out around his boots.

"Stoney, you have the wildest looking dogs I have ever seen, but that one has to the weirdest looking of them all. Look at those eyes," the office manager said.

"I remember him," the cute receptionist said. "Stoney gave me one of his brothers and he doesn't even resemble this one."

While Stoney sat down to wait for Betsy to finish with a client, Pecos scooted underneath his chair, his head sticking out one side and tail the other.

Phillip came out of his office.

"Hello Stoney," he said. "Still playing cowboy I see." Stoney was wearing his usual: western hat, boots, and nicely pressed Wranglers and shirt. Betsy liked what he wore and always took his good clothes to town to be laundered with heavy starch.

"When are you going to move back to town so that Betsy doesn't have to drive 40 miles every day."

"What's the matter Phillip?...You buying a new boat or something and need more of Betsy's hard earned commissions?"

The girls in the front office buried their faces in their work to keep from laughing. Stoney couldn't figure out why he said that to Phillip. He had never had a smart mouth and would generally just smile and take it when someone would lay a taunting remark on him.

Phillip's face turned red; he was ready to counter when he noticed the dog.

"Stoney, you know I don't like pets in the office. Why do you insist on bringing..."

He stopped short as Betsy came out of her office.

"Well hi! Who is that under the chair." Pecos immediately recognized the sweet voice and his tail made quick thumping noises on the floor.

She bent down revealing a nice set of breasts from her low-cut blouse; Stoney was quick to notice that Phillip certainly was enjoying the view.

She whistled softly and said, "Come here little guy."

Pecos walked slowly, almost crawling to her. A few drops of pee hit the carpet before he finally reached her and lay down beside her while she scratched him.

"Phillip... isn't he the best looking puppy you have ever seen?" She winked at Stoney.

"Humph," was his reply.

"You're just in time for lunch. Phillip and I were just leaving," she said.

"You two go on. I have to be back early and I know how long your lunches take," Phillip said, and walked out the door, visibly irritated.

Stoney and Betsy went to "The Steak House". They made a good-looking couple. Betsy was 50 and attractive, with almost the same cute figure that she had when they first met at college where she was a drum majorette. Stoney's hair was turning a distinguished grey, but he was still flat-bellied and nice looking.

Many of the people in the restaurant knew them and they exchanged pleasantries with them as they weaved through the tables to their favorite booth in a corner. Actually it was just a few of the older business people that knew Stoney but many of the rest knew Betsy since she had gradually taken Stoney's place as a public figure and had chaired several of the local and state organizations and civic committees. After they had moved to the ranch Stoney had given up a short, but promising career in politics and now most of Clovis knew him as Betsy's husband.

"What are you doing in town in the middle of the day?" Betsy asked him after the waitress had taken their order.

"Have to go to the bank. We need to re-stock and need some operating money. Travis called this morning and he's found some cows. They sound like they would work."

After twenty-five years of living with her husband Betsy knew his moods well and could easily tell it was worrying him. She turned her head to the dining area, then, after a couple seconds back to Stoney.

With a wave of her hand she said firmly, "You won't have any trouble."

She was not a nagging wife by any means and never showed any outward signs of worrying. She and Stoney were not just man and wife, as well as lovers. They were also each other's best friends.

She tried to remain as cheerful as always, but inside she was beginning to worry. They owed a lot of money and she had a gut feeling that small operators in agriculture were in for an even tougher time. She had been raised on a small ranch and although she loved the life, she also knew the heartaches. Her father had lost their ranch while she was in high school; only by working part-time and earning scholarships was she able to finish three years of college.

There was a time when she believed that if they could live nicely on her earnings and reinvest whatever the ranch made back into it, they would have a nice retirement and something their daughter and grandchildren would be proud of.

Low cattle prices, high interest rates, and the drought changed that. More financially farsighted than her husband she had, in the last year or two, begun to invest in a few rentals, annuities and mutual funds. She had tried to discuss with Stoney their long range plans but he had merely shrugged it off, saying their situation would be better in a year or two.

Changing the subject, she entertained Stoney through the meal with stories about her work, who she was working with, and funny things that had happened at the office. It had the intended effect. He deeply loved and admired his wife's charm and beauty. Just sitting across from her and listening to her bantering was enough to raise his spirits.

She gave Stoney a twenty-dollar bill to pay the check and he took it, although it bothered him. He seldom carried even a small amount of cash since he seldom came to town.

"Let me know how you get along, "she said when she pulled alongside of his pickup in front of her office.

They always went in Betsy's vehicle since she drove a nice new car and dressed neat and in style; Stoney's truck, besides showing five hard years of wear and tear on the ranch, was always filled with ropes, pliers, halters, bailing wire, dust and dog hair.

"Okay," he replied. They reached over and gave each other a short kiss.

"Are you going to work late again tonight?"

"Yes, I am sorry," she answered, "I have another appointment. I have to show some big homes to the new doctor that's coming to town."

"Well..., make a sale. You want me to fix supper for you?"

"No, I'll just grab something before I go."

"Okay, see you later sweetie." He headed for the bank feeling better, but the good feeling began to vanish the closer he got.

CHAPTER 4

"Hi Doris, I see he made it back." Stoney said, and started to walk into Bud's office.

"Just a minute Stoney," she said, lifting up the phone. The corners of her mouth turned down and she raised her eyebrows.

Setting the phone down she said, "Sit down cowboy, he said he would be with you in a few minutes." She turned back to the files she had been working on. Stoney could tell that she did not enjoy her new boss.

Stoney sat down in one of the chairs in front of Bud's office and watched the comings and goings of the bank. Alex walked by, looked at Stoney without so much as a nod then entered his office next to Buds. Alex and Stoney had not been on good terms ever since Stoney ran against and ousted him from his county commission seat. Stoney picked up a magazine, glanced through it, put it down for another one and became more uncomfortable by the minute.

Fifteen minutes later Doris's phone buzzed and before she even lifted it up she whispered, "You can go in now. He probably just finished his article on 'How to Play Mister Big and Make Your Secretary Miserable.'" She laughed, then her expression changed as she said, "Good luck Stoney."

"Hello Stone," Bud said motioning him to sit down. He did not rise and ignored the hand that Stoney offered him.

A feeling of anxiety immediately tightened the muscles in his body, a feeling that he had a pit in his stomach; a feeling that he hated and occurred whenever a confrontation was imminent. When he received the perfunctory greeting all of his prepared speech began to fade. He felt his heart rate quicken and hated himself for it. He wondered if that was one of the little tricks they taught at that banker's school. Let them sweat it outside and make them so apprehensive that you, the banker are in control. "I've had your file on my desk for a week, just been so busy I haven't had the time to call you in." Stoney had a flashback about being called into the principal's office while he was in junior high..

"It's been twelve months since you paid on any principal…and little on interest. All I see that Joe did is renewals. So…, what are we going to do about this?" he inquired, thumping the file with the class ring.

"Well…, I hope the next time you pull that file it will look a whole lot better. It looks like this is going to be a good year and I have been able to hold on to fifty of my best cows, but I need some more. Travis has found me a hundred and fifty cows that will calve in the next ninety days and…"

"I am more interested in today than I am tomorrow." Bud interrupted. "How much are you going to pay on your note today? Then we will talk about tomorrow."

"Bud, you know I can't pay anything today. I am running a cow-calf operation. Fall is the only time I have anything to sell."

Bud opened up Stoney's file. "Let's just go over this," he said. "You have five thousand acres of deeded land and three thousand acres of state lease. You said last year the fee land was worth $100 per acre, that's five hundred thousand dollars. Has that figure changed?"

Stoney's mouth was dry. "Well..., the price has been dropping on grassland. But these corporations are coming in and what with the water underneath it I am sure it would bring more, but I would never sell it."

"Okay, let's say $90 per acre, that's four hundred and fifty thousand dollars. You had 200 cows when you filled this out, worth you said eight hundred fifty apiece. How many do you have now and what are they worth?"

Stoney looked up on the credenza behind Bud. There was a stuffed prairie dog staring at a coiled rattle snake. Someone had probably given it to Bud trying to get on his good side. The taxidermist had done an excellent job, even somehow, capturing a terrified expression on the prairie dog's face. Stoney wondered if he might not have the same look.

"Fifty," he said, still looking at the rattlesnake.

"Fifty" Bud said, his voice raised. "What happened to the rest?"

"I sold them over a year ago."

"What did you do with the proceeds?"

"Bud," Stoney's breath began to shorten and he could feel the anger rising within him, "I brought every last penny of it in here. In fact I brought you the check and you had me endorse it and turn it over to you." He knew Bud remembered this.

Bud shuffled through the file. "Here it is, I loaned you back five thousand of it for feed, made your land payment for you, paid up your state lease and applied the rest on interest."

"The fifty you have left, they're worth about six hundred and fifty a head."

"No," Stoney replied. "Those are really good young cows, my foundation stock. I wouldn't take eight hundred for 'em.

Bud paid ignored him. "Let's see, fifty times six fifty, that's thirty two thousand, five hundred."

"You had 20 head of horses down at thirty thousand." Bud's face had turned a crimson red and he glanced up at Stoney. "Just so we understand each other, let's set things straight. Joe is history: I am your banker now and I am telling you this bank is not in the horse business. I am going to plug them in at seven hundred and fifty dollars a head. That's fifteen thousand."

"You owe the Farmers Home Bank two hundred thousand and you owe us eighty-five thousand. Last year you owed us ninety thousand." He punched on his calculator. With 16% interest that's roughly a hundred thousand. He continued punching the calculator.

"Your net worth is three hundred and seventy seven thousand. Your last financial had a net worth of six hundred and eighty three thousand.. That's a loss of three hundred and six thousand ."

He leaned back, closed the file and began thumping his ring on the desk.

"Your net is about half as much as the last financial statement Joe had you fill out. Looks to me like we have a problem. A big problem."

Stoney turned cold. The pit in his stomach had turned into a chasm and he thought he was going to throw up. He knew he had taken a beating the last couple of years but couldn't make himself put it on paper to see how bad it really was.

"Bud, most all of that is paper loss. Anybody that's in agriculture and especially in the cattle business around here is taking a loss but it's going to come back in a couple of years. The ranch didn't actually lose that much money. Interest has to come down and the market will be back. Look, I've taken good care of the grass, it looks great and my statement will look a whole lot better in twelve months."

"What are your plans?" Bud said coldly. His eyes were looking past Stoney to the lobby and fantasizing about one of the cute secretaries that the old man who owned the bank kept around for his own entertainment.

"Okay, I can get a hold of these cows worth the money, their calves, plus the ones from the cows I have and I'll have six or seven two year old, broke horses to sell. That will put the ranch breaking even. Then buy another hundred head of cows the next year and we will be in good shape."

"How many dollars are we talking about?" He was still watching the activity in the lobby, acting bored. Stoney took out his pocket calculator. "The cows will cost a hundred and twelve thousand and I'll need about five more bulls. That will be a hundred and seventeen thousand. I sure would like that note to be set up on a three year pay-out." Stoney felt a glimmer of hope and decided to roll, even though he knew Bud was only half- listening to him. "I would like ten thousand for operating, that will be for just ten months , till I sell the calves."

Then he came to the part he had been dreading.

"Bud, I didn't make my land payment to the FHA in December. I sure wish you could catch me up on that."

He had all of Bud's attention now. "What you're begging me for is roughly a hundred and fifty thousand. Is that not right?"

"Yes sir…I guess." Stoney couldn't help lowering his head a little, the word begging went all over him..

Bud looked up at the ceiling. "You know what you ought to do. Plow up that grass. You said you got good water out there."

"Bud, I am no farmer, I tried some of that years ago. Besides that, I don't think that water out there is going to last another fifteen or twenty years. Then what have you got? Another dust bowl in the making." He felt himself beginning to panic.

Bud's complexion turned another shade of red.

"Okay, this is the deal," he said. "I am not a cow-calf man, so forget about a three year payout on some old cow. Your place should run seven hundred yearlings, easy. A three hundred pound calf will cost us three hundred dollars, plus or minus. That's two hundred and ten thousand. You'll get thirty five thousand for your cows. So you you'll need a hundred and seventy five thousand. I'll loan you that, plus make your land payment and some operating money. You should be able to pay it all back in at least nine months. But, I want a second mortgage on the ranch that includes the horses and everything else. And, I want a second on all your wife's property."

Stoney was stunned. He just set looking at the banker trying to think of something to say.

"That's cow country Bud, not yearlings, I..."

"Take it or leave it, makes no difference. In fact I would be better off if you didn't. Just pay up and find yourself another banker."

His phone buzzed and Stoney knew he was being dismissed when he heard him say "I'll be right out."

"Let me know in a day or two, no later. I will have to adjust this file for the bank examiners," he said and stood, waiting for him to leave. Stoney was so weak-kneed he didn't know if he could walk.

There were two men waiting for Bud that Stoney did not know. One of them had pushed aside some papers and was sitting on the corner of Doris's desk. He was about thirty and had on western cut gabardine pants, boots, and a western hat with a large colored hat band with a feather in it. That was enough to tell Stoney he was not from these parts. That was not all that gave him away. His face didn't have the ruddy tan or the crow's feet around the corner of his eyes that most ranchers and farmers acquired at an early age in this country of dust storms and searing sun.

He could tell Doris was not enjoying the conservation. She had little time for braggarts or people trying to be someone they were not. After forty years of dealing with cowboys, farmers, and ranchers she could spot a fake the minute he walked through the bank doors.

The other was about the same age, only dressed big city style, briefcase and all.

You would have thought they were bank examiners themselves the way Bud was making over them.

Stoney walked to the teller window and cashed a hundred dollar check which almost wiped his account clean. But he figured that no more than he came to town he could get along with that much for a couple of weeks or more.

As he left the teller's window Doris called him back.

"Mister Thurman would like to see you in his office again," she said, with heavy emphasis on the Mister. Then she whispered, "you're about to meet the county's newest movers, shakers and ass holes."

Bud introduced them. Stoney, getting a little hard of hearing, failed to catch their names and could have cared less when he learned they were from Taylor Farms.

"These are your new neighbors Stone. They bought that grass just east of you and they just purchased the Chalk Hill Feedlot. I told them you might be needing some calves and they were telling me they have a good source..."

"Eddie here," he said pointing to the one in the hat, "said he would be glad to help you..., for a little commission of course." The three of them chuckled.

"Well..., I really hadn't made up my mind about the calves and anyhow I have a good friend that's been doing my buying and selling for years. But I appreciate the offer."

Bud's face turned red again.

It would be a cold day before that pumpkin would buy cattle for him, Stoney thought to himself.

"Bud tells me you have some good water under your land. I would like to visit with you sometime. Maybe we could work a deal Mister Stone," the one in the suit said.

Stoney acknowledged the statement with a short nod. "I better let you all get on with your business. Nice to have met you: if you're out my way stop by. I'm most always out there, somewhere." He turned and left the bank feeling sick.

Pecos was standing up in the seat, his head hanging out the window waiting for him. He reached through with both hands and fondled the pup around the neck before he opened the door. "Son-of-a bitch, son-of-a-bitch, son-of-a-bitch, what the hell are we going to do Pecos?"

They started back to the ranch, Stoney deep in thought. Pecos, standing with his front feet on the dashboard was relishing every moment of the ride.

Half way home Stoney said, "Hot damn Pecos." Pecos turned his head, tilted it and looked at him quizzically.

"I need a drink… like bad."

They turned around and headed to the City Limits.

CHAPTER 5

Stoney pulled into the parking lot and did not recognize the other two parked vehicles.

"We must be a little early, Pecos." He took the pup out and set him in the bed of their pickup. "You'll have plenty of company pretty soon."

This was to be his first lesson on being a good country dog. To stay in the bed, and not jump out until told to. Some dogs have to tumble out many times before it finally sinks in, but it seems almost natural for heeler or heeler crosses to ride behind the cab. Soon there would be other pickups lined up in the lot and most of them would have from one to three dogs in the back. For the most part they would be red or blue heelers, border collies, Australian Shepherds or a mix of the three breeds.

The City Limits Bar did not attract many tourists, maybe a hitchhiker, but no tourist of any monetary means. The building was an old barracks that had been bricked up halfway, any repairs that were made and those were few, were made of anything cheap and handy. The inside mirrored the outside, but it did have atmosphere, or at least its loyal patrons thought so.

A jukebox stood in one corner and a pool table was towards the back of the building, next to the not-too-sanitary bathrooms. Like most barracks, the building was longer that it was wide and the bar itself ran almost half the length of the long side. The rest of the space contained a small dance floor, two pool tables, and several high tables with four bar stools around each. One exception was towards the front where there was one long special table. It always started the evening with ten stools but usually ended up with more.

Stoney took a seat at this table. The patrons that usually sat at the table would be drifting in about four o'clock and then in and out till late in the evening. They were an assortment of farmers, ranchers, cowboys, cow buyers, hired hands, truck salesmen and others that, one way or the other, made their living in something related to agriculture.

Whatever their vocation, and almost without exception, they had several attributes in common: they were honest, hardworking and enjoyed a drink, or drinks, in the evening with their friends. Not everyone was invited or had the grit to sit at this table.

Stoney did not take the chair at the head of the table. That spot belonged to Ben Green. Ben was about seventy and one of the most successful and respected farmers and ranchers in the county. He had made it the hard way, through hard work and perseverance. He was also fair and honest with everyone and had a work ethic that all admired. He had never forgotten his past and could still work, play and drink with the toughest.

There were two young cowboys at the end of the bar visiting with Janie Mims the bartender. She acknowledged Stoney with a smile and a nod when he came in and cut her conversation short. Without asking she mixed his bourbon and cola, brought it to him and sat beside him.

"Where you been Stoney? It's been weeks since you been in."

"Busy I guess… and not getting a damn thing accomplished," he replied.

"My God, you look like you lost your best friend. Troubles on the home front…I hope."

Stoney was looking down at his drink; he looked up her and grinned. "Nope, sorry about that, on the money front."

Janie and Stoney had been high school sweethearts. When Stoney went to college the romance faded. Although every once in awhile the old flame was fanned, both of them knew it could never be rekindled.

"I am just kinda down today; things are getting a little tough out there." His fingers fumbled in his shirt pocket.

"So, tell me something new." She took a package of cigarettes from her apron, lit one and handed it to him. Stoney was always trying to quit, but whenever he was down and drinking in earnest he had to have one.

"You wanta' talk about it?"

"No, not really." He looked at her, after thirty some years she hadn't changed that much. When her hair had started to grey, she changed from brunette to blond.

Three failed marriages, a few more pounds and a lot more wrinkles vouched for her work hard- play hard philosophy. In spite of all this, she still retained much of the same attractive, seductive image.

"I'll bet you can't guess who came in today," she said.

Stoney wasn't in the mood for guessing games and she quickly caught on to that. "Jim Bob Nuckols."

"You're kidding, I haven't seen or heard from him in two or three years." Stoney's mind quickly changed from depression to interest. "The last I heard from him he was a hunting guide and dude wrangler up at Red River. How did he look?"

"Put on some weight around the middle, other than that, just fine. He went to college with you didn't he?"

"Yeah, for a little while. Too confining for him. He's a mess," Stoney replied. "If you didn't know better, you would never guess that he and Travis are brothers."

"Just their size, they are both so damn big," Janie said. "Even at that I bet he outweighs Travis by forty pounds."

"I wonder if Travis has seen him?" Stoney asked. "They've been on the outs for years."

"Not any more. They came in together and acted just fine."

"No shit." Stoney stirred his drink. "Well…, I am glad."

"They were looking for you."

"Yeah, Travis found me some cows…"

"It wasn't Travis," she interrupted. "It was Jim Bob. He acted like he was in a hurry to find you."

"Well…,guess I'll just have to stick around and see if he comes back." He emptied his glass and relished the feeling of the whiskey when it hit the bottom and began to flow through his veins. With just one drink his outlook on life abruptly changed.

The door swung open and Ben Woods came in with one of his hands. Janie asked the young cowboy what he wanted then left to fix his drink and Ben's customary Wild Turkey and water.

"Bring Stoney one," he called to Janie while seating himself at the end of his table.

Two hours later Stoney was drunk. Not falling down drunk but a hair past being tight. The table was filled by then with the 'Special Group'. Four different conversations going on at the same time and everyone, hands and all, vying to buy the next round..

Stoney, deep in a friendly argument about the good and evil of coyotes caught a glimpse of Pete entering the establishment with Emmett a step or two behind him.

They were not part of the group. In fact Pete was not particularly liked by any of them. No special reason, except maybe Pete's bully kind of attitude.

"Hey Pete," Stoney said. "I see you're wearing your trophies." Pete had on a rattlesnake hatband and belt. "I thought snakes gave you the jitters."

"You got a smart mouth," Pete stopped and glared at him. "In fact I think you're a fuckin' little smart aleck."

"What the hell is the matter with you?" Stoney asked. "Your air conditioner on the tractor go out today," Stoney giggled. He was tight enough that he didn't realize how mad Pete was getting. "You just gotta' learn to take it easy."

The table had suddenly become quiet and the group was watching for Pete's next move. Stoney had turned back to the table and started lighting a cigarette.

Pete watched him, stood up from his stool and started to take a step toward him. Emmett grabbed his arm to hold him back.

"Let it lie, Pete," Ben Green said coldly. "Stoney didn't say a damn thing. Just go on about your business."

Pete looked at Ben and started to say something. Then he looked at the table where a couple of men had started scooting their stools back, ready to jump in if thing got sticky.

Pete read the situation correctly, jerked his arm away from Emmett and returned to the bar.

Stoney was oblivious to the near fracas he had almost started and the conversation immediately returned to such topics as: cattle prices, rodeo results, weather and gossip.

By eight he knew he had enough. He bought a round of drinks telling Janie to leave him out. She returned with the drinks; he tipped her five dollars, gave her a hug,and a kiss then went out the side door where Pecos was anxiously awaiting him.

"What'a you say big guy," Stoney leaned over the bed of the pickup nuzzling and talking to the dog. Pecos smothered his face with kisses. He lifted Pecos up and out of the truck and started to unlock the door. Then he had a thought. "Come on Pecos, us go get a bottle to take home."

He walked around to the front of the building and into the package store where he purchased a fifth of Jim Beam, a large bottle of cola and a package of Salem's.

"Hell Stoney, I thought you were going home," one of the farmers sitting at the table called out when Stoney came through the bar instead back out the front door.

"I am..., just had to get some groceries," he replied holding up the sack. Besides, I wanted you all to see my new partner. I bet you all would trade your pick-up for a dog like this."

Pecos was going around to everyone at the table, ears laid back in a friendly way, his long bushy tail sweeping the floor. Everyone petted and talked to him and Pecos, smiling from ear to ear was fully enjoying himself.

"My God I don't think I ever saw and uglier dog," Ben said.

The rest concurred as Pecos made his rounds. Leaving the group he began making his acquaintances with other tables and those sitting at the bar.

Most of those at the bar had turned around and were watching the dog... all but Pete who was trying to get Janie's attention. He had a crush on Janie and had tried to take her out more than several times, to no avail. Pecos, head lowered, was sniffing each set of boots as the continued his tour.

He came to Pete's, took one sniff, and started to go on. But then he stopped, took another long sniff, and hoisted a leg, laid his ears back in satisfaction as he unleashed a long, steady stream of pee on Pete's three hundred dollar python skin boots. The whole room broke out in laughter. Pecos was finishing with some fancy squirts when Pete turned to see what the commotion was. He saw the dog lowering his leg and realized what had happened.

"You son-of-a-bitch, I'll kill you, you fuckin' mongrel." He kicked savagely at him but Pecos was too quick. He jumped aside and stared at him, ears laid back in defiance this time. His lips curled up and exposed young, but menacing, canine teeth. He just stared at Pete, not growling, just glaring at him and waiting for Pete's next move.

Just then Spence, the owner of the City Limits came in. Instantly he sized up the problem and said, "Stoney, damnit to hell, how many times I gotta' tell you to keep your cotton-pickin' dogs outa' my bar. City Hall and State Health is just lookin' for a reason to pick up my license."

Stone had already called Pecos and was headed for the door.

"Sorry about that Spence, I keep telling you that you need a good pissin' post outside."

He opened the door and stepped out. Making sure Pecos was in the clear he opened it up again and shouted inside.

"Sorry about that Pete, son-of-a -buck, it must have been all them snake skins you got on."

He hurried to the pick-up and could still hear the crowd laughing when he shut and locked the door with Pecos safely inside licking his face.

Stoney drove carefully knowing he had too much to drink with Pecos snuggled against him and listening while his man talked. It did not make any difference what Stoney was talking about, the inflection of his voice told him his master was happy, and that made his dog happy.

He turned off the highway on to the dirt road leading to the ranch house. They hadn't gone two hundred yards when Stoney shut the pickup down, turned the lights off, got out, leaned up against the pickup and took a much needed leak. Pecos jumped out and did the same. It was a beautiful night and even though it was still early in the evening, it was cool, and the sky was already filled with stars. He finished his chore.

"Pecos, just smell that sage. Have you ever seen anything so peaceful and quiet? I believe I'll just make myself a drink."

He fumbled behind the seat and found an old, much worn-heavy jacket and a plastic mug that had Allsups Store inscribed on it. He poured a good helping of Jim Beam in it topping it off with warm Coke. Letting the tail gate down to sit on, he pulled out the package of Salem Lights, took a deep puff and began to review the days happenings and what he could do about it, or at least he tried to. His mind, under the spell of the soothing whiskey and the perfumed night just would not let him concentrate on problems.

Finishing his drink he went home and stepped inside just as the phone was ringing.

"Hi-low." That was all he had to say for Betsy to know he was drunk.

"Where you been?" she asked.

"Just messing around. And you?" Trying not to slur his words.

"I wished you would have called. I was finished with my appointment early and the girls wanted me to go by the Holiday Inn and have a drink with them. I guess I should have gone by the City Limits." She paused, knowing that few ladies visited the bar. Stoney knew it was a kind of jab and could feel the irritation in her voice.

"How did it go with the bank?"

"Well..., okay I guess," he lied. "I might have to change our operation up some." The whiskey high quickly vanished. "I'll talk to you tomorrow about it. What time will you be home?

"I don't know; I am beat. I had one drink and someone just ordered the table another round. I'll finish it but I am so tired I might spend the night with Mickie, if you don't mind."

Mickie was their daughter and he knew how much little Bobbi loved to have her grandmother spend the night. He was about half glad she was not coming home. He did not want her to see him in the shape he was in and wanted to get his thoughts together before telling her Bud's ultimatum. The down side of it was that he needed her tonight and her staying in town was beginning to happen more often.

"No, go ahead, see you tomorrow."

"Love you." When he did not reply she said, "Your okay aren't you?"

"Yeah, I am okay..., love you too."

Stoney's young horses at the tank where he found the coyote. Ranch house in background.

CHAPTER 6

It was seven o'clock and the sun had been up for an hour when Stoney awakened. He rolled over in bed and saw a Blue quail on the windowsill. It was pacing back and forth; every so often it would stop, preen itself and then give a short call.

He watched the quail for a while, relishing the peaceful moment He wondered how many other people would enjoy this picture, the quail not six feet from where he lay. Stoney loved his Blue quail and except for a few relatives and close friends would not allow any hunting on his place, and then, only on specific coveys around the ranch in order to keep the birds genetically healthy.

"The bird is looking for his mate," he thought. "Not a lot of difference I guess between myself and him."

Then his mind swung suddenly from this beautiful moment to his other world; the world of pressing problems, the guilty feeling of having a hangover, lying in bed at this hour, morning chores undone. "It's not worth getting drunk anymore," he said to the quail. The bird looked in to see who had spoken to him and fluttered to the ground, then walked away clucking to itself.

It took him awhile to remember what all happened the night before and why Betsy had stayed in town. Then he heard a pick-up turn into the driveway and Pecos barking. Looking out the window he saw it was Travis's.

"Shit," he said to himself and jumped up, embarrassed that someone was going to catch him in bed at this hour; especially Travis.

He heard two sets of boots stomping across the deck as he pulled his boots on.

"Damn him, why in the hell can't he go the front door and ring the bell like most folks."

He heard the back door slide open and Travis's booming voice.

"What the hell's going on, anybody home?"

Stoney came out of the bedroom buttoning his shirt. Travis and Jim Bob Nuckols were standing there grinning at him. They reminded him of two big honey bears that had caught the bees away from the hive.

"You look like shit. Where did you go when you left the Limits? You still had the place in an uproar when we got there."

Stoney ignored Travis's question.

"Hello Jim Bob, it's been awhile." Jim Bob stuck out his huge hand and Stoney grabbed it.

"About ten year if I remember right," Jim Bob replied.

Jim Bob had a briefcase in one hand. That was most unusual for him, and immediately aroused Stoney's curiosity.

"We looked for you at the Holiday. Betsy was there and we told her what your dog pulled off at the Limits."

"Thanks a lot partner, I'll return the favor first chance I get," Stoney replied.

"Jim Bob and I carried her around the dance floor all night. Damn, I wish you would teach that women how to dance."

Stoney looked at him and grinned. Betsy loved dancing, and never lacked for a partner..

"Travis, why don't you go over to the pens? There's a pie-bald roan colt over there and if you'll saddle him up and make a circle or two around the arena I think he might blow a lot of the bull-shit out of you. And while you 're over there throw those horses some hay. My heads kinda' under my arm this morning."

"Okay, now tell me what you been up to Jim Bob," Stoney said as he put the coffee pot on the stove.

Jim Bob brought him up to date: trading cattle in Mexico, gambling in El Paso, guiding and packing hunters and dudes into the Pecos Wilderness and other capers he had been into.

Stoney was observing him closely as he told of his escapades. Jim Bob was the same age as he was and he could tell, sadly, that like him, the edge was gone and he had begun to mellow.

Finished, Jim Bob laid the brief case on the breakfast bar. Travis got up and started nosing about the room, inspecting its contents as usual, and then stepped outside. Talking to Pecos he watched the mares and colts grazing behind the house.

"How's your memory," Jim Bob asked.

"Not worth eight eggs," Stoney answered.

"You remember about twenty years ago," Jim Bob continued. "We got drunk at a little Mexican bar in Questa. You were up there buying killer cows for Winton Packing."

"Shit Jim Bob, you and I got drunk in so many places back then…, yeah, now I remember, you conned me out of five thousand dollars. That's been more like twenty-five or thirty years ago.. Betsy was pregnant with Mickie. Damn I caught hell when I got home."

Jim Bob looked hurt at the word 'con'. Stoney continued, hoping to make it slide off.

"If I wouldn't have made it back on that little bunch of yearlings you scouted for me, Betsy would have really been mad."

"I'll tell you what I'll do," Jim Bob said, leaning over the bar and pushing his hat to the back of his head.

"I'll give you that $5,000 back, with interest, or you can stay in the deal."

"You mean that gold mine," he asked hopefully. "Did you finally hit pay dirt?"

Jim Bob leaned back in the stool and grinned smugly.

"The Goose Creek Mine, owned jointly by Bill Stone and Jim Bob Nuckols. That was the deal, if I remember right. I prove up on it, you put up the $5,000 I happened to need at the time, and we would be partners, 50-50."

It all came back to Stoney. The hot dusty road that ran through the little mountain village and the one old gas pump that he had pulled up to, a real gas pump. The kind that you pumped the gas into a large glass container that sat atop it. It had a long handle that you manually pumped. When it was full you put the nozzle in your tank and the gas gravity fed into it. When finished, you read the amount of gallons you had taken from the graduated measurements on the glass. Simple and reliable, no electricity needed.

An old Mexican had come out of the cabin that served as the station and watched Stoney fill up. When he replaced the nozzle back in its holder he handed him a twenty. The old man smiled, shook his head and made Stoney understand that he didn't have change. He motioned toward the cabin. It was then that Stoney noticed the small sign above the door that said, 'CANTINA'

He followed him into the dark interior. The room was fairly large, with an old roll top desk on one side with an assortment of fan felts hanging above it. On the other side a half dozen tires, a few inner tubes and a meager assortment of tools. On the backside of the room there was a bar with four or five stools. A lone cowboy was sitting on one of the stools hunched over a bottle of beer. There was something vaguely familiar about the man's long broad back. At the end of the bar was a red and white Coca Cola cooler.

The old man walked behind the bar to get his change while Stoney opened up the cooler where the top of Cruz Blanca beer and a few Pepsis were sticking their necks up through the cool water. He popped the lid of a beer with an opener that was tied to the handle of the cooler with a long string and turned around admiring the old pictures on the wall of bullfighters, beautiful senoritas and horses, all of them advertising different kinds of Mexican beer and brands of tequila.. He took a seat at the bar where the owner was counting out his change.

"I'll buy his beer," a loud voice said, just as fifty-cent piece clanged between Stoney and the old man. It startled Stoney and the old man alike. The he recognized the voice. Sure enough it was Jim Bob whom he hadn't seen since college.

It was 11 am when Stoney had pulled into Questa and 2 pm when he and Jim Bob emerged from the bar, with a fifth of whiskey and a case of Coors. They got into Stoney's pickup and left Jim Bob's at the side of the building where it would stay until the old man's son could come along and fix a couple flats on it. The pickup swung out toward Red River. Jim Bob had convinced Stoney that he knew where there might be some yearling steers he could buy. Jim Bob thought they could be bought right, and anyhow he wanted to show Stoney his camp.

They passed through Red River, and drove some 40 miles to part of the old Sontero Ranch. The ranch manager drove them to the yearlings. After thirty minutes of haggling over price and shrink he bought them and they agreed on a delivery date. After leaving the ranch headquarters they turned back toward Red River. They hadn't gone far before Jim Bob told him to slow down and to turn back west on a rugged, seldom used road.

"That's Goose Creek," he said, pointing to a small stream no more than five inches across and hardly noticeable among the tall grass and rocks that held it in bounds.

"Any fish in that river?" Stoney asked half joking.

"You'd be surprised," was the answer. "If you know where to look, some of the holes hold the fattest, best tasting little brook trout you ever had."

After a mile of bumps, turns and high centers, spilling the beer that they had been sipping onto their laps, they finally came to a more level and broader place in the road. Jim Bob had him stop, and he jumped out and removed an old log and motioned Stoney to drive into a small rocky feeder canyon. After the log was replaced they drove up the small, heavily wooded canyon for a little over a hundred yards. There they had to walk the last hundred yard to the camp. About fifteen acres had been fenced off with aspen rails and live pine trees. A smaller creek flowed noisily through a corner of it and furnished water for two stout saddle horses and a pack mule.

Further up the side of the canyon stood a one-room cabin. It backed into the rocky side of the canyon wall. The three walls were made of stone, and a heavy canvas strung across poles was adequate enough to serve as a roof during the summer. Some twenty feet from the cabin was the entrance to a well concealed tunnel.

Just before dark they walked down to the stream and caught several of the small native trout. After a supper of trout, fried potatoes, Dutch-oven biscuits and lots of whiskey, Jim Bob brought Stoney up to date on his current problem.

He had dropped all his money in a poker game with the group that leased the Sontero Ranch where he worked as a guide during the hunting season. He told Stoney that he needed $3,000 to square him and another $2,000 as a grubstake.

He explained how he found this little hidden piece of paradise while retrieving an elk for a rich hunter. While dressing out the elk he had noticed some interesting and unusual pebbles and put several in his pocket. After the hunting season was over he had them assayed and they showed some traces of gold and silver. It was enough that he was able to get a mining claim on the Federal Land. He fulfilled the government requirements by putting in a hundred dollars' worth of labor a year and proof that there was some valuable mineral on the claim. He then showed Stoney a little sack of gold that had come from the ore he had taken to the smelter in Pueblo, Colorado. By the time they finished the bottle, Stoney had written out a check for the $5,000. He was also the drunk, but proud, owner of a half-interest in the claim called, after a lengthy argument, the Goose Creek Mine.

..————..

"Now what?" Stoney asked, snapping back to the present.

"I said it's not gold that's going to make us rich," Jim Bob repeated.

"Okay, what is it, that's going to make me rich beyond my dreams?" Stoney asked.

"Molybdenum," Jim Bob answered. "Did you fall asleep or something?"

"No, just reminiscing. Sorry about that. Okay, so what the hell do they use molybdenum for and what is it worth?"

"Lots of things. It's a heat resistant metal, space shuttles, stuff like that. But it's not really molybdenum that I am after. The vein isn't thick enough to make much money. It's the rhenium in it. I think it's really rich in rhenium."

"Losing me again Jim Bob."

Jim Bob smiled, "Rhenium is a scarce metal, so scarce that they really haven't done much experimenting with it. Except lately. Did you ever hear of smart bombs?"

"Nope," answered Stoney, thinking that this was going to be another one of Jim Bob's wild dreams.

"They're working on these bombs with little cameras in the nose. A fighter plane can toss 'em in the general direction of, say a building, and while the pilot's flying away he's guiding this bomb right through an open window and down the hall..., picks out any room he wants to and then boom!"

"Come on Jim Bob," Stoney said, shaking his head. "I am too old for your tales."

"I'm not shitting you. They hope to have them ready in five or six years, by the early 90's. That's what they tell me up at the smelter. They have all these scientists and military people up there snooping around. They think they have to have this rhenium to make it work.

Anyway people that oughta know what they are talking about tell me it's one of the ten most expensive metals on earth. Maybe the most expensive."

"Okay," Stoney said. "So what do you want from me?"

"Are you still in, or do you want a check for five? If you want a check you might have to hold it awhile."

There was a sly smile on his face as he gave Stoney that last little bit of information.

"Well..., I think I'll stay in. The troubles I got... five thousand's not going to do me a lot of good. Especially a check that's going to wear out in my billfold."

He smiled at Jim Bob. "Somebody's liable to steal it before its cashed."

"Done," Jim Bob said. "I knew I could talk you into it. Just sign your name to these papers and we are on our way."

"What are they?" Stoney asked. He loved Jim Bob, but sometimes, you had to ask him these things. It seemed like every once in awhile he had a habit of forgetting some important detail.

"One of them is the application of ownership for the land the claim is on. I have proved up on two hundred acres of it. By the way; we will owe the Government five dollars an acre so you owe me five hundred. The other is an affidavit of citizenship. The last one is from the smelter."

"What bank you want your checks sent to?"

"I don't want the checks sent to any bank, Jim Bob. Send them to me."

"They won't do that Stoney. They send them to the bank so they know you won't come back later and say you didn't get it."

"Whatever," Stoney said. He was not really expecting anything anyhow. He finished signing the papers, reluctantly giving the Merchants and Farmers Bank address.

Travis came in just as Stoney went into the bedroom to get his billfold. Opening it up he was surprised to find only twenty dollars in it.

"Son-of-a-bitch," he said to himself. "It must have been a hell of a good party: I can't believe I went through a hundred dollars that quick."

Then, a miserable thought came to him. "Shit! Jim Bob said five hundred, not fifty."

He sat down on the bed dejectedly. "How in the hell can I come up with five hundred when I don't even have fifty."

"Betsy has it but I am sure as hell am not going to ask her for it."He thumbed absently through his billfold. "Credit card," he thought. Betsy and he used different credit card companies, and he since he seldom used his, neither she nor the bank would ever know.

"Loan me five hundred Travis," he said sheepishly when he came out of the bedroom.

He knew Travis always carried a large roll of bills and he could pay him back as soon as he could find an ATM machine in town. Sure enough, Travis reached in his pocket, unfolded five one hundred dollar bills from a fat roll and handed it to Stoney shaking his head.

"Thanks, "Stoney said, handing the money to Jim Bob. "Don't let me forget I owe you."

"I'll try not to. So, how about the cows?"

Stoney looked down and shook his head, "Can't do it Travis. I am changing my whole operation, as requested by Merchant and Ranchers Bank. They say I have to sell my cows and buy yearlings."

"What the shit. This is cow country, not…"

Stoney held his hand up interrupting him. "I know that, but I am in a corner and it's the only way they'll go with me for another year. Why don't you see if you can find me a buyer for the cows and find out what those yearlings out of south Texas are going to cost? You been getting some out of Grosbeck haven't you?'

Travis nodded then looked out the glass door at the horses. Both he and Jim Bob could tell Stoney was really worried and didn't want to talk about it.

"Us go Jim Bob," he said. "How much you want for the cows?"

"All you can get me. You know those cows as well as I do," Stoney answered walking out to their pickup with them.

"When can I pay my banker off with all that rhenium Jim Bob?" Stoney shouted as they were driving off.

"Jim Bob laughed and replied, "It might be awhile."

"Yeah," Travis said. "Like maybe five or ten years."

Stoney watched them till they made the turnout in his driveway. "I am sure you're right Travis," Stoney said to himself. He tested the wind. It was out of the southeast and clouds were already building over the Pecos River fifty miles to the west. A sure sign of rain, and it smelled like it too. He reached down and petted Pecos who was sitting beside him, face upturned and tail sweeping the ground.

"You crazy son-of-buck, you liked to got us killed last night."

The dog looked up at him, ears laid back in affection and with complete innocence in those strange eyes.

Stoney went back into the house, drank a glass of instant breakfast, and then drove over to the pens. He saddled three colts. The saddles were old and in rough shape from colts laying down and rolling on them, rubbing up against fences, and anything else they could think of to remove them from their back. He hobbled them and left them to figure things out by themselves. Pecos stayed busy trying to catch the numerous cottontails that stayed around the corrals competing with a large covey of quail for grain spilled by the horses.

Stoney then saddled his favorite horse. Leo was a fifteen-year-old sorrel gelding that had been born on the ranch and had been Mickie's barrel racing horse. With Pecos following close behind he rode out to check the cows.

Everyone of his cows had been born on the ranch and they were his pride and joy. He had started with good Hereford cows and Black Angus bulls and now his entire herd was made up of black baldies. He was crossing them with Polled Hereford bulls this year and had just turned them out with the cows so they would calve in February the following year.

To the average person a herd of black-baldy cows look like just so many black cows with white or mottled faces. But not to the rancher that has raised them. To the rancher, each cow was different in some small physical characteristic or personality. They in turn knew Stoney and paid no attention to him as he slowly rode thru them. They were however, a little worried about Pecos being around their calves. Stoney generally had two or three dogs following him, they knew those dogs and were not worried about them., but Pecos was new to them. The spring rains had already brought the early season grasses and they were lush, a bright green and already heading out. The baby calves, laying in last year's taller bluestem and side oats couldn't be seen unless you were almost on top of them.

A cow off by herself was a sure sign that she was either calving or babysitting. If she was in charge of the nursery there would be anywhere from six to a dozen babies hidden close by. It had always been a mystery to Stoney how the cows figured out whose turn it was to baby-sit while the other mothers were off grazing.

The farther Stoney rode, the more heartsick he became. To sell these cows off the ranch they were raised on would be the most agonizing experience he would ever have to endure.

The heavy roll of thunder brought him out of his despondent mood and he nudged Leo into a fast lope to the corrals. Arriving just ahead of the approaching storm. Rider and horse both had enjoyed the long gallop, jumping the sagebrush and yuccas, and running up the side of sand dunes and off the steep side in an unfaltering stride.

Stoney unsaddled Leo and the colts, turned them loose and jumped into the saddle house just as the first few heavy drops of rain hit. A few soft hail stones hit the ground and broke a part, the were followed by a nice steady rain. Pecos had stopped to investigate a fresh badger den and now came in shaking water all over Stoney who had pulled up a chair to the door where he could enjoy the rain and watch his horses. No one, he thought, had ever made a perfume that could compete with sagebrush and desert grasses awash in a fresh rain. The horses with the Alpha personalities were under the shed. Those on the lower end of the pecking order were standing with their hind ends backed to the cool light wind that accompanied the rain. Their heads were lowered and noses almost touching..

As the rain continued and the skies darkened, so did Stoney's spirits. There had to be a better way. He took a pencil and a small notebook out of his shirt pocket and began to figure. An hour before dark the rains let up. He fed the horses and went to the house, still without coming up with a way to hold on to the cows. He dreaded facing Betsy that night. and telling her that they must sell the cows and, place a second mortgage and assignments..., not only on the ranch, but on all the rentals and investments that she had worked so hard to accumulate.

"No! Absolutely no, Stoney," she said firmly.

They were sitting out on the deck across the table from each other. He had grilled lamb chops and opened a bottle of wine. They had finished eating before he told her the banker's ultimatum.

"It's enough we have to sell the cows, and I am sorry for you and me both. I love them as much you do. But I am telling you we have to keep something clear if..," she hesitated and said what she had wanted to say to her husband for some months,..."If we lose the ranch." She knew it would hurt him...and it did. But it was something he had to face eventually. She knew he was having a hard time facing reality, but sooner or later he had to.

She continued talking fast, trying to get through to him.

"Look how old we are. I don't have many productive years left in this business and then I am through. If we lose the ranch we won't have anything. You don't have any kind of retirement fund and little Social Security. You're not alone. I don't know of many farmers or small ranchers that have made enough money to pay into Social Security."

"You know we had always figured that if I made enough money to live off of, and pay for Mickie's education we could put everything the ranch made back into it. It would be our retirement. Stoney, listen to me,... it's just not working. I know it and you know it."

She was right and he knew it, but he still had to play the game, selfishly, for his benefit.

"That will never happen. Maybe Bud is right. If we have two or three good years with yearlings we can get a lot of this debt paid off," he reasoned, standing up gathering the plates from the table. She helped take the dishes into the kitchen and went into the bedroom, neither of them saying another word.

When he finished cleaning up the kitchen Stoney entered the dark bedroom . He knew she was awake. She lay on her side of the bed with her back to his side. He slipped into the bed and said, "I love you."

"I love you too," she replied. He could tell she had been crying.

There was a large space between them on the king size bed. For thirty-five years they had always slept cuddled close to each other. There were some nights, after a minor tiff that this space would be empty... but by morning they would be cuddled together. Not so, this next morning...the first of many.

Mickie and Leo work the barrels.

CHAPTER 7

With sad resoluteness, Stoney started the ranch on its new course.

The next day he was back at the bank. He told Bud he would have the cows sold in two or three weeks, and Travis would start buying the light yearlings. Bud objected to Travis and told him he would prefer Taylor Farms cattle buyer to purchase the cattle. And, since it was the bank's money that was the way it was going to be.

Stoney reluctantly nodded his head, but there was one stipulation from their previous meeting that he was going to refuse to do.

"Everything is settled then but the second mortgage on the ranch and an assignment on the stat land and on your wife's property," Bud said. It was a good feeling, dominating Stoney.

"Can't do that Bud. A second on the ranch is fine. But an assignment and second on my wife's stuff aint' gonna' happen. It's all in her sole and separate estate and me or anyone else is not gonna' talk her into it. Besides, what with all the peanut and dairy people are paying for this land you got more than enough collateral."

Bud's ring tapped the table a few times and he leaned back in his chair. He was enjoying this feeling of power.

"Okay, trouble at home, huh." He smiled solicitously.

"Bring that money in here as soon as you sell the cows. On a second thought, have them make the check out to both of us. The bank and you. When I get the check I'll make out one to the Federal Land Bank and have the second on the ranch ready for you sign."

Stoney set up straight in his chair.

"Bud, I never cheated this bank, or anyone else out of a dime in my life. No one has ever asked me to have the banks name on any check I ever got."

"Sorry, that's the way I do business," he said.

He swiveled in his chair and picked up the Wall Street Journal.

"I'll call you when it looks like I got the cows sold," Stoney said, and started walking out.

"Tell Betsy hello for me, and tell her to come by and visit some time. I foreclosed on a couple of houses the other day and I might let her have the listing on them," Bud said,.. not lifting his eyes from the paper.

Stoney walked out, so mad that he didn't even stop to chat with Doris.

It wasn't a week till Travis found a buyer for the reputation cows. As delivery date approached Stoney's congenial personality began to change even more and Betsy found more reasons to stay in town.

Before sunup on delivery day Stoney was saddling Leo as Travis and two of their mutual friends unloaded their horses.

Stoney had asked Mickie if she wanted to help. He had always said that she was the best cowboy that he had ever worked with. But she turned him down saying she grew up with those cows and couldn't stand to see them loaded up and hauled away. He knew how she felt.

The four of them rode out of the corrals as the first promise of sunlight began to brighten the horizon. This point of most roundups are filled with lots of talk and joking before the riders split up to start the gathering. Not so on this one. Not a word was spoken. They all knew how this was tearing Stoney apart. His somber mood affected all of them.

Three hours later the cattle began entering the pens and by the time the new owner and the state brand inspector arrived the sorting had commenced and the pens turned into an organized melee of; bawling cattle, dust, Pecos's yapping, snap of whips and the shouts of the cowboys.

By noon the final calf had been pushed into the last of the four large pot-bellied cattle trucks and the check was exchanged for a bill-of-sale. Stoney paid the inspector, thanked his friends and promised to buy a drink later at the City Limits.

Stoney shook hands with the buyer and wished him luck. Travis stayed after the others followed the trucks out the dusty road.

"What do I owe you Travis?" Stoney asked.

"Not a damn thing. I got my commission from the buyer," he replied sourly.

They were facing each other, leaning over the hood of Stoney's pickup. He reached in, got a checkbook off the dash' and wrote out the five hundred he had borrowed and handed it to him.

"Hold on to that till I have time to get to the bank and cover it."

Travis folded it and stuck it in his shirt pocked without glancing at it, instead he looked out across the empty pastures shaking his head slowly.

Pecos was stretched out in the shade of the pickup. He had taken a swim in the large stock pond and was covered with sand he had rolled in. He was still hot and tired, but happy, after all the work he had done that morning. One could not say he was a good cow-dog yet, but he was learning such rules as: you're not to stand in the gate when the cowboys were trying to push cattle through it, there is a time to chase and a time not to, and other tricks of the trade.

Pecos had his feeling hurt several time for being in the wrong place at the wrong time. After being scolded, and with anything handy thrown at him he would find a place out of the way to lay down and sulk. He would watch the proceeding for a while and after he thought he had it figured out, would jump right back into business. All things considered he was feeling mighty proud of making a hand and had a wonderful time doing it.

"It looks mighty empty," Travis said.

Stoney followed his gaze to his grasslands. He felt a large lump in his throat and a heaviness in his chest. He couldn't answer. Just nodded his head in agreement.

"Let me tell you something," Travis said, looking back at Stoney. "Those calves that Taylor outfit buys come from southeast Oklahoma. Half of them are sick when they buy 'em and what isn't, gets sick. They oughta' be arrested for the way they handle them. You're gonna' have hell keepin' 'em alive. Don't be so damn stubborn, call me, I'll come help. There's a hell of a whole lot of difference in those and the ones I get out of Grosbeck."

Stoney had told Travis why he had to get the calves from the Taylor outfit. Travis didn't like it but understood.

"Appreciate that Travis, I am going to need some help. It's been a long time since I handled shipped in calves."

Travis reached down, unbuckled his spurs and laid them on the hood. He started playing with the rowel on one of them. The spurs were hand made with his brand on them.

"I'll tell you somethin' Stoney. These calves are too high. I don't like the looks of the market this comin' fall. In fact, it could be a wreck."

"Well…, "Stoney replied. "I can't do much about that now, can I? Besides, I 'm already in a wreck."

Travis looked at his friend. "No I guess you can't. Let me hear from you."

He reached down, patted Pecos and walked over, loosened the cinch on his horse, loaded him and drove off without saying another word.

Stoney took the check to Bud that afternoon.

"This check's not made out to both of us," Bud scowled, his face turning red. "I thought we had an understanding."

"Guess it was an oversight. Anyhow you got it. What difference does it make?"

Bud said nothing; he just started pushing papers over to Stoney to sign. He handed him an open-ended note.

"This will be for the cattle and operating expense. You can start using it as soon as this check clears."

He leaned over the desk shaking a finger at Stoney.

"I want'a warn you. I'll be watching every damn check that comes in here. If I find just one that I think is frivolous I'll be on your ass."

Stoney was completely taken back. No one had ever talked to him like that and it took every ounce of self-control to keep him from getting up and slapping the banker. Instead he started reading the note hoping to regain his composure. Then he received his second shock.

"18.75% interest! Bud, you gotta' be kidding I can't pay that kind of interest. Nobody in agriculture can. You know that as well as I do."

"Sorry. Hadn't you heard? President Carter wants us to tighten up the credit and…, this is a high-risk loan."

"Yeah, but…," Stoney started to protest but Bud cut him off.

"Look, I am about ready to call the deal off anyway. You want it, you sign it. Otherwise pay up and find yourself another banker.."

Stoney signed.

CHAPTER 8

The cows were gone and it was too early to receive the calves so Stoney spent his time working with the yearling colts and 'riding fence'. This was a never-ending part of ranch life, making sure the barbwire strands and post were all in good shape, replacing staples that had worked out and splicing broken wire. He used to enjoy it and used is as a good opportunity to halter break and exercise his yearlings. Lately however he began to dread riding his north and east fence lines. Those were the boundaries between the ranch and land rapidly being turned into farm land by large agriculture corporations growing subsidized crops... such as Taylor Farms.

Corporate agriculture procedure was simple, cheap, and effective but sadly devastating to all the many creatures that were unfortunate enough to call that particular part of the planet their home. First, after plowing a fire guard around the perimeter of their project they would set the grass on fire. Few of the inhabitants of the sandhill grasslands could escape the inferno as the fires were always started during periods of high winds that are frequent in Eastern New Mexico and West Texas. Four wheel drive pickups with an employee riding in the back and hanging over the sides with butane burners could start a fire a mile long in a matter of minutes. After that came the bulldozers with their large blades filling in the blowouts and leveling grass covered sandhills. Next the huge, thumping tractors pulled their king size plows turning all vegetation and small animals that had escaped the fire beneath the sandy soil.

The corporation's tractor drivers had little concern and regards for whose fences happened to be next to their turn rows. When wheeling their cumbersome machine around, and whether turning too fast and late, or half asleep, they could take out twenty feet of fence without their tractor making a shudder. They couldn't care less: they would just laugh and leave it up to somebody's cowboy to spend a half a day repairing it.

This was not the only reason that he dreaded riding his fence lines. A couple weeks earlier he had found an antelope that had become entangled in the fence while trying to escape the fire with her fawn. Unlike deer that jump fences, antelope try to go through a fence. This one had not made it before the smoke had ended her life. By following the tracks Stoney could tell the fawn had made it through the fence but returned to its mother's side and died of starvation.

On this day he found the fences on the north and east in good shape and turned Leo and the yearling back toward the pens in order to return the colt to the corrals and replace it with another. He was almost to the pens when he noticed a strange set of tracks. He prided himself for being able to not only find hardly discernable tracks but also to identify them. These tracks were two parallel lines that carefully went around clumps of sagebrush and yucca. Dismounting and following on foot he finally figured out that it was a coyote pulling a drag trap.

For many years coyotes have challenged ranchers over their right to inhabit the grazing lands of the southwest. Stoney accepted their rights to make a living in the sandhills as he did; however, he would, on occasion, thin out some packs that had developed an appetite for his calves. But he detested traps and considered them indiscriminate, cruel and unfair. He especially detested those that trapped for a sport. Some of those checked their traps so seldom that the victim died of starvation before the so called sportsman would come along ending their pain with a bullet to the head. Many of them would take the carcass and string them on fence-posts along some busy road to attest to what they considered a skill, but Stoney thought it more of an immature macho thing.

The tracks were headed to the ranch headquarters. He quickly mounted and striking a lope he hurried to the pens anxious to find out why. Tying Leo and the yearling to the saddle house hitching rail he followed the tracks as they skirted the corrals and up the banks of a large stock pond. There he found her, a large beautiful female coyote. She was still carrying her luxurious winter coat which was full and smooth, more a light gray than the usual brown. From that he could tell she had just reached maturity. She was the prettiest coyote he had ever seen. It was apparent from the tracks that she had gone down to the water and the drag had become ensnarled in an old cottonwood log. The trap had snapped around her left front leg above the ankle. The trap itself was attached to four feet of chain then the drag device made of two steel four-inch prongs which were welded onto a six-inch rod. The prongs had made the two mysterious lines in the sand. The coyote had given up and just lay there accepting whatever fate had been chosen for her.

Stoney just stood there admiring this beautiful animal. Pecos was completely enthralled by her, smelling the trap then the coyote, deciding her gender then moving on up to where the trap had torn into her leg. He stopped there and began to lick her wound. Stoney watched in amazement as Pecos laid down and continued to clean her wound.

Thoughts flooded Stoney's mind. Upon approaching her his first thought was to retrieve his 30-30 from the pick-up and end her suffering, but now he wasn't so sure. Because she knew exactly where to come to quench her thirst, he was almost certain she had been born on the ranch, and spent her young life there. She knew the rolling sand hills and grasslands as well as he did.

"We are two of a kind, arent't we little girl? We are both in a trap and don't know how to get out of it." He thought about the agonizing walk she had just made.

"I'll tell you one thing. You're a tough little gal".

He turned and instead of going to the pickup he went into the saddle house getting a heavy saddle blanket and picking up a can of wound dressing. Then he had a second thought and putting it back, deciding that Pecos cleaning the wound would probably do more good than anything he could put on it.

Neither the coyote nor Pecos had moved since he had left. Moving a reluctant Pecos aside he carefully laid the heavy saddle blanket over the coyote's head, in case she might snap at him. Then carefully he tried to squeeze the trap open. It didn't work. It was old and rusty, plus with the angle of the trap, and with the coyote laying on her side, there was no way he had the strength or the leverage to open it. He marveled that she had still not moved a muscle.

"Pecos, I don't think I can do it without cutting her foot off." He looked at Pecos who was sitting on his haunches watching. He tilted his head toward Stoney as if trying to understand why he couldn't do it. Or was he pleading with him?

Stoney looked into those crazy eyes. "Okay, I'll figure something out."

Standing up, he looked at the two of them. The coyote, unmoving except for an occasional deep breath, and Pecos, sitting on his haunches shifting his eyes from the coyote and back to his master.. Stoney could hardly believe the empathy that he could see in Pecos's eyes and action. He went to the box car where he kept his tools, not knowing what exactly he was looking for; then he spied two C clamps hanging on the wall.

Returning to the trap, he placed the clamps on the sprung steel. Carefully tightening each one until there was enough room for him to remove the trap. He lifted the saddle blanket. The coyote had not moved, her eyes were still closed, and except for the breathing, one would have thought she had died. Stoney had another thought.

After taking the blanket back to the saddle house he went to the bunkhouse, which was a small trailer house that was seldom used. He did stock it with a few cans of vegetables, canned meat, salt and pepper, and flour for an occasional, hungry wetback that came through looking for work. The word had passed among them that one could always rest up at this rancho, get something to eat and maybe a few days' work at good pay from the patron.

Opening a can of pork and beans and grabbing a paper plate he hurried back to the coyote wondering if she would still be there. She still laid there and Pecos had resumed his cleansing of the wound. He emptied the can on the plate and carefully placed it not far from her nose. He quickly withdrew his hand when her eyes suddenly opened. He looked into those stunning yellow eyes and that he believed were in some strange way communicating some sort of gratitude.

Coaxing a reluctant Pecos back to the saddle house, he turned the yearling back into the corral, haltered another, and then continued riding fence. Three hours later they were headed back to the pens with Pecos leading the way. The dog went immediately to the pond with Stoney following. No coyote and the plate had been licked clean. Pecos ran to the highest part of the bank and stared off in the directions of the thickets. He was still there when Stoney whistled for him after he had finished his chores and was ready to call it a day.

THE THICKETS
Pecos' Hideout and the barn where Stoney and Pete have their last confrontation.

CHAPTER 9

Stoney spent the next few days breaking his colts and getting ready for the calves. He knew processing these young southern calves and keeping them alive was an art all its own. Stoney visited with several of his friends, who received thousands of calves each fall to find out what kind of vaccine and medicine were working. It seemed to change every other year.

After being shipped hundreds of miles by truck these freshly weaned calves would be extremely stressed out. Getting them to eat and drink as soon as they were unloaded was the trick. Some of them would have already gone without food or water for two or three days, either because it wasn't available or the quality was so poor they refused to eat or drink. "Shipping fever" was the name given for a combination of dehydration, pneumonia, shock and a whole host of exotic diseases.

The first truck bearing the Taylor logo, a quarter circle over a T, arrived at the ranch shortly after midnight carrying 160 calves. While Stoney was directing the driver backing to the chute the strong smell of ammonia stung his nostrils: urine, it meant that the calves had been on the truck too long. After several tries, the driver finally got the truck backed up square with the chute. "Where in the hell have you been?" Stoney demanded as the driver descended from the cab. "You were supposed to have been here ten hours ago."

"I got held up in Amarillo, flat tire." Stoney could smell liquor on his breath.

While the driver unloaded them Stoney counted the calves off under the outdoor security light that stood beside the chute and illuminated the pens.

"Where are the rest of them? I counted 156. Supposed to be 160."

They found them on the floor of one of the compartments, still alive and sick. The driver started hitting them with the hotshot, he had two of them on their feet when Stoney stopped him.

"Let'em be, you can take them home with you or stop by the Chalk Hill Feedlot and let them have 'em."

"I was told to bring 160 to this place and that's what I intend to do," he said, viciously jabbing the hot shot into the eye of one of the calves. Stoney felt like he could feel the shock when he heard the buzz and the agonizing bawl of the calf. He did something he had not done since he was a freshman in college. He threw a punch.

In the dim light he was hoping for the man's head. He connected. The driver went down into the mixture of manure and urine. Stoney had thrown so much of himself into it that his feet slipped out from beneath him, so he went down in the liquid mulch. He was on his feet first thinking of some way to protect himself. He was certainly no fighter and although they were the same size, the driver was thirty years younger. Stoney knew he was overmatched and quickly grabbed the hotshot, breaking it over his knee. Holding the halves in each hand he pointed the sharp points of the fiberglass hotshot at the driver.

"Come on, you son-of-a-bitch, I'll jab your eyes out."

"I don't want anymore," the kid said, getting groggily pulling himself up.

Stoney followed him out of the trailer. As the driver climbed back into the cab Stoney said, "I got four more of these loads coming. You had better not be behind the wheel of any of 'em. You tell the rest of the drivers that if they are so much as thirty minutes late the front gate is going to be locked. I don't care if they have to drive those trucks on the rim to get here, they better be here on time."

"You understand me you son-of-a-bitch?"

The driver nodded and put the truck in gear. Stoney tossed the remains of the hotshot into the truck as it passed.

He let the calves into four different pens where they would have shade, and protection from the wind. There, they would find feed in the troughs, water and fresh oat hay that he had scattered around the lots so they wouldn't have to move but a few feet to find something to eat. There wasn't anything else he could do for them that night.

He pulled off his boots and clothes that were beginning to stiffen from the ooze in the trailer and threw them in back of the pickup where Pecos immediately rolled on top of them, trying to get some of that good smell on himself.

As he opened the door of the pickup he suddenly felt sick. He stared shaking and threw up. As if in a dream he drove to the house. Stepping up on back deck of the house he peeled off his shorts, leaving them on the back porch. He headed straight to the liquor cabinet, fixed himself a strong helping of Jim Beam, rummaged through the catch-all drawer, and found a half pack of Salem's. He was bent over his drink, soaked and shaking when Betsy, awakened by the commotion, came into the kitchen.

"Stoney! What in the world happened? You look terrible.

He took a big drink. "That damn driver and I had an argument."

"Did you have a fight? Are you hurt?"

Stoney started telling her what happened. She listened until he got to the part of hitting the driver'… there she had had enough.

"What in the world is happening to you? You have haven't been in a fight since you were a kid. You're changing so much sometimes I wonder if you're the same man I married and have lived with all these years."

She turned on her heels, and with a look of disgust, went back to the bedroom.

Stoney finished his drink and fixed another. The chills and shivering gradually left and reality begin to set in. He couldn't believe what had transpired that night, how Betsy had taken it and what she had said to him. She was right. He was changing, but it was not just him; she was changing too. He felt his whole life was shifting and it was slipping into some unknown and dreaded conclusion. Complete exhaustion set in. He made himself move out of his stupor, put the whiskey back in the cabinet and dragged himself into the shower.

He collapsed in bed and snuggled up as close as he could get to Betsy. As soon as he touched her she immediately moved away. It hurt. If ever he needed to lie close to her it was this night. Stoney desperately needed some support and solace. He turned over with his back to her and tried to sleep but sleep would not come. Visions of sick calves, drunk truck drivers and fat greedy bankers kept going through his mind until an hour before daylight; fatigue finally took over and he drifted to sleep.

A younger Stoney and Kenneth at their last rodeo.

CHAPTER 10

He awoke with a start. He had overslept. Betsy had left without awakening him, either because she wanted to let him sleep or because she didn't want to talk to him. Stoney was afraid it was the latter. Daylight poured through the window and he could hear the newly weaned calves bawling a half-mile away. He jumped up and dressed. Not stopping to grab himself his usual instant breakfast he hurried to the pickup, lifted Pecos up and into the bed and rushed over to the pens.

Most of the calves were milling about the pen but a few were just standing with saliva drooling from their mouth, side's drawn in, and eyes sunken. Keeping Pecos at his side he began to gently ease the sick ones out of the pens and into the alley. Then, with Pecos's eager help, he moved them toward the working chute to give them electrolytes and combiotics to hopefully stave off shipping fever.

As the noon hour came and went, Stoney and Pecos were still at it. After taking care of the sick ones and moving them into a separate pen, he began to work the others, moving them a small group at a time to be branded, vaccinated, dehorned and castrated. He was moving the last little bunch up the alley when he saw a cloud of dust coming down the county road and then down the half mile of lane to the pens. Immediately he was mad. He didn't like anyone driving that fast down the county road and especially down his lane.

He had the calves in the crowding chute when the driver stepped out of the shiny new pickup with the quarter circle T on its side... a logo which Stoney was beginning to despise. The driver was Eddie, the one he met at the bank with a feather in his hat. Stoney began working the calves.

Eddie watched for a while, getting no acknowledgement from Stoney. Then he climbed up on the alley gate, hooked the heels of expensive red boots on one of the rails and said.:

"Nice looking bunch of calves aren't they."

Stoney ignored him and continued working the calves. He placed the hot branding iron on the hip of one of the calves and the solid puff of smoke with the acrid smell of burning hair blew directly into Eddie's face.

Eddie coughed and tried to be heard over the bawling of the calves and roar of the butane burner heating the branding irons.

"I understand you and my brother-in-law had a little disagreement last night."

Stoney let the calf out of the chute, turned off the butane, and said, "Now, what did you say?"

"I said you and my brother-in-law had an argument last night."

"Who in the hell is your brother-in-law?

"The truck driver. And I damn sure don't appreciate you beating him up with a club."

"I didn't use a club and if I ever see the son of a bitch on my place I'll use more than a club."

"Now get your ass off my damn gate and follow me. I don't know where you were raised but my two-year-old Granddaughter knows better than to sit on the swinging end of a gate. They're made to open and close, not for some dumb fat-ass to use as a squatting post." Eddie turned a beet red but followed Stoney down to the sick pen which now held 20 calves. One had just died and lay next to the water trough.

"Now what do you think of your Okies?" Stoney asked.

"They don't look so good," Eddie replied. "You oughta' doctor them."

"Don't look so good? I'll be lucky to save 5 of them out of this pen. You go back and tell your cattle buyers, and your damn truck drivers, if they don't do a better job I'm going to turn every truck back, and you and Bud can go to hell."

Eddie didn't say a word, just turned on his heel and walked back to his pickup. Pecos was standing by the gate when Eddie opened it to let himself out of the alley. He kicked at the dog, infuriating him. Pecos ducked the pointed- toed boot and immediately started snarling with his lips curled up showing his teeth; those, and his crazy eyes were enough to send his antagonist climbing back up the gate. Stoney, hearing the ruckus and figuring out real quick what was happening, came sauntering back up the alley in no hurry.

"Damn, what is it about gates that you can't keep off of em?" He giggled.

"You better call that damn mutt off or I'll kill him."

"Seems to me you would have to get off that gate first. He'd be mighty hard to reach from where you sitting."

He called to Pecos who quit barking and happily followed his laughing master back down the alley. Stoney watched as the pickup recklessly fish-tailed around and roared down the lane in a blur of dust.

Stoney and Pecos returned to the house just as the sun was bathing his sandhills with the last bit of light. Both were famished and dragging as they stepped up on the back deck. He was hoping Betsy's car would be parked in the garage when he pulled up. Instead of the smell of cooking that he was wishing for, the ringing of a telephone greeted him in the darkening house.

It was Betsy.

"Hi, what are you doing?"

"Just walked in."

"How are your calves?"

Everything used to be ours, we, or us... now it's mine or yours, Stoney thought to himself. "Not good," he replied.

"Oh, I am sorry. I'll bet they will be all right. I am working late again so will stay with the kids again tonight. Hope you don't mind."

"Naw, go ahead."

"Well, I'll see you tomorrow. You go ahead and fix yourself a good supper and get to bed early, you sound tired. Love you." Click.

Stoney fixed himself a drink and sat down in his favorite chair without turning on the television. He lit a Salem and took a drink. “I remember when I never worked calves without her right beside me, making as good a hand as I could find and loving every minute it”, he thought to himself.

He stubbed the cigarette out and quickly fell asleep in the chair.

Stoney was back to the pens before light. Two hours after daybreak found him dragging three more dead calves behind the pickup and into the thickets. The thickets were in a corner of the ranch. It was seldom used by the cows because of its lack of grazing, it also had one large barren sandhill that was slowly, steadily creeping east away from the prevailing west wind. The area other than the sandhill was heavily populated by salt cedars, that thrived on the abundance of water that lay just below the surface. Large cottonwoods and locust trees also enjoyed the shallow water and in the middle of all this were the remnants of an old three room house, an outhouse, a windmill tower lacking its fan, and what remained of an old barn and corrals. All this was evidence of a misguided homesteader that settled in the Blackwater Draw and tried to turn the sandy soil, with its lush grasses, into something that it was never intended to be,... a dryland farm. He might have coaxed two or three pitiful crops out of it before the drought of the thirties, galloping on the back of fierce winds blew throughout the region. It turned his hundred and sixty acre homestead and dreams into blow-outs and sand dunes... forever to remain unproductive.

The coyotes, foxes and other, what some called varmints, loved the secluded wild area and Stoney knew that the carcasses would disappear within a couple days. While unchaining the carcasses he noticed Pecos, standing in the bed of the pickup, and staring intently toward the old corrals. Stoney looked in that direction and saw a large coyote watching them. When the coyote saw that he was looking at it,... it started walking off without taking its eyes off Stoney and Pecos. The coyote was limping on her left front foot.

"Well I'll be a son-of-a-buck. Pecos, that has to be the same coyote you doctored."

He looked at Pecos, his tail making long sweeps from side to side, was still watching the coyote.

On his way back to the pens and going by the house he was surprised to see Betsy's Cadillac parked in the open garage. His heart felt lighter as he turned in,... thinking she had come home to have lunch with him. Pulling his pickup beside her car he hurried into the house. He could hear her in the bedroom and startled her.

"Hi sweetie, what are you doing home in the middle of the day?"

His raised sprits fell as he glanced to the bed and saw an open suitcase. She had some clothes in her arms, dropping them as he spoke..

"Oh, you surprised me. I thought you would be over at the pens with your calves."

"There goes 'yours' again", he thought.

"I am sorry. You going on a trip or something?"

"No, not really." She forced a small laugh. "I just came out to get some things. I have a really hectic two or three days ahead of me so I'll just stay in town with Mickie."

Stoney didn't say anything as he watched her close the suitcase.

"You have time for lunch?" he asked.

"No, really I don't, but thanks." She looked up and into Stoney' saddened eyes. "I am sorry hon. I promise, I'll be back Friday night and we'll have the weekend together." Stoney nodded his head and picked up the suitcase.

"Go ahead and put it in the trunk, I have to show some houses as soon as I get back and the whole family wants to go. I'll need all the room I can get."

Pecos was waiting by her car sitting on his haunches with his long tail stirring up a small dust storm. She patted him on the head and told him to take care of his master. She got into the car and lowered her window.

"Stoney… I have something to tell you. Yesterday I had a Chamber of Commerce luncheon. I was late and the only empty seats were at a table where Alex Maynard and Bud Thurman were sitting… so we had to take it."

"Who is we?"

"Phillip and I."

Stoney immediately became short of breath and felt himself getting sick and turning red.

Betsy sensed his distress.

"Now wait just a minute. They were real nice; it was Dutch treat and they picked up my ticket."

"I damn sure hope they could afford it."

"Stoney! Damn it, just settle down. I can't understand you anymore. I told you they were really nice."

"And so?"

"Did you have some words with some of the Taylor Farm people?"

He just stared at her. His heart began pounding and he wondered if she could hear it.

"Anyway they were talking to Phillip about Taylor Farms moving a bunch of people in here and building several more dairies. They really think a lot of Phillip and they hinted that they might swing all of Taylor's real estate needs over to us. It could be a really good deal for both of us."

"You mean Phillip and you."

"Oh Stoney! Don't be that way"

He could tell she was losing patience with him.

"Anyhow, Bud said something about you and some of Taylor's men having some sort of an argument, or something, and about you not being very nice to one of them."

Stoney turned his head and looked down toward the thicket.

Betsy looked up and saw that he was not going to reply.

"After we left, Phillip wanted to know what it was all about and said he hoped you didn't screw things up for us. So honey,... please try to control yourself. One of the reasons I married you was because of your temperament."

"You tell the son-of-a-bitch to kiss my ass."

He turned and whistled for Pecos to follow and started toward his pickup. Betsy put her car in reverse and turning it around started out of the driveway. Stoney barely heard her say "I love you Stoney", as she raised the window and sped away.

CHAPTER 11

In a three week period he had received 730 head of the light calves. His message to the truck drivers and buyers of the Taylor outfit must have been delivered. The rest of the calves arrived in better condition, but the damage had been done.

Normal death loss for shipped in calves runs two to four percent. Stoney, with the help of Travis had been able to keep the death loss to under four percent on the balance of the loads. But the first truck load had been a disaster in spite of all could do. Of the 156 unloaded only 80 were alive after thirty days. A dozen more would be lucky to make it through the five months grazing period. That made a thirteen percent death loss. The calves had cost $330 apiece so he had already lost $30,000 and the grazing season had just started.

The rains continued, not enough to make the grass washy, but enough to keep it nutritious and growing. The healthy calves were doing great. Stoney was horseback every day roping and doctoring the sick ones and riding down two or three horses a day in the process. When it came time to ride fence he used the two year olds; taking them on long lopes to build their strides, and teaching them what hobbles are for when he stopped to repair fence.

Pecos was his constant companion and turning into a seasoned cow dog. He had lived through the usual calamities that befall all ranch dogs: being kicked by horses and cattle, falling out of the pickup, a run in with a temperamental porcupine, and the painful removal of quills, learning that when a skunk stands up on his front legs and turns his back to you, it's time to look for other sources of entertainment. It wasn't until after he was bitten on the nose by a rattlesnake and laid under the deck for a week without eating, that he learned that it was not necessary to stick his nose into everything that looked as if it needed investigating.

They seldom went to town during this time. When they did, Pecos enjoyed the ride. After falling out of the bed a time or two he had figured out that; he should not lean out too far and should watch his balance. From that time on, riding in the back was more fun than in the cab. He could bark at other dogs and be out of reach of Stoney's hand. What really excited him was another pickup with a dog in the back. That would start a barking contest.

After many miles following Stoney a horseback across the sandhills, Pecos was in superb shape and a natural athlete to boot. One afternoon, in town, they pulled up at a stop-light next to a brand new, shiny pickup with a well groomed city dog in the back. Before the light had changed Pecos had jumped out of his truck, into the bed of the other and had the dog down and cowered beneath him in seconds. Their owners were driving off before they were aware of what was happening and were astonished as Pecos made a flying leap from the stranger's pickup back into his own. Neither dog was barking as they drove side by side down the street. One dog was embarrassed by being put down by an unkempt, musky smelling, country dog in an old, dirty, battered pickup. The strange looking dog was standing proud and innocent in a bed full of old ropes, barb wire, posts, baling wire and other miscellaneous items necessary for ranch life.

It was mid-summer by then and their marriage seemed to be in a sort of hiatus. Betsy's business was doing well and she stayed busy. Stoney had by now grown used to her staying in town two or three nights out of the week. She did make it a point to be home most of the weekends. It helped that Mickie, her husband, Scotty, and Bobbi would spend Saturdays with them at the ranch. Stoney would usually take Bobbi in the pickup with him while the other three would have a nice horseback ride around the ranch that they all loved.

During these summer months, after the calves were straightened out and doing well, Stoney was enjoying what he loved most: checking the cattle, working with his young horses, fixing windmills and doing just general ranch work. They had started going to church again. Betsy would drive into Clovis to attend services with their family while Stoney, not wanting to be gone from the ranch that long, preferred a small country church a few miles south of their ranch. The congregation was made up of farm and ranch people and he knew everyone there.

One of the members that Stoney especially liked was Sadler Yates. Sadler was twenty years younger than Stoney and had inherited a small place a few miles south of Stoney. The ranch was not large enough to be an economical unit and Sadler day-worked for other ranchers, and hauled hay to make ends meet. A few years back when he was trying to buy a truck Stoney had taken him into his bank, and introduced him to Joe. Joe had taken a liking to the tall young cowboy, loaned him the money and Sadler had been a customer of the bank ever since. Stoney had helped Sadler in other ways; by buying hay from him and introducing him to other horse people and potential customers.

He had two small children, a girl six and a three year old boy who he named Bill, after Stoney. Sadler taught Sunday School, did not drink and was honest to a fault. He and some of the neighbors including Stoney had built a small arena at Sadler's ranch. Together they purchased some Mexican steers and on Sunday afternoon would practice their roping and train their young horses.

One Sunday late in July Stoney had attended church and noticed that Sadler seemed preoccupied. After the services Sadler asked Stoney if he was coming over that afternoon. Stoney acknowledged that he was and asked him if something was the matter. He answered with a nod and said he would talk to him later. After church Stoney fixed himself a quick lunch, gathered two young horses and decided he would ride over to Sadler's in order to warm up the young horses before their roping lessons. With Pecos lagging behind he cut through his south pasture and the thickets, crossed the backside of a neighbors ranch, and rode across a freshly broken out corporate farm and onto Sadler's place. He covered the five miles in just over an hour. Pecos sauntered in almost an hour later, went straight to a drinking tub and then to the shade of large cottonwood where he stayed until Stoney was ready to go home.

One of the other ropers told Stoney that Sadler wasn't feeling well and wouldn't be playing with them that afternoon. Later the cowboys called it a day. Stoney told them he would take care of the roping stock, feed and water them. As the last trailer left Sadler walked outside.

"Thanks Bill." Out of respect he never used his nickname and in fact Stoney had to remind him to drop the Mister Stone and simply call him Bill if he was uncomfortable with Stoney.

"What's the matter Sadler?"

"I got problems, lots of 'em and big problems."

Stoney tied his horses up.

"Us go over here in the shade." Stoney said motioning to the large cottonwood where Pecos lay watching them, his long tail wagging back and forth.

Sadler squatted down and Stoney sat leaning back against the trunk. He could not help thinking how he used to be able to eat his lunch squatting down and never lose his balance. But the knees had begun to feel their age, especially after too many times thrown from his young horses.

"Let's hear it." He said rubbing Pecos's neck.

"You know I bought another hay truck."

"Yeah, I noticed it when I rode in. Nice lookin' rig."

"Well, I haven't got the other one paid for yet. Almost, but not totally."

"Maybe not too smart. Who did you borrow it from."

Merchant and Ranchers."

"Bud?"

"Yeah"

"Oh shit."

"Yeah, I know."

"What's he charging you?"

"20%"

"A damn bandit."

"I know, but everything looked good then."

"Well...., you'll make it, you're a good, hardworking operator. Don't sweat it so much."

"Stoney."

This surprised him since he never called him that before.

"Little Bill is sick."

"What do you mean he's sick"

"He has an inverted sternum. Have you noticed that his chest is kinda sunken in? Anyhow it's affecting his lungs and heart. It's real bad, and unless we get it fixed he's not going to live very long."

Stoney stopped stroking Pecos.

"What'a you mean, not gonna live very long?"

"It's real serious Stoney. And it's going to take an operation in Dallas or some other big town."

"Well then get it done."

"Stoney! It's going' to cost a lot of money and I just ain't got it."

"Like how much are we talkin' about?

"Thirty, maybe forty thousand."

"Son-of-a-buck. Lotsa' money but we'll get it. So what do you want me to do?"

"Will you go with me to talk to Bud?"

"Well sure, but he and I aren't on the best terms. But if you think it will help, I'd be glad to."

They agreed to meet that morning at the sale barn restaurant and plan on how they were going to approach the banker before going into his office.

Stoney mounted his horse, gathered up the lead rope of the other, he whistled for Pecos and headed home in a stiff trot. After they crossed the plowed land and back into grass-land he pulled his horses to a stop. Looking at the tracks that they had made previously he noticed a second set of canine tracks. They were much narrower than Pecos's big wide foot and he had no trouble figuring out they were coyote tracks. Following the tracks at a walk he could see that sometime Pecos was stepping in hers and other times she was stepping in his.

"Pecos, look's like to me you had some company. No wonder you were late getting there. Don't suppose it could be the little lady we set free could it?"

Stoney nudged his horse back to a trot, keeping it up until they were into the thickets. He pulled up to a walk again so he could watch the tracks. He saw that they both had gone off the trail. After leaving the thickets, Pecos's tracks resumed without his companion.

When he crossed the county road in front of their house he saw Betsy's car returning from town. He hurried to the pens anxious to visit with her and tell her about Sadler and little Bill.

The next morning Stoney and Sadler met at the sale barn. Sitting down at a table they tried to figure out the best way to approach Bud. It was hard to do because other cowboys kept dropping by the table to visit. Finally giving up, and without a plan, they drove to the bank.

They took a seat next to Doris's desk for their usual thirty minute waiting period. They watched Bud in his glassed in office. He had no one in the office and was trying to look busy, shuffling papers back and forth and talking on the phone. Doris looked at them and shook her head in disgust. Eventually he looked up and motioned for them to come in. Bud neither rose nor offered his hand as they entered.

"Okay, what do you want?" he inquired arrogantly and dispassionately.

Sadler explained the situation to him and how much he needed. Bud's face was expressionless.

"How my steers doing Stone?"

It went all over Stoney, not only calling the calves his, but treating Sadler that way. His hands were shaking and he was trying his best to control his temper.

"Bud, you have to help us out here. I'll co-sign the note."

"You....co-sign? Talk about the blind leading the blind. You want that to go against your credit line or what's left of your credit line? I'll tell you what I will do. How big is your ranch Sadler?"

"I got about two and half sections of deeded land and a half section of state land."

"Ok, that's 1600 acres deeded and 320 leased. I'll take a mortgage on the deeded and an assignment on the state lease and loan you the money at 19.3/4 percent."

"Bud! That land is worth a bunch more than that and you know it," Stoney said half rising out of his chair.

"Stone you better stay out of this."

Sadler hung his head and thought a minute.

"My folks left that place to me free and clear I hate like everything to place a mortgage on it. But I need the money right now. We're leaving Wednesday for Dallas to check into Baylor Hospital Thursday morning."

Bud reached behind him to a credenza and pulled out a blank note and mortgage.

"Just sign here Sadler," motioning to a line at the bottom of each.

"I know you got a lot to do, getting ready and all. I'll just fill these out later and you can start writing checks on your account right now."

Stoney could not believe what was happening and could almost see the gleam in Bud's eye.

Furious, he stood shaking his head and walked out as Sadler was signing the papers.

"That son-of-a-bitch," he muttered as he passed Doris. She looked up and shook her head in agreement.

Stoney was leaning against the bed of his pickup playing with Pecos when Sadler came out of the bank.

"Sadler."

"I know, I know, I know Stoney, but I just had to do it. I just had to."

"Ok...Enough said. Do you want me to feed for you?"

"Thanks, but I hired Carl Beavers to drive the old truck for me and he'll take care of my stock."

Stoney just nodded his head. He knew Carl and had even worked him building fence. He wasn't too impressed with him and had caught him drinking while on the job. People in the area hired him for short term work, and only if they were in a jam and couldn't find a more reliable hand.

"Fair enough," Stoney said. "I'll be praying for Little Bill." He paused. "And your whole family too."

"Thanks Bill I am going to need it. See you down the road."

"Bueno," Stoney replied.

It was a too early for lunch but he decided to drop by the office and see what Betsy was doing. Maybe they could meet later for lunch.

After greeting the secretary, who told him Betsy didn't have anyone in the office, he opened the door and went in. Pecos went straight to her and she petted him while talking on the phone. Stoney took a seat across the desk and looked at all her awards, the photos of the two of them, their horses and cows and many photos of Bobbi that covered the walls. Finally hanging up she asked him how they got along at the bank.

"He got the money." Stoney didn't go into the details.

"See, those guys aren't so bad after all," she said. "I have something to tell you but you must promise me not to tell anyone."

"Ok."

"Tommy Kirby called me this morning."

"Really? How's our Congressman?

They had gone to college with Tommy and he had been one of Betsy's suitors. He had been successful in the oil business in southeast New Mexico and six years ago had run for Congress. His first race was close but the last two had proved to be almost a walk in. Stoney had been active in his first campaign and had helped him carry Curry county. He had done it more as a favor for Betsy than any real liking for Tommy. Stoney had then dropped out of civic life and Betsy had become his county campaign manager for the other races.

"He wanted to know if you were still in the cattle business. I told him you had sold your cows and were running yearlings," she paused making sure Stoney was listening.

"Go on."

"He said, bad choice!'"

"So what does he know about the cattle business?" His voice was tightening up and Betsy knew he was becoming resentful.

"Stoney! He's trying to help you. He said that something was coming down in congress that wasn't going to be good for the cattleman. And that you need to sell those yearlings as soon as you can."

"Okay. Tell him thanks for the information." He rose, too upset to ask her about lunch. You coming home tonight?"

"Yes. Don't fix us anything. I'll just stop and get us Pizza. I might stop by and pick up Bobbie too."

Stoney nodded and Pecos followed him out of the office.

It was cattle sale day at the auction barn and he decided to watch the sale, have lunch and visit with some other cattlemen to get their thoughts on the fall markets. Everyone had their own ideas but all agreed that the near future for agriculture looked bleak. Someone said that the price of milk was so low that even the dairies were running in the red. Stoney asked how? And why in the hell were they still building so many in the area? No one had an answer.

After three hours he had had enough of the depressing talk of his peers. On the way home he tried to figure out what to do. If the markets stayed the same in the fall as they were at the present his yearlings would just about break even. Should he sell now and take his lump, as Tommy recommended, or wait till fall? They would be heavier and the market could come back. But Tommy, no matter what he thought of him, had always been honest and above board with them, and he just might be right about this.

At a break even scenario, it would mean a summer of good grass wasted and in the same plight as he was a year ago, except no cows and no calf crop for the following year. Things did not look good, in fact they looked down right bad, he thought.

He went straight to the pens and saddling a two year old, leading another, and with Pecos taking his usual position behind them, he struck a high lope across his place. This had always made him feel better when he was depressed.

CHAPTER 12

Four days later, Sadler called and told him little Bill had had a tough post-operative time but was doing a little better. His family had to stay in Dallas longer than they expected but he was coming home in a couple days. The operation cost him more than he had planned for and the expense of keeping his family in Dallas that much longer had really got him in a hole. He said he had not been able to get a hold of Carl and was worried about his trucks. He would be catching the bus home as soon as he got his family situated.

Stoney was staying busy with his two year olds. For the last couple of years he had sold them to a horse trader out of California. He was using a Hancock, Easy Jet cross for a stud which gave his colts speed and toughness. The was just what the calf, jerk down, and team ropers were looking for. The trader was coming back to Clovis for the fall horse sale and Stoney had promised him he give him first chance to buy them. Stoney wanted them in the best possible shape and was hoping the market on horses would hold through the fall.

He was getting low on good horse hay and had tried to call Sadler several times after he heard he was home, but could not get an answer. He decided to take a couple of the young horses and lope over to the Yates place and see if could catch him. When he stopped to open a gate to cross the plowed field he became aware that Pecos was no longer following him.

"That son-of-a-gun. I bet he stopped by the thickets to visit a spell with Miss Gimpy," he said to the young horses who were watching him intently. He tried to imprint all of his colts within a few hours of their birth and talked to them all the time. Just the sound of his voice was reassuring and soothing to them.

No one was around the Yates place when he arrived. Tying the horses to a hitching rail he loosened their cinches to let them blow, then sat in the shade of the cottonwood tree. He was hoping that maybe someone might drive in. After a half-hour wait he started cinching up his horses when he saw a cloud of dust coming down the lane to the house. When it drew close he could see that it was Sadler in his old truck.

"Where's your new truck?" he asked as Sadler climbed down from the cab and slammed the door. Stoney had no trouble telling that he was mad; he had never seen him that way before.

"It's wrecked."

"Wrecked! How?"

"That damn Carl got drunk down by Las Cruces and totaled it. I told the son-of-a-bitch not to drive it, take the old one. I'm damn lucky no one was hurt but if he ever gets out of jail I'll be tempted to kill him."

"Well...You got insurance on it."

"Hell no."

"Bud told me he would take care of the insurance. I got proof of liability but never got nothing on the comprehensive. I called him and he said I misunderstood him that I was supposed to get the comp insurance. I been paying for it, but never got it."

"The lying son-of-a-bitch," Stoney said.

"Yeah, and there ain't a damn thing I can do about it. I went in to see him and he was in some kind of conference so I asked Doris to find that note and contract. She looked in the file where it was supposed to be and finally found it beside his typewriter. Sure enough at the bottom it said I was supposed to put the comprehensive on it. Bill I swear it wasn't on there when I signed it."

"You still got your copy. Don't you?"

He looked down at the ground. "I was so excited about getting the loan I just walked out without even asking for it."

"She showed me something else. You know when we were in there and he just told me to sign a bunch of papers and he would fill them out later."

"Oh shit."

"Yeah..., all my notes were combined into one and down at the bottom it said, 'due on demand'."

"Bill, I'm screwed. There's not a way in the world I can pay out of this without that new truck. I couldn't haul enough in this old rig if I drove it all day and all night."

"Sadler...I'm sorry, I don't know what to tell you."

"I know Bill. I didn't want to bother you with all my troubles. I know you're having it tough too. I'll think of something."

"If you need some hay I got about 20 bales left on the truck. But I need to make another run to Artesia and get a load. Can I just unload them here and you pick 'em? We'll settle up later."

Stoney agreed and started back to his place. When he got to the thickets there sat Pecos in the shade of some locust trees. He looked about half embarrassed as Stoney pulled his horses to a stop.

"Pecos....You been up to something."

Pecos stood, yawned, stretched and looked up at him, his tail wagging. Stoney had heard that a male dog would occasionally cross with a female coyote. He wondered if this might be one of those rare instances.

"Us go home and load some hay," he said as he nudged the young horses into a lope.

Stoney didn't hear from Sadler for three weeks. The Sunday roping's were called off and he never showed up at church. He heard some things, things he didn't really like. Someone told him that Sadler was working day and night but seemed to be on a perpetual high. He also heard that the bank had called his notes in and given him thirty days to come up with the money.

The sale barn in Clovis had cattle sales on Wednesday and Friday, and Stoney would come into town on those days and try to catch Betsy for lunch. For the last couple of months he had been unsuccessful. He would then go to the sale, and try to get some glimmer of hope for the approaching fall. After the sale he would go to the City Limits bar to pick up on the gossip. There was talk of a dairy buyout but most thought it was just a rumor. The dairy people had overproduced, and milk prices were dropping every day. Their lobby, one of the strongest in the nation, was asking the government to bail them out by buying up thousands of milk cows at an inflated price and dumping them on an already depressed beef market. The beef producer was one of the few agriculture businesses that were not subsidized by the government, and they were no match for the dairymen in Washington.

Stoney finally figured out that this was what Tommy was talking about with his warning to Betsy. He couldn't figure it out. "If the milk boys were in trouble, how come the powers in Washington were letting them build so many new dairies, letting them break out new land then helping them level it, putting sprinklers on it and calling it conservation," he thought.

A new squadron was being formed at the Air Base and many more military personnel were moving in. The real estate business was booming and Betsy was spending more nights in town and most of the weekends. Stoney was drinking more…, if not out at the City Limits then at home, by himself. One Saturday morning he got a call from Sadler. It was three hours before daylight and not a good time to get a phone call. It frightened him thinking something might have happened to Betsy, who was spending the night with the kids.

Sadler apologized for calling at that hour. Stoney could hardly recognize his voice. He was talking fast, like he was excited.

"Bill, I got a load of hay I'm gonna drop off at your place. I'll be there in an about an hour."

"Sadler, what are you talking about. I can't take a full load. I'm almost out of operating money and still have some hay left."

"You can pay me later."

"I don't want to do that."

"Okay but can I put it in your stack lot? "I gotta go back for another load as quick as I can get it unloaded."

Stoney reluctantly said okay then was surprised when Sadler told him he was coming in from the back way and hung up before telling him why.

There were two large ranches west of Stoney's. The farthest one was adjacent to a Farm to Market Highway and was used almost exclusively for agriculture related businesses. A locked gate off of the highway opened onto a ranch road that wound its way through the sandhills and the two ranches, each with their own locked gates before ending at the county road that ran through Stoney's. He, the other two ranchers, and some trusted feed deliverymen including Sadler were the only ones that had keys.

Stoney had stayed too long at the City Limits the night before, but he got up and made a pot of coffee. He wasn't much of a coffee drinker but figured Sadler was going to need some. He kept trying to figure out what was going on. Why was he coming in the back way?" It was much longer, with the real possibility of getting stuck in the sand. The neighboring ranches did a fair job of maintaining the road but it had been a while since Stoney had used it and didn't know what kind of shape it was in. "Why didn't he just take it to his place? What was he doing out at this time of night?"

"I got a lotta' questions for that boy," he said as he pulled on his boots and talking to Pecos, who had started sleeping in the house when Betsy wasn't home.

He drove to the pens, gave the horses some early morning grain then climbed up on the corral fence to wait for Sadler. The pens were bathed in the soft glow of the security light. Kenneth, his old, retired saddle horse finished his grain, walked over to where Stoney was sitting and stuck his head over the fence. Kenneth was born on the ranch when it was just over a thousand acres, and had never spent a night off of it throughout his 21 years. Stoney put his arm over Kenneth's neck and began to rub him. Leo, finished his oats, walked over and put his head next to Stoney on the other side. Pecos was laying just on the outside of the corral fast asleep.

"You guys," Stoney said, playing with each of their forelocks. "You all and that crazy looking dog down there are my best pals. Somehow, someway we are going' get through this storm…I hope."

He looked to the west and could barely make out headlights headed his way. It was just a brief sighting, gone and then coming into view again before it went behind another sandhill. It took another half hour before it stopped at the last gate. The eastern sky was beginning to lighten up when the truck started moving again on the county road.

Stoney directed Sadler to where he wanted the hay stacked. Neither spoke as they unloaded the large double-axle truck. Sadler was agitated and Stoney didn't figure it was the time to start asking questions. It took a little over an hour to unload 240 bales and stack them the way Sadler wanted them. After the last bale was put in place, Stoney told him to leave his truck there, get in the pickup, and they would go to the house and some steak and eggs. Sadler objected but Stoney insisted, telling him Betsy wasn't there and he needed some company for breakfast.

Stoney had breakfast started when Sadler came out of the bathroom. He handed him a mug of coffee motioned him to sit at the kitchen bar, then brought him an ash tray. Sadler took a long drag off a cigarette. He looked bad and hadn't shaved for several days. He was shaking so bad it took both his hands to hold his mug.

"That's not the kind of hay you been getting. Where did it come from?"

"Fabens, down below El Paso."

"Yeah, I know where Fabens is. I went to some roping's there when I was in college at Cruces. It's right across the river from Mexico."

Sadler nodded.

"Did you steal this hay? Look at me Sadler! Tell me the truth, Sadler."

"No! I swear Bill, I didn't steal it. It cost me over five hundred. Really, I'm not lying to you."

Stoney passed him his plate of steak and eggs. Not another word was said as he wolfed it down. Stoney could tell he hadn't eaten for some time and cut off half of his own steak and shuffled it onto Sadler's plate. Sadler looked at him and nodded.

When they were through eating, Sadler lit another cigarette and finished his second cup of coffee.

"Bill, I can't tell you how good that was and how much I appreciate it. There will be a truck in next week from Kansas to pick up that hay. They'll call you; I gave them your number."

"Kansas! That's' an awful long way to haul hay." He got no response from Sadler. He asked him about Little Bill and was told he was getting along great and his family would be home in a week.

They drove back to the pens and before he could get out of the cab Stoney wanted the answers to two more questions.

"Why did you come the back way?"

Sadler looked out his window and Stoney knew he was searching for an answer.

"I had to drop a few bales off at the Rocking K Ranch."

"Sadler! Remember, I helped you unload that truck. You couldn't have more put one more bale on it."

Sadler sat looking out the window.

"Why didn't you take it over to your place?"

He looked back at Stoney. There was a tear coming down his cheek.

"Bill, thanks. Thanks for everything," he paused. "If something should happen to me would you kinda watch out for Brandi and my kids."

Before Stoney could respond Sadler was out of the pickup and gone. He wasn't surprised when the truck turned back west on reaching the county road; back through three locked gates and a rough ranch road.

Stoney never saw Sadler again.

CHAPTER 13

The next Wednesday Stoney was having lunch with Travis and a couple cattle buyers at the sale barn when one of the cowboys he roped with pulled up a chair.

"Did you hear about Sadler," he asked.

"What do you mean? What about him?"

"He's been running dope I guess. Been hauling it in his hay. Anyway, I guess they got wind he was coming through with some of it and they set a roadblock up this side of Oro Grande, between El Paso and Alamogordo. He ran the road block and they shot out his tires and he run off the road, turned the truck over. It threw him out and rolled on top him. Killed him. They said he must have been doing eighty."

"Hell, I didn't know that old truck could run over fifty," one of the cattle buyers setting at the table remarked.

Stoney was visibly shaken and the others could see it.

"Where did you hear all that crap?" he demanded.

"My wife just called me. She's training to be a dispatcher over at the sheriff's office and they got word on it. Wanted the sheriff to take some deputies out to the Yates place and look for a load he was supposed to have brought in last week."

Stoney shoved his plate aside, threw down a ten dollar bill and left for Sadler's home. Hoping he could get to Brandi before the sheriff could.

Saddlers yard was full of cars and pickups. Stoney had been stopped by one of the deputies as he turned off the highway and only after the deputy radioed the sheriff was he allowed to proceed down the dirt road to the Yates headquarters.

Randy Roberts was the sheriff and a good friend of Stoney's. They had been high school classmates and had traveled to amateur rodeos together. Stoney roped and rode bareback while Randy was a rough string rider, competing on bulls, saddle broncs and barebacks. Both had given it up at the insistence of their brides. They always enjoyed getting together and reminiscing about those fun days and the adventures they were involved in.

There were four units from the sheriff's office, that many state police cars, and more non-descript looking sedans with federal license plates. Some pickups were parked closer to the house. Stoney went to the house tapped lightly on the door and was ushered in by the preachers wife. She told him that someone had taken the kids into town to entertain them and that they had put Brandi under sedation and she was laying down. They had sent for her folks from Oklahoma and expected them in three of four hours. Seeing there was nothing he could do for her he went outside.

There was much activity. Sheriff deputies and federal plain clothes officers were searching the whole area: barns, corrals, chicken shed and all the outbuildings. There was a group of them tearing apart the thirty or forty bales of hay that were left in Sadler's stack lot.

Stoney saw Randy talking to an official looking younger man wearing a shoulder holster and had his shirt sleeves rolled up. Randy saw Stoney walking toward him and motioned for him to wait. Stoney walked over to the shade of the cottonwood tree where he, Sadler, and the rest of their buddies held lots of bull sessions, and enjoyed home-made ice cream, while their horses and stock rested up from their Sunday roping's.

He watched as Randy and the man talked. He was surprised when the stranger shook his finger at Randy and Stoney thought to himself that was not a smart thing to do. He had seen Randy take men to the ground for less than that. Their voices were raised and Stoney had no trouble telling they were in an argument. Randy turned away, saw Stoney sitting by the tree and joined him.

Randy set down beside him, took his hat off, revealing his receding, gray hair, and wiped his brow with the back of his sleeve before replacing it.

"I think I'm getting too old for this stuff," he said while pulling out a package of cigarettes and offering one to Stoney.

Stoney turned it down and told him if he would quit those damn things and quit trying to fill that thing, pointing to Randy's ample girth, he might last another ten years on the job. He then asked him what they were looking for and, even though he had a good hunch, why they were ruining those good bales.

"Powdered cocaine bricks."

"Oh shit!"

"Yeah."

"Let me tell you something Stoney. You remember that kid that used to rodeo the same time we were? Lived up north of Clovis..., think he went to high school at Wheatland. Donald Clark, his family were big farmers up there."

"Yeah I remember him he was a little older than we were. Must be close to sixty by now."

"Would have been. I had to go up there yesterday. Suicide. I understand the banks were putting a lot of pressure on him and he was about to lose his place."

"Damn," Stoney replied, looking down and shaking his head.

"While I was that close, I drove on over to Dallam County. Buck Young is the sheriff over there and we get together and compare notes ever so often. Anyhow, we got to talking about how tough things are for you guys trying to make a living in agriculture.

He told me he had two farmers over there that couldn't face the facts, got to drinking and lost their places. Both of them were good size operators and instead of downsizing or whatever, they just couldn't be realistic. Just ignored what was happening till there was nothing left."

"After we compared notes we figured there are four different ways that you guys are taking this. One, go out like Donald Clark did. Two, hit the hoot owl trail and doing something illegal like peddling drugs..., like

Sadler did. Buck had to arrest one of his old friends the other day for taking that route. Three, go to drinking, thinking things will be better *manana*. Or face facts, that it's just another bridge to cross, do what you have to do and get on with your life. Don't just keep fighting a losing battle."

"Are you trying to tell me something Randy?"

He put his hand on Stoney's shoulder. "I know you're having a tough time Stoney, and I hear things. You're beginning to kinda hit that bottle pretty regular too, aren't you?"

"Well....probably more than I should I guess, but I'll watch it Randy, really I will. I'm ok."

Stoney was anxious to change the subject. "How's the election coming?"

"I guess we will know in about six weeks. I'd like to get four more years in before I retire, but that young guy I'm running against says I'm getting too old and don't know how to fight all these drugs comin' in. Say's I don't work with the narc's like I should be. Maybe he's right. I sure couldn't get along with that one, "he said, pointing to the one he had been arguing with. "Anyhow, it's gonna be the closest race I ever been in. Not enough of the old timers left."

One of the deputies was motioning him over to the pens. "Stoney you take care and remember what I been tellin' you."

"Bueno," Stoney replied and they shook hands.

On his way back to the pickup he saw Randy's chief deputy getting himself a drink at the windmill. He walked over to him and asked him if he had a minute. The deputy knew him and knew he was Randy's good friend. Stoney asked how much drugs Sadler was hauling.

"Plenty, he had about thirty kilos hidden in that hay. Didn't take but ten or twelve bales to hide it and he had it stacked in the middle of the whole load. Pretty slick."

"How much would that be worth?"

"Close to half a million. But that ain't all. Packed inside each of those cocaine bricks, they had packed about a quarter kilo of herion. They don't know if Sadler knew that. They get a lot more for hauling heroin than they do cocaine. That whole load was worth about three quarters of a million dollars. Sure beats hauling hay, don't it?"

Stoney agreed and asked him if they thought there must be more hidden around here.

"Yeah, the narc's informant told them that Sadler had hauled another load a few days ago. Said it was over twice as much as he got caught with."

Stoney thanked him and walked off shaking his head.

Pecos had jumped out of the bed of the pickup and crawled under it to be in the shade.

Stoney opened the door and made him ride in the cab. They headed to the City Limits.

CHAPTER 14

Stoney had lots to think about. For the last two months, and since he and Betsy were spending less and less time together he had got in the habit of discussing his problems with Pecos. Although a good listener, he seldom commented, with the exception of a yawn or two.

"Now don't that beat all Pecos? Here we are about to lose our place, I have just enough money in my pocket to buy a couple rounds of drinks, and there's almost two million dollars setting out in our stack lot. Enough to get us completely out of debt and buy a place twice as big as ours…, and stock it too."

He was silent the rest of the way into town. First thinking about Sadlers family and how tough it was going to be then…, fantasizing about setting up a scholarship for the Yates children…, going into the bank and paying them off, with a few choice words to Bud…, which neighboring ranch he would buy before the corporations break out the entire draw, buying his cows back..., the make and model of his new pickup and the options he was going to have on it and... what kind of gifts he would give to Betsy and his family.

By the time he walked into the bar he had the money spent. He had a good time..., a real good time. By midnight he was feeling no pain, his worries about money over, he had, after borrowing a hundred off of Janie Mims who always seemed to have a fist full of them, bought more than his share of drinks. Stoney's drinking buddies were kidding him about feeling so good and asking if he discovered oil out in the sandhills. He would just grin and order another round. Most of them had left by the time Janie told him she thought he had enough, and he better go home before she put him in her car and took him home with her.

To get from town to his ranch he had to go through the stockyards on the south edge of Clovis, and then across a railroad track. It was not a busy track but a branch that ran off the Santa Fe's main track from Kansas to California. This single track had only one main job: to bring potash from mines near Carlsbad and then, after reaching Clovis, to destinations across the United States. The crossing was on a farm to market road that had minimal traffic, especially late of night or early morning. The waits were long for the many railroad cars to pass..., sometime as long as twenty to forty five minutes. Over the years Stoney had spent many hours waiting for the crossing to clear. With nothing to do but watch the cars slowly roll by, he often wondered what it would be like to catch a ride on one of the cars like the hobos. Most of the cars were hoppers for hauling the potash but occasionally there would be a box car.

This night, one of the trains was just pulling out of Clovis headed south as he approached the track. He turned the motor off and humming to the western music on the radio, he opened a bottle of Coca Cola, emptied out part of it and filled it from a bottle of Jack Daniels he had bought before leaving the bar.

Stepping out of the pickup and leaning against its front hood he watched the cars slowly creep by. He walked down the track a little ways to see how long he was going to have to wait. He couldn't see that far, but could see three regular boxcars approaching him. Now's my chance he thought, I'll just catch one and ride it a little ways, then jump off.

Carefully setting his bottle down, he caught one of the ladders as it came by and climbed up a couple rungs. That was easy enough he thought. Believe I'll just climb up to top of car and see what that's like. He did so and sitting on top of it on a beautiful moonlit night was quite entertaining. He didn't notice that the train, with the cars empty, was picking up speed faster than he had anticipated. All of a sudden he became aware of it and started down the ladder. Half-way down and with the lurching of the train one of his boots slipped off the metal rungs. He barely caught himself and looked down at the railroad ties whizzing by.

"Son-of-a-bitch," he said above the racket. "I done got myself in a mess."

Cautiously he climbed back up to the top of the boxcar. He was beginning to sober up real quick by now. Trying to figure out what a man in his mid-fifties, who sometimes, supposedly, had some sort of semblance of intelligence was doing on top of a boxcar doing some fifty miles an hour rocking along in the sandhills at two in the morning. He came up without an answer.

"Okay," he thought. "This is the deal, I got myself into this and now I got to get out of it. So here is what I'll do. Hopefully this thing will slow down when we go through Portales, I know it won't stop but maybe it will slow down enough that I can jump off without breaking both legs Then I'll call Travis to come pick me up."

Having solved that problem for the time being he got to thinking about his new found fortune. The more he sobered up, the more he disliked what he had been thinking about.

He had a cousin who had a wonderful, beautiful daughter with a future that knew no limits. She had become addicted to drugs while in college. It had cooked her brain and she would probably be forever to be in a sanitarium. He thought of Bobbi. What would he do to some low-life that would talk her into trying, just once, some of that stuff that was fixing to make him rich.

The train was pulling into Portales. He waited until it was right in the middle of town, and probably going as slow as it would ever go. Climbing down to the lowest rung he jumped. A younger and more agile person would have had no trouble keeping his balance as he hit the ground running. Stoney couldn't, and went sliding across the gravel and cinders ripping his shirt half off of him. His hide suffered likewise..., peeling the skin off in several places on his chest, arms, hands and face. But at least he escaped the wheels. His hundred dollar

Stetson wasn't so lucky. One wheel ran directly over it before casting it aside.

He lay there for some time making sure nothing was broken then set up looking around to see if anyone was watching. There was an Allsups Convenience Store nearby, it was almost three in the morning and he startled the clerk when he walked in.

"My gosh! You scared me. You must have been in some kind of fight. You want me to call an ambulance?"

Stoney told him he had a little accident but that he would be alright, he just wanted to use his phone and his bathroom to wash up a little. He had just enough money left to call Travis who, after lots questions, said he would pick him up as soon as he got dressed and could make it down. As soon as he hung up he realized he had forgotten to ask Travis to check on Pecos and his pickup. After he cleaned up, as good as he could, he walked out of the bathroom and asked the clerk if he could have a cup of coffee and would pay him soon as his ride came. The clerk told him to go ahead and get one, and there would be no charge. But in exchange he wanted an answer to one question.

"What in the hell happened to your hat.?"

The mirror that had hung in the bathroom had long since disappeared and he had no way of knowing what it looked like. Taking it off he thought," that could have been my head." The train wheel had run down the middle cutting the crown in half without making so much as a dent in the brim which now held the two halves together. He just shook his head and put it back on. He took the coffee outside and sat on the curb. He thought about what he had just been through and what he was going to do with the treasure sitting in his stack lot. By the time Travis drove up he had made his mind up.

"Damn you look terrible. What happened to your hat? That's the funniest looking thing I ever saw."

Worried about Pecos and his pickup he asked Travis if he had come through the stockyards. When told he had come another way and wanted to know why, Stoney told him the whole story and Travis laughed till tears were coming down his face.

"Just wait till I tell the guys at the sale barn about Bill Stone's midnight train ride." Stoney had to agree that it would be a good story and knew Travis would enjoy telling it. But he just hoped Betsy and his daughter didn't hear about it. A mile from the crossing they could see the bouncing blue and red lights of law enforcement cars.

"Oh shit." Stoney said and slunk down into his seat.

It was Randy's unit and another unit from the sheriff's office. Two of the deputies were walking down the track with their flash lights. One of them had something in his hand.

"Okay Stoney, what the hell goes?" By then Randy was close enough to see how he looked.

"My God! What the hell happened to you? And what in the world happened to your hat?"

"It's a long story Randy."

Travis was leaning against his pickup giggling.

"Yeah, I bet it is, and a good one too. Your cotton-pickin' dog won't let us in your pickup so we can't move it. I called Betsy awhile ago and she's headed this way.

One of the deputies walked up and handed a Coke bottle to Randy, it was half full, he took a smell of it.

"Hmm, Coke and whiskey. I used go down the road with a fella that used to drink his whiskey this way. You know anybody that still does Stoney?"

Travis was bent double by this time.

Betsy's Cadillac pulled up, and she and Mickie came running over.

"What happened?" when she was close enough to see Stoney's condition.

"Stoney! Are you hurt?"

He assured her that he was all right and just kinda skinned up.

"Daddy! What did you do to your hat?" Mickie exclaimed.

Both deputies were there by now and all of them were looking at him waiting for an answer. Even Pecos, who had jumped out of the window when he heard Stoney's voice, was standing beside Betsy, and looking at him as if he too deserved an explanation for being left in the pickup for so long. Travis was driving off saying he had all the fun he could stand for one night.

Stoney looked at all of them. The emergency lights were still flashing, the headlights were on him. He felt like he was on a stage, in front of a crowd and had forgotten his lines.

Randy had explained that one of the deputies had got a call from the dispatcher about a pickup blocking the road at the crossing with no one around but a dog sitting in the cab.

They had called in the license number and, after finding out that it was Stoney's, they had called Randy.

"We are waiting!" Betsy demanded.

With no way out, and not one simple explanation, Stoney told the whole story.

When he was through the deputies walked to their units hardly able to control their laughter. Randy asked him if he was sober enough to drive home. Stoney was adamant in saying he hadn't had a drink in four hours and was dead sober.

Randy left. Mickie begged him to come home with them so they could clean him up and make sure he got a good night's sleep. He said he just couldn't do it, he had too much to do tomorrow. Betsy was silent. When Mickie finally gave up and went to the car. Betsy folded her arms and looked at him.

"Stoney I love you very much but you have just about pushed me too far. One more of your stunts and I am all through."

"Betsy…I."

She held up her hand. "I am telling you. You have changed so much that I am not sure I want to be around you anymore."

She left him standing there. Her window was open and Stoney thought he heard her sob as she slowly pulled away.

He looked down at Pecos who was looking up at him wagging his tail.

"Us go home Pecos, and don't be asking me what happened to my hat."

CHAPTER 15

Stoney doctored himself as best he could, put Band-Aids on places that might bleed. He was exhausted and quickly fell asleep. At ten the next morning Pecos awakened him by placing a large paw on the side of the bed. Rolling over he lay there for another twenty minutes until it was clear in his mind how to resolve his dilemma.

Before he left for the pens he had placed a call to Randy. Apologizing for the night before, he asked him to come out to the ranch. He had something important to go over with him, and to come out in his old pickup and not his official unit. Randy asked him if he could do it tomorrow, but Stoney insisted. Randy told him it would be about two hours but he would be there and meet him over at the pens.

Stoney was too sore to work with his horses so he went to the bunkhouse and heated up some pork and beans. He felt better after getting something in his stomach and laid down on one of the beds thinking about what was fixing to come down.

When Randy drove up Stoney motioned him over to the stack lot where he had pulled up a bale of hay next to Sadler's stack.

"What's going on Stoney, I hope it's important cause I got a lot to do, if I'm going be sheriff again next year."

They sat on the bale of hay.

"You know Randy, I used to be a pretty good politician and I think I still know how to win elections."

"Go on." Randy said acknowledging that what he said was true.

"See that stack of hay. There's something in it that's going to win that election for you."

"Stoney you hadn't been hitting the bottle this morning..., have you?"

"Nope, last night I make up my mind that I'd never get drunk again. Other than a sociable beer, I 'm all through. Randy...there is, I bet, over two million dollars' worth of drugs in that hay."

Randy jumped up. "You better not be kidding me Stoney!"

"That's Sadler's load of hay that you guys and the feds are tearing up the country looking for. I figured Sadler thought they might be watching for him at his place so he calls me the other night and wants to put it here. He came the back way,, and left the back way so I know damn good and well that hay has got the dope in it."

Randy agreed and when Stoney told him there was supposed to be some people from Kansas coming down to pick it up, they started figuring out how best to handle it. If just Randy and his deputies could pull this off by themselves without any help from the feds it would silence the talk about him being too old for the job and unable to handle the drug trade. They spent the next two hours on how to accomplish it, with the least chance of someone getting hurt.

Their final plan was to wait until Stoney received his call. Let them load the hay on their truck or if they tore into the bales and removed the drugs, either way, Randy and his deputies would ambush them after they had turned onto the highway. The tricky part was the ambush.

On the Farm to Market highway to Clovis there was one small draw a couple miles past the Blackwater Draw Site; at the bottom of draw the road crossed a small bridge over a dry creek that might run for a few hours every ten years or so. The crossing was obscured from drivers coming from the south until about 500 yards from the bridge. It was a perfect place for an ambush. There was even a windmill close by that would be perfect for a sharp shooter to lay on the platform and cover the area. While they were at the stack lot, Randy and the deputies would haul in two wrecked cars and place them on the bridge. There would be several sheriffs cars, an ambulance, a wrecker, all with emergency lights going to give the appearance of a major collision. Stoney would be on one of his windmills that was some distance away from his pens, but with his binoculars he could monitor them. He would also have a radio informing Randy of the drug runners progress. The success of the ambush depended on one thing; that the runners would turn north toward Clovis, and not south toward Portales.

To cover that Randy would place a couple deputies on the city limits of Portales where they could call for back-ups from that towns police force. Although it wasn't critical to the ambush it would be better if they had a truck full of hay, then there would be no place for them to turn around.

There was one other thing that Stoney made Randy promise… whatever happened he was not to tell anyone that the hay came from his place and that he had absolutely nothing to do with it. He was to make his deputies swear that it would forever remain a secret.

The following morning Randy received a phone call from Stoney. The outlaws were to arrive the next morning. They would telephone Stoney from Clovis. At that time Stoney would tell them that he was just leaving for the hospital to check on his granddaughter who had an accident. He would give them directions and unlock the gate to the pens.

Things went as planned. At noon the next day he lay atop his windmill platform watching two laborers loading the hay. He radioed Randy and told him the good news about the truck. There were two men loading the truck that looked to be laborers, they didn't appear to be armed. There were also two Mexicans accompanying them in a gray four door sedan. They appeared to be the leaders and were not helping with the loading. They also had shoulder holsters on and walking around with what looked like shotguns.

Two hours later Randy got the call he had been waiting for. The truck was almost loaded and would probably be leaving in a matter of minutes. He immediately set up the ambush; hauling in the two cars, placing the ambulance and tow truck in position. He also set up roadblocks on each end of the highway to keep traffic out of the way.

The next radio call was the one he had been most worried about. A spotter reported that the truck had indeed turned north. The ambush was on.

The gray sedan rolled over the small rise with the truck behind them, with no time to stop or turn around. There was an officer standing in the middle of the highway slowing them down and others that looked as if they were trying to extricate someone from one of the cars. When they stopped the officer walked up to the window.

"It will be a while before we get this mess clear. You'll just have to wait."

The driver nodded his head and the officer walked quickly back to the wreck. It suddenly occurred to them that they could not see any of the deputies or emergency personnel. The officer they had talked to had disappeared behind one of the wrecks. Just as quickly there was a bullhorn blaring at them.

"Out of the car and on the ground with your hands behind your head!"

The two men looked at each other, and the passenger reached for his weapon as the driver attempted to swing the car around. Randy had chosen the site well. The borrow ditches were deep sand and the car, with tires spinning, quickly became stuck while the passenger was firing at the concealed officers who were firing back. The sniper on the windmill quickly placed a bullet in the head of the driver. The passenger opened the door still firing and was immediately riddled with a barrage of bullets.

It was over that quickly. The laborers were cowered on the ground yelling for mercy.

Stoney drove up as they were cleaning the mess up. He just stayed in the pickup, Pecos was standing up in the bed looking around the cab watching the activity. Randy saw him and walked over.

"Well...Looks to me like you've had a busy afternoon."

Randy nodded, "Looks that way don't it. Thanks Stoney."

A car with Clovis News Journal in bright colors drove up on the other side of bridge. It was followed by a van with KOB TV logo plastered all over it.

"Man...they sure got here fast. Wonder how they heard about it so quick," he looked up at Randy.

Randy winked and with a big grin replied, "Guess they just got a nose for action." Stoney you sure you want your name out of this? There's plenty of good press to go around."

"Not on your life, and Randy, you promised me."

"You got it amigo. Guess I better get busy."

"See you down the road, sheriff." He put the pickup in reverse till he could find a solid place to turn around.

CHAPTER 16

The next morning he remembered that he had borrowed a hundred dollars from Janie Tims "Son-of-a-gun," he thought. "I hope I got enough in the bank to pay her back. I don't think it would be a good idea to ask Betsy for it." After he had finished the chores Stoney went back to the house and placed a call to Doris at the bank.

"Hi Stoney, have you heard about your old buddy Randy?"

"What?"

"He made one of the biggest drug raids in the state. It's been all over the news, radio, TV. Everyone is talking about it. They're calling him the Silver Fox, they say the feds are mad as hell cause they weren't in on it."

"Well son-of-a-gun, I am tickled to death for him. Guess I'll have to turn on the radio." He let her finish with the story and then she asked him what he needed.

"Doris, I think I'm overdrawn or close to it. Can you look at my account up and give me the bad news?"

"Be glad to. But unless you have spent ninety eight hundred since yesterday, you're a long way from being overdrawn. Hold the phone, I'll get the overnight and let you know."

She put him on hold before he had a chance to ask what she was talking about. "Ninety eight hundred? There's got to be some mistake," he said to Pecos who was lying beside him while he was sitting in his easy chair.

She was back on the phone in five minutes.

"You have ninety eight hundred and," she laughed and emphasized, "forty cents."

"Doris as much as I like that figure there has to be some mistake. Where do you think the ninety eight hundred come from?"

"I know where it came from. As soon as it came in the girls downstairs sent it up to Bud. He wanted me to put it in escrow under the banks name and I convinced him he couldn't do that. Said he'd figure out a way and laid it on my desk. I deposited it into your account and he is mad as hell at me. Stoney, if you need it, you better get it out of there before he figures out he can freeze your account."

"Well where did it come from Doris?"

"It was from Capitan Precious Metals and drawn on a big bank in Denver and it has, 'for royalties' written on it. Do you know anything about it or them?"

He thought for a minute then it all came back. The Goose Creek Mine!

He told Doris that it was his. An old investment he made years ago might finally pay off. He asked her what was the quickest way to get the money out of the account.

"Just come in and cash out what you want, but don't let Bud see you."

All the loan executives had glassed in offices and they could watch everything that goes on in the lobby and the cashiers windows.

"So how do I do that?" he asked.

"He has a lunch meeting with Phillip, some of the big wheels from Taylor Farms, and..., and your wife."

"Now ain't that something," he commented.

"He's real excited about it, thinks he has arrived in the big leagues. I think that's one reason he forgot to freeze your account. He will be leaving here around 11:30 and said he'd be out about two hours. So if you could be here between 12 and 12:30 it would work.

"I'll be there, and Doris I really appreciate you taking care of me."

He changed clothes and put on his old hat with the crown he had laced together with a string of leather. He looked at himself in the mirror and had to admit that it was the funniest looking hat he had ever seen.

"Pecos," who was standing beside him and admiring himself in the mirror, "old Stoney he got himself some money and we're going to town, buy us a brand new sombrero, then we'll go to the sale barn and split the biggest T-bone they got."

He was feeling better mentally than he had in months and was even whistling when he turned on the radio to catch the noon news. The number one story was all about the sheriff and the biggest drug bust in the state's history. It was determined that the two laborers were from Amarillo and been hired by the drug runners to haul a load of hay to Kansas City. They had no idea that they would be hauling heroin and cocaine. They were released on their own recognizance. The feds were upset because the sheriff would not give them the name of his informant. The sheriff responded, saying he had been cultivating this person for years and would in no way jeopardize his confidence.

Stoney's mood changed after the local news. The national news reported that despite the protest by the beef industry the president signed the controversial Dairy Buyout Bill.

The reporter droned on, "Several Economist believe that it will be an unmitigated disaster for the beef industry. They predict the price of fat cattle and feeders will drop fifteen to thirty dollars a hundred and cost the industry upwards to one billion dollars, breaking many cattle producers and feeders. The cost to the taxpayers will be close to 1.8 billion. Representative Tom Kirby of New Mexico was one of the prime sponsors. He was quoted as saying that…" Stoney turned the radio off.

"Jim Bob," he thought, "if you ever going to come through, now is the time."

Stoney's first stop was the bank. He gave the teller a check for ninety eight hundred and made out to cash. The teller looked up from the check then to his hat.

Stoney smiled, "Pleased don't ask, it's a long story, and as soon as you give me my money I'll go buy a new one."

"I'm sorry Mister Stone but that's a lot of money I'm going to have to get someone to okay it."

She locked her cash draw, left her cage and headed toward Bud's office. Stoney watched as she looked in his office and then went to Doris who looked across the lobby at Stoney, smiled, and gave him a little wave. She took the check, initialed it and handed it back to the teller. The teller returned and Stoney told her one hundred dollar bills would be fine.

After she finished counting the money out she said," Mister Stone that just leaves you .42 cents in your account." He acknowledged that, and threw Doris a kiss as he left the bank.

His first stop was Joe's Boot Shop where he picked out a nice 10 X beaver hat. After much quibbling with Joe they agreed on a price, with the condition that he could hang Stoney's old hat on the wall where he had collection of old, used ones. While he was blocking the hat, in the particular style that characterized Stoney's hat's, he asked him if he had heard the news about Randy.

"That old fart," Joe said. "He's smarter than a fox and his timing was just perfect, everybody will vote for him now. Wonder who his informant was? Most people that come in here are betting its somebody local."

Stoney wasn't responsive, thanked him and left for the stockyards.

He caught Travis as he was finishing his lunch.

"Sit back down Travis, I need to talk to you."

Travis said he would be right back, that he needed to make a phone call.

Stoney ordered his steak. Most of the customers had gone back into the sale.

"Did you find some place to go with my steers?" he asked when Travis returned.

"Sorry Stoney. I been trying to get someone on them for two weeks now and everybody was waiting to see what the president was going to do. Now that he's signed the bill I bet you couldn't get a feedlot to look at a feeder, at least for a week or two. The futures market on fats and feeders fell their limit two minutes after he signed it. It's a damn wreck."

The waitress brought him his T bone but he had lost his appetite. They visited a while longer until Travis said he had to go back into the sale and buy some canner cows for Winton Packing Company.

"Ok," Stoney said, "But keep trying. The cattle are doing good right now, but frost is just around the corner and I need to go with them before then. I sure don't want them to lose their bloom."

Travis nodded, "I know, I'll do my best. You know I will."

"Travis, I need to get a hold of Jim Bob real bad. You know where he is?"

He shook his head. "I got no idea. I haven't seen him since we were out at your place. I guess if he's not a guest in someone's jail he's up in the mountains someplace. Seriously, I wouldn't have any idea how to get a hold of him. Sorry."

Stoney wrapped the almost untouched steak in napkins, paid his bill, and walked out to his pickup. Pecos was laying underneath the pickup.

"Get in the back" he ordered and Pecos jumped in with one fluid motion, just barely touching the top of the tailgate. Stoney threw the steak in after him and they drove to Betsy's office. He was going to tell her about the check but decided he would wait and see how things played out.

As he and Pecos walked across the lobby to Betsy's office, he could hear her laughing with Phillip and another man whose voice sounded familiar. They came into the lobby and all three acted surprised to see Stoney and his dog.

"This is my husband," she started the introductions. "This is Eddie, he is with Taylor Farms."

"I know who he is. The gate setter."

Eddie started to shake hands with Stoney but jerked it back when Pecos bared his teeth and started growling.

"Pecos!" Betsy scolded. "You quit that! What is the matter with you? You've never acted like that before? Has he Stoney?"

Stoney shrugged his shoulders. "Aw...just to people that ain't trust-worthy," he said in his best redneck kind of voice. He looked over at Phillip who could not have shown his displeasure more.

"Your lookin' good Phillip."

Stoney went into Betsy's office and in a few moments, Betsy came in and shut the door firmly.

"What is wrong with you Stoney? I just sold him an eighty thousand dollar home. That's four thousand dollars commission for me."

"OK, I'm sorry. But he and the calves he bought are going to lose a lot more than that."

"I have an appointment and I am already late for it. I'll be home tonight and pack some things. I think I forgot to tell you that the Realtors National Convention is in New York and a bunch of us are going. We will drive to Lubbock day after tomorrow and catch the plane."

"Yeah I guess you did. I'll fix us something for supper."

"That would be nice." She gave him a little kiss, picked up her briefcase, and walked out the door.

Since Betsy had been spending most of her time in town, Stoney, being short on cash, was low on groceries. He went by Albertson's and stocked up on everything he thought he might need for at least a couple weeks. He passed by the liquor department, had a second thought, and picked up a quart of Jim Beam and a carton of Salems. That was something he had never done before. Maybe a fifth of whiskey and a couple packs would be the most.

Stoney wanted that night to be something special so he fixed a small pork roast with all the condiments. After they had finished their supper they sat in the glider on the back deck with their after dinner drink. It was like old times when they had sat close together and visited about their dreams for the ranch. This time they were silent, each lost in their own thoughts. Later they made love, the first time in a long time. They cuddled together and Stoney slept better than he had in months.

That morning they walked together to her car and kissed goodbye. She said she would be gone for about a week and would keep in touch. Just before she pulled out of the driveway, she said something to him that completely set him back and spoiled what they had accomplished the night before.

"Stoney I forgot to tell you. Yesterday I had lunch with Bud, Eddie, and some others from Taylor Farms. They were talking about quail season that will be opening soon and how much they enjoyed it. I told them how many birds we had and invited them out anytime to go hunting. Hope that's ok. I'll call you when we get to New York."

With that, she drove off. Stoney was shocked at what she had just told him. She knew how much he cared about his Blue quail. He was so surprised he could not respond.

Stoney and Leo waiting for Travis to bring more cattle out of the Thickets.

CHAPTER 17

Stoney could not believe how fast his small world was changing. As he watched her car receding down the county road he felt as if something had taken the air away from him and his life was draining away into the grass covered sandhills he loved so much. He turned back toward the house and stumbled over Pecos who was lying at his feet. He gave him a kick and yelled at him for getting in the way. Pecos could not believe that Stoney would kick him for just being beside him and ran under the deck. Stoney was as surprised as was Pecos. Surprised at himself for kicking what was now his closest companion and surprised that his first thoughts, after watching Betsy leave, was to get drunk.

He went to the deck and coaxed Pecos out. Stoney sat on the ground and put his arm around him, loving and talking to him. He soon had Pecos wagging that long tail and licking him in the face.

"Come on big buddy. Us go for a little ride." Pecos immediately dashed to the pickup completely clearing the tailgate as he jumped him.

Stoney saddled Leo caught one of his young colts and left the pens in a lope with Pecos happily running behind. The yearling cattle, with the exception of three, were all fat and in great shape, their coats were as slick as show steers. The three would have to be classified as unmerchantable; they were thin and carrying lots of dead hair. Stoney figured he had given them too much antibiotics trying to keep them alive and it had killed the good bugs in their rumen. His head count of the others gave him 635 deliverable yearlings. He estimated their weight to be right at 700 pounds, if he could ship them in the next 10 to 15 days.

Headed back to the pens he marveled at the therapy a ride on a good horse, among fat cattle on a beautiful fall day could do to one's attitude. He unsaddled Leo, cooled him off with a water hose and gave him a good brushing. This was something that they both enjoyed and he gave him an extra helping of oats after turning him into his run.

Feeling somewhat better he drove to the house hoping to catch the market news, which he was sure had to be somewhat better or had at least had stopped its free fall. Just as he turned on the TV the phone rang. It was Doris.

"Stoney, I have been trying to catch you all morning. Bud told me to try every ten minutes till' I got a hold of you. He is hot."

"Oh crap Doris, I'm real sorry for getting you in trouble."

"Forget it, nothing makes my day like seeing the fat turd frustrated. But seriously, you better get in here. Like *muy pronto.*"

"I'll be there in about an hour and thanks Doris…., for everything."

An hour and a half later he was sitting in Bud's office. When Stoney had walked in, Bud told him curtly to shut the door. This surprised Stoney since Bud had never shut the door at any of their conferences.

"You been holding out on me Stone and I am not very pleased about it."

"I don't know what you're talking about…sir," Stoney replied giving added emphasis to the last word.

"You know damn well what I am talking about and don't start playing smart with me. I am talking about the check you got yesterday."

"Oh…, that check."

"Yes, that money you were in such a hurry to get out of your account. If I had a damn secretary worth a flip you would have never gotten that cash. That money belongs to me."

"Uh…, you mean the bank's, don't you?"

Buds face turned red. "Same damn difference, and I want that money back in that account. You owe it to us. You signed a financial statement over to us that listed all your assets and we got a mortgage on them. What kind of royalty was that and what from."

"Well…," Stoney slouched back in his chair, taking his hat off, looking at it admiringly. He turned it around to see if the brim was just right and carefully placed it on the chair next to him with the crown down. He leaned back and locked his hands behind his head. "Well it's a long story." He was enjoying seeing Bud getting more frustrated by the minute.

"I got time. Spit it out," Bud said, his ring drumming rapidly on his desk.

"Well…., first of all when I filled out that statement it wasn't an asset. I guess you bankers would have said it's more of a liability, and that money wasn't really mine. It like, belonged to another fella' and I gave it to him and he's long gone. I just see him once every couple years, but the next time I see him I'll sure tell him you'd like to visit with him." Stoney was getting a real kick talking with a back country accent, and for some reason he couldn't figure out, he was more relaxed in front of Bud than he had ever been.

"What's his name and what's the royalty for: gas, oil, coal or what?" Bud asked, as he took a yellow pad from the corner of his desk and a silver Cross pen from a breast pocket on a shirt that had begun to show perspiration soaking through it.

"Smokey, yeah, that's his name alright, Smokey Bob. Yes sir, Smokey Bob. I never knew him too well. I used to run across him in a few bars across the state when I was pimp'in for the Amarillo Cattle Auction. You would have liked him Bud. Big fella but gentle as a lamb…, when he was sober, and in a good mood. He told me he had a mine up in the north part of the state but didn't have a permanent address or bank account and asked me if he could use mine."

"What was in the mine, Stone?"

"No it wasn't stone, it was. Oh, I am sorry, you were calling my name, weren't you. I thought you meant like a rock or somethin'."

Stoney knew then he was about to push Bud too far and decided he better slack off.

"I think it was gold or maybe silver, Bud. I'm not too sure. Smokey wasn't the kind of fella' you would want to ask too many questions. And that's all I know about it Bud, honest injun'."

"You're trying to be cute aren't you?" Bud replied, "Well let me tell you something cowboy. If you think I am not about to check all this out, you're mistaken little friend. And mister you better be telling me the truth. Now then, what about the steers, when do we get our money?"

Stoney was tired of his little game and became serious.

"I have to sell them first Bud and I'm really trying. You know what the market is. I know you do. I'm not the only one in this trap and you keep up with the markets. It's tough as hell out there. I haven't been able to get anyone out to even look at them."

"When do you need to go with them?" Bud asked.

"I really need to ship them in the next ten days or two weeks."

Bud started clearing his desk, "You can go now. I gotta' conference. I'll send someone over from Chalk Hill. We are financing all of Taylor Farms business, and I happen to know they are in the market."

A very disgruntled Stoney was dismissed.

That afternoon Stoney was working with his colts when a pickup going fast and raising considerable dust turned off the county road and sped down the lane toward the pens.

"That better not be who I think it is," Stoney said to Pecos who was laying in shade watching him curry his young horses.

Sure enough it was Eddie climbing out of the cab. On the other side was Pete Benson.

"Afternoon gentlemen," Stoney said, climbing over the fence, and determined to be civil, and not to lose control of himself.

"Bank sent us out to buy your yearlings," Eddie said. Stoney could tell from his voice that Eddie had his guard up and Stoney was wondering if maybe that was why he brought the big Pete with him.

Pecos was standing beside Stoney. He wasn't growling, just watching with the hair on his back rising every so little. This was unusual for Pecos; he generally was pleased to have company and would greet everyone that would drive in with a little love croon and a wagging tail.

"Ok, us get in my pickup and we'll drive through them..., or I'll saddle some horses and we can ride through them. That way you can get a better look at all of them."

Before Eddie had a chance to answer, Stoney said, "Pete I didn't know you were cattle buyer too."

Pete had a sour look on his face and was watching Pecos. Before he had a chance to answer Eddie said, "He's in charge of our farming operations now, and I wanted to show him how the country lays out this way. And I don't have to see all the cattle. We saw enough driving in, and if you'll remember I'm the one that bought them for you."

That familiar pit in Stoney's stomach returned just as quickly as his demeanor changed. "How in the hell could I ever forget it. I want 58 cents a pound for them, delivered over my scales with a 2% shrink."

"Hadn't you got a radio out here? We ain't got no market," Eddie replied. "I'll give you 53 cents with a 4% shrink and pick 'em up day after tomorrow. Take it or leave it. Just remember, you're not the only one that's got any say about this."

"Did you see that rafter S on the hip of those cattle? That's my brand and that means they're my cattle. Now, if your're through here I got chores to do."

Eddie turned on his heels and motioned Pete to follow. They got in their pickup and spun it around, and rolled down the window. Stoney was walking away and Eddie slapped the side of his pickup to get his attention. Pointing to the forty or fifty quail that were scratching around the horse corrals he said, "Keep feeding those birds. We'll be out when the seasons opens and we want them nice and fat."

They spun out and Stoney could hear them laughing. He looked around for something to throw at them and finding nothing he gave them the finger and yelled, "You son-of-bitches." He could see Pete turning around, laughing at him and throwing the finger back at him. Pecos was following them and barking, something Stoney had never seen him do before.

After he had finished the chores he went back to the house and mixed himself a whiskey and cola. Sitting out on the back deck he lit a cigarette and tried to relax as the sun was going down. This had always had a calming effect on him but not this time. When he finished his drink he went back inside and tried to call Travis. Joann answered and told him he hadn't come in yet and that he said something about Bill Bleiker being in town and they were probably at some bar. Without cleaning up Stoney and Pecos were on their way to the City Limits.

He saw Travis's pickup in the parking lot and pulled up next to it. Travis was setting behind the wheel with the door open talking on a radio phone.

"Getting' pretty fancy for just an old cattle buyer aren't you? How many of those do you have in that truck? "Stoney said motioning to the phone.

"I just had it installed this morning and you'd be surprised the miles it has saved me. Fact of the matter is I was just calling you to see if you would come in. Bill Bleiker is in there and I think he's a buyer for your yearlings."

"Us get it on," Stoney replied and told Pecos to stay in the bed of the pickup. The sun was just about to disappear and it had cooled off considerably.

Bill Bleiker was an old friend of Stoney's and Travis, and had just recently renovated an old feedlot at Texline in the Texas Panhandle. He was now stocking the lot and needed some feeders. Travis had told Bill and he was only too glad to help Stoney out. He offered a full dollar a hundred over what he was paying others. They agreed on $56.00 per hundred with a two per cent shrink delivered day after tomorrow. That was going to amount to a little over $10,000 more than Eddie's offer.

The morning of delivery came. In the past, delivery day was a day of harvest, a day that brings the reward for a year's hard work, a day to rejoice and celebrate with family and friends. In the past all of the Stoneys family would help in the delivery and it became a tradition to have friends over in the afternoon for a barbeque.

How quick things can change in a year. Only Bill Bleiker, Travis, the Brand Inspector and Stoney were saddling up a half-hour before daybreak to gather the yearlings. It wasn't in the inspector's job description to help in the gatherings but he always enjoyed riding one of Stoney's well broke horses and would do so at every opportunity.

The delivery went smoothly, the three unmechantables were cut out, and the rest were weighed, loaded and on their way to a feedlot. The cattle, that had lived, had done exceptionally well, grossing 730 and paying on 715 pounds. Pecos had taken a cooling swim in the stock pond and lay in the shade of Stoney's pickup while Bill and Stoney were settling up. They all congratulated and bragged on Pecos for becoming a really good cow dog and a job well done. He relished the attention and his tail kept on wagging, even though he was almost asleep by the time the cowboys were shaking hands and saying their goodbyes.

Grabbing something to eat, and a shower, Stoney and Pecos were on their way to town. After waiting twenty minutes Bud motioned Stoney into the office.

"I was just going to have my secretary call you," Bud said before Stoney had a chance to sit down. "Eddie told me he made a good offer and you turned him down. So..., what are you going to do?"

Stoney laid the check on his desk with a copy of settlement weights, number, and price. He set down while Bud studied the check and the figures.

"Texline Feeders, never heard of them. This check damn sure better be good. Let me tell you something... cowboy. I have always found that it's better to do business with somebody you know than some damn stranger. Especially when we are talking that kind of money."

"You dumb, immature, fat ass hole," Stoney thought to himself. "You're thirty six years old, couldn't tell a heifer from a steer, and you're telling me how to do business."

"It's good," Stoney said.

"Won't take long to find out," he replied, yelling to Doris to come in. Giving her the check he told her to call the Dalhart bank it was written on and find out if they would honor it.

Opening Stoney's file he said, "Ok let's see how you came out."

He compared some papers with the settlement sheet. "I got down 760 head of calves and you're just showing a sale of 635 head. Where in the hell is the rest of them?" He looked at Stoney accusingly.

Stoney had had it. "Three of 'em might bring $50 apiece at the sale next Friday, the rest are dead. Thanks to that damn Taylor outfit. It's a miracle that any of them are alive, the way they were dropped off at my place."

Bud looked up at him. "You should of looked after them better. And if you didn't know how to doctor 'em you should have called in someone from Chalk Hill Feedlot to show you how. Now let's figure this out."

Bud pulled over his desktop calculator and started punching in the numbers, every so often he would stop and thump that ring on his desk, shake his head and continue.

Stoney had known days before delivery that the yearling operation was going to be a disaster, but he couldn't make himself sit down and crunch the numbers.

Betsy and even Randy Roberts had been right; he just couldn't face reality. Now he was wishing he had so he would have been better prepared for this day of reckoning.

"Well Stone, you got yourself a real problem, a real bad problem. You owe us $335,000 plus $66,000 interest. That's over $400,000. You brought me a check for $252,000. That leaves roughly $150,000 you owe us."

"What are you going to do about it? Except for some horses, the only asset you got is a ranch that might be worth, or might not be worth $450,000 and you still owe the Federal Land Bank almost $300,000 on that with a $20,000 plus payment due in two months. Boy, you got yourself in one hell of a mess."

Stoney just sat looking at Bud, making no comments.

"Now this is the way the bank examiners are going to look at this. A couple years ago you had a financial statement showing a net of $683,000, last year it was $373,000. This year it's..., zero, zilch, nada. You're broke Stone, broke."

"How old are you?" Bud continued, enjoying himself. "You're getting close to 60 and nothing to show for it. I am in my 30s and worth almost a half million. All you got left is what you're wife has made."

Stoney continued to stare at Bud, seething inside. He was thinking of going to his pickup, getting is .30.30 and killing the bastard.

"I can tell you got no answers," Bud said. "I'll call Betsy and have her come in and we'll see if we can work something out." As an afterthought he said, "You might be able to get out of this with your pickup," he gave a short laugh.

"No," Stoney said, very softly and very coldly.

"No, what' a you mean no," a very surprised Bud replied.

"I mean you're not going to call Betsy. You're not going to talk to Betsy. You're leaving her completely out of this. Do you hear what I am telling you?"

Something in Stoney's voice and the way he was looking at him made Bud reconsider. "Well, if you got any ideas, let's hear them."

Without thinking Stoney said, "Bankruptcy, I'll take out bankruptcy." His own words shocked him. He had never, ever, considered losing the ranch, much less taking out bankruptcy.

"What happened," he thought. "How could this be happening? And how could it of happened so quick? Three years ago he had a great little ranch stocked with the best cows and the best horses; a beautiful wife and family. a respected reputation. And now it was gone. It was all gone."

"Bankruptcy, bankruptcy," Bud repeated bringing Stoney back to the moment. Bud laughed. "Your wife is going to love that. This is a community property state. You take out bankruptcy and all her investments are gone, including her reputation as a real estate agent."

Bud looked at Stoney and didn't like the way Stoney was looking at him. "I'll tell you what you can do. You can just sign over everything on that financial statement to us, in lieu of foreclosure, and be on your way. Or…, today is Thursday, I'll give you till Wednesday, next week, to find someone that will take you on and you can pay us off.

Stoney rose, "I'll see you next Wednesday."

On leaving the bank Stoney's first thought was to go to the City Limits, but he changed his mind. He didn't want to talk to anyone, not even Betsy. He just wanted to be out at his ranch, his place. He didn't want to be in town: he didn't like towns, any of them. He wanted to be with his horses, to watch his quail. To sit on his deck and watch his beloved mares with their babies coming into to water at the close of day. Pecos was dozing under the pickup. Stoney told him to get in the cab, he wanted someone near him, not saying anything, just close to him.

As he slowed down to make the turn off the highway onto the county road that led to his ranch, he saw two men digging a posthole. They were on the corner of the freshly broke-out field where he had his first run-in with Pete. Pulling up behind their pickup he recognized Emmett. Emmett came from a dirt poor farm family and his little sister had idolized horses. When Mickie had outgrown her pony Stoney had given it to Emmett's family. The pony had become a member of that family and lived a long and pleasant life.

"Hi Stoney," Emmett said as Stoney and Pecos got out of their pickup.

"Hello Emmett," he acknowledged the other man with a nod.

"You fixing to set a corner post? I thought you farmers didn't like fences the way you keep plowing mine up."

Emmett laughed. "No we're fixin' to set that sign up so you'll have to pull clear out on the highway to see if anything's coming." He pointed to a large sign, professionally done, that was laying in the bed of their truck.

As Stoney walked over to look at the sign Emmett whistled to Pecos. "Can I pet him, Stoney, he won't bite will he?"

Stoney looked at Pecos to see what his attitude was. Pecos was putting on his best smile and wagging his tail. "Sure, go ahead, he likes you."

Stoney read the sign:

'SITE OF TAYLOR FARMS NEWEST DAIRY'
'A SIGN OF PROGRESS'.

Stoney shook his head and walked back to where Emmett was squatted down, petting and talking to Pecos. "I have always wanted to pet him Stoney, ever since I first saw him. He's got the strangest eyes I ever saw. What's his name?"

"I call him Pecos, but I think your buddy Pete has another name for him," Stoney answered.

Emmett laughed and proceeded to tell the other Taylor hand about what Pecos had done to Pete's boot, laughing all the time. He then turned to Stoney and said, "He ain't my buddy, he's my boss, and delights in giving me all the shity' details that comes along. He thinks it's funny."

"Well..., I understand he got promoted. You guys take it easy and I'll see you down the road."

"Stoney, could you help us out? This damn outfit is too cheap to buy a pickup that runs. This piece of junk will only start every other time, and I forgot and turned the key off. Could you give me jump? I have some cables in the back somewhere."

Stoney got their pickup running and went to the pens where he stayed until the sun was almost down. He curried every horse that was up, talking to them; he spent a lot of time with his Leo and Kenneth, his two old friends. Time slipped away from him and it was dark when he turned into the driveway of their house.

Betsy called just as he was sitting down on the back deck with his bourbon and coke. She wanted to know how the delivery went. He told her it went good, that the steers weighed more than he expected. Then he told her of his meeting with Bud and his ultimatum.

"Stoney, I am so sorry, I am coming home right now," she told him.

"No, no," Stoney replied. "I have lots to think about and I am tired. Let's both think this thing over tonight and we'll get together tomorrow and maybe we can come up with some ideas."

Betsy agreed, told him how much she loved him and they could and would work through this. Just as he placed the phone back in its cradle it rang again. It was his California horse buyer telling him that he had taken sick and was going to be laid up for a year so he wouldn't be out to New Mexico for the fall horse sale. Stoney thanked him and this dismal night just got a little darker.

Stoney mixed himself another drink, lit a cigarette, and returned to the back deck. He just couldn't believe what was happening or how it happened. Finally it started sinking in. There were three reasons why and how this happened. First was the drought. There is no market for cows in a drought, he had to sell most of his cows on a low market. Second, a banker that had forced him to the yearling route and to buy calves from a less than reputable source. Third, the dairy buyout, a conspiracy of a strong, well-heeled lobby and greedy politicians. There was nothing he could have done to prevent a drought. The second one he could have, if he had the fortitude to stand up to his banker and moved his business somewhere else.

"But that was yesterday and yesterday is gone," he said to Pecos who was lying beside him. He was beginning to use this cliché more and more. "The question is what do we do now."

He went into their bedroom, opened the drawer of his bedside table and brought out an old revolver. It had belonged to his grandfather who had taken it off the victim of Clovis's most famous feud some seventy years earlier. Despite its age it was in excellent condition, Stoney would take it out every year, shoot it a few times, give it a good cleaning and oiling, and return it to its lamb's wool sheath.

He spun the cylinder to make sure it was loaded and went back to his chair on the deck. Sitting down he laid the gun on his lap and leaned back and let the thoughts roll. All of them were sad thoughts; what would happen to Pecos, what would happen to his horses, how about his family? Some of them would be better off without him he thought, and others wouldn't. He sat for a long time, getting up once to mix himself another strong drink. When he had finished the drink and his last cigarette he put Pecos inside the house, telling him he would be back shortly. He was going to do some shooting and knew that he did not like the noise.

He drove the pickup slowly out of the driveway and onto the county road while sipping on a fresh coke and bourbon. Turning the cab light on, he dug around into the ash-tray till found two or three cigarettes that had just a few puffs taken off them and then were gently stubbed out in the tray. It was another beautiful night with just enough light of a crescent moon that he could drive without lights. When he reached the highway he stopped and smoked one of the stubs while waiting for an automobile to come by. When its taillight had disappeared he got out of the pickup bringing the revolver and his 30.30 Winchester with him. Leaning up against the pickup he lifted the .38 up and without hesitating put six, .38 special bullets through Taylor Farms brand new sign. With the click of the hammer on a spent shell he laid it on the hood. Picking up the rifle he levered a shell into the chamber and fired until five more holes appeared in the sign. It was very, very quiet after the shooting, then a coyote howled on a distant sandhill and that brought out yapping from several more coyotes scattered around the area. It made Stoney feel good.

"Thanks for the applause sports fans. I thoroughly enjoyed it too," he said out loud, in response to the coyotes. The chatter quit just as suddenly as it had started as if the coyotes had understood him. He could still smell burnt powder as he put the weapons back in the cab. Lighting the last cigarette stub he leaned back against the pickup, finished his drink and went home.

The next morning Betsy and Stoney met for breakfast at the Rounder's Restaurant. Stoney was first to arrive and shortly after a breathless Betsy came in. Stoney could not help but admire how pretty she was and wondered how she kept on becoming more beautiful every day.

"Stoney I have it all figured out," she said after giving him a kiss. "Two weeks ago I sold a house to a loan broker that just moved to town and, far as I know he is the only one in Clovis. He told me he does lots of agriculture loans. So, here is what we'll do. Last night I put together my financial statement and along with yours, I know he can broker it somewhere and we'll start all over again. What do you think?"

The waitress came and took their order. He could hardly take his eyes off his wife. When the waitress had left they reached across the table and held hands.

"I love you so much Betsy and I appreciate you wanting to risk all your hard work for me and the ranch, but you were right all along when you said I was not facing reality. The way things are going a little ranch with a high debt load just isn't going to make it. Especially on these high interest rates, it's time to check out and I know it. Unless you got a better idea on how to close this thing I'll just sign it over to the bank."

"Stoney, I just can't believe we are going to lose the ranch. All the hard work we have put into it. I know how much you love it. I do too. Isn't there anyway out of this."

Stoney, unable to speak for fear of breaking down, just shook his head.

The waitress brought their breakfast but it remained untouched as they both just sat there.

"How soon do you think we'll have to move," Betsy asked.

"Well...," Stoney replied. "I'll have to find someplace to go with our horses. I think he'll maybe give us a month, but if we have to do it, us do it and get it over with."

Betsy reached across the table and grasped Stoney's hand again. "I have a condo that's coming vacant next week. We can move into it until we can get something bigger."

"How 'bout Pecos? There's no covenant about dogs is there?"

"Betsy looked down at her plate, "They have to be twenty pounds or less. Stoney we can board him in a kennel or maybe one of your friends that live out in the country will take him. He'll be all right."

Stoney didn't say anything, just looked across the room. Betsy buttered a piece of toast, then put it back on the plate.

"We have till Wednesday, maybe something will change by then," Stoney said. He was thinking of the Goose Creek Mine and Jim Bob. Maybe, just maybe, he could sell out his interest for enough to pull them through this.

"Are you ready to go?" he asked. She nodded. Stoney put a ten-dollar bill on the table. They got up to leave and he grabbed a strip of bacon. Other than that, their breakfast remained untouched. As he was getting in his pickup a sheriff's deputy pulled up.

"Hi Mister Stone, the sheriff wants you to come by his office. He's been trying to call you this morning and told us to keep an eye out for you."

Stoney thanked him and drove to the courthouse. He visited with the dispatcher until Randy called him into his office.

"Sit down, I got something for you," Randy said motioning toward a chair. He wheeled around and spun open a medium-size safe. Turning back he handed Stoney a thick brown envelope.

Stoney opened it and pulled out a large handful of twenty dollar bills. He looked up at Randy.

"There outa' be a hundred of those little fella's in there," he said, a big grin across his face.

"I don't understand," Stoney said.

Randy explained to him that the feds had set up a reward fund for anyone that tips off law enforcement, if it results in a successful drug bust. The amount of drugs have to be quite large and Stoneys reward was the largest ever for New Mexico. Randy went on to explain that he had a hell of a time pulling this out of the feds since he didn't bring them in on the ambush, nor shared the name of the informant. He wanted to take him to lunch later but Stoney took a rain check telling him there was something he had to do.

Stopping at Feed and Ranch Supplies and picking up a half-dozen bags of oats he headed south on his mission. There were two pickups with the Taylor logos and a deputy sheriff's car pulled off the highway at the intersection of the county road leading to his house. Slowing down he recognized Pete Benson and the deputy looking at the riddled Taylor Farms sign. He also saw Emmett pick something off the county road and putting it in his pocket.

"Shit," Stoney thought. "I bet he found my 30.30. casings". He drove on by.

Four miles down the highway he turned into the lane that led to the Yate's place. Brandi's car was parked in the drive along with a four-door pickup with Oklahoma license plates. No sooner had had he pulled to a stop besides Brandi's car, and shut the engine off than Sadler's little girl followed by Little Bill came bursting from the house. Pecos had jumped out of the pickup and met the two children, covering their face with his tongue.

Amid their giggling the little girl shouted at Stoney, "Guess what Uncle Bill! We're moving to Oklahoma and going to live with Grandma and Grandpa. Can we take Pecos? Please, we'll be real good to him, please." Brandi had opened the door and motioned to Stoney. She told the kids to stay outside and play with Pecos.

Brandi introduced him to her parents whom he immediately liked and the feeling was mutual. Brandi then gave him the sad news. The bank had taken everything; the ranch, all improvements, what little money they had in their account, Sadler's pickup, even his horses. All they left her was a twelve year old car and what little furniture they had accumulated.

"Even the horses?" Stoney said unbelieving. "What did they do with those?"

Sadler had two horses, they were old but still had a few good years left and were good cow horses. Sadler always kept them fat as ticks and they had a good life.

"I don't know," she replied. "The kids cried and cried and I had my hands full with them and didn't get a chance to ask Luther where he was taking them. He just said he would find them a good home."

"Luther…,Luther who?" he asked. He felt himself grow cold.

"Oh, you know. That horse buyer."

"You mean Luther Hartzog."

"Yes, that's him."

"When did he pick them up?"

"Last week. I think it was Wednesday. Why?"

"Just curious," Stoney said. He wanted to get to a phone right away. He told Brandi that he had a meeting and needed to run, but before leaving he had something for her and handed her the brown envelope with the two thousand dollars reward money in it.

"This is yours, Brandi. I talked to Sadler a couple days before the wreck and he gave this to me. He said if anything happened to him to wait a few weeks and then give it to you. He also wanted me to tell you that he loved you very much and to please forgive him."

Brandi had stood up and was crying. Stoney walked over and gave her a kiss on the forehead.

"I have to go Brandi but I'll be in touch. Let me know if there is anything I can do."

He walked outside and gave the kids a kiss. The little girl asked again if they could keep Pecos. Pecos had already jumped in the bed of the pickup when he saw Stoney coming out of the door. He told them Pecos better stay with him but when they got settled he promised them they would come for a visit.

He drove as fast as he dared to his house, ran in, and looked up Luther Harzog's telephone number. Stoney was praying that Luther was home.

Luther was not well liked around the stockyards. He called himself a horse trader but almost all of his business was killer horses. He bought horses and sold them to the horse slaughtering plant in Morton, Texas. The talk around the stockyards was, when he couldn't find horses to buy he would get them by other means.

His wife answered the phone and said that Luther was just walking out the door. In a minute he picked up the phone. Stoney asked him if he still had the horses that he picked up at the Yates place.

"Hello Stone," he replied. Naw, I took them over to Morton the same day so they would have 'em for Thursday's kill. Boy were they ever fat, they made...."

Stoney slammed down the phone. He felt sick, if he had only know in time.

He called Travis and asked him if he had heard from Jim Bob, that it was real important that he find him. Travis said he still hadn't heard a word.

The next call was to Mickie. He told her that he had to be out of town for a couple days and asked if she would mind bringing Bobbi out to the ranch to spend a few days so she could take care of the horses and watch things. She said she would love to, and knew that Bobbi would have a ball. He also asked her to tell Betsy in case he couldn't get a hold of her. That done he packed a few things. Then he and Pecos were on their way to the Goose Creek mine.

Stoney giving Bobbi a ride on Kenneth and taking one last ride on their ranch.

CHAPTER 18

It was after dark when Stoney turned into a motel in Cimarron, New Mexico. Cimarron is a small town lying in the eastern foot hills of the Sangre de Cristo mountains. A beautiful little village, boasting a year round population of 800 or so inhabitants. Stoney and Pecos stepped in the office, which was actually the front room of a residence. A small bell on the door announced his arrival to a rough-hewn mountain woman that looked like she was in her seventies but who Stoney guessed actually to be in her early sixties.

"Whata' you want hon," she said brushing some strands of mixed grey and blond hair from her eyes and stubbing out a cigarette that had been hanging from her lips.

"I need a room for the night. Just me and my friend here. You do take dogs don't you"?

She peered over the counter and looked at Pecos who was sitting on his haunches looking up at her as if waiting for her answer.

"Sweetheart as good lookin' as you are you can bring your dog, horse or camel with you…, if you got one."

Stoney grinned back at her, "Well…, I left my horses at home and don't have a camel so it'll be just me and Pecos here."

"That'll be forty five dollars," she said, looking down at Pecos. "Aint he got the craziest looking eyes you ever saw? Gives me the creeps, but he act's like he's friendly don't he?"

Stoney agreed and handed her the forty five dollars. She ignored the cash register and put it in the pocket of her soiled frock.

Stoney asked her where he could get something to eat and she pointed toward the door.

"Sounds like the St. James is still open" The sound of western music, laughter and loud talk was seeping down the street and through the open door.

"But darling,' you be careful over there. Cimarron didn't get its name for nothing."

"What does Cimarron mean?" he asked.

"It means wild and unruly. And baby it ain't changed a whole hell of a lot."

He thanked her, found their room. Telling Pecos, who had immediately jumped on the bed, and laid his head on a pillow, to stay, he walked down the street to the St. James Hotel.

The St. James was one of the oldest hotels in New Mexico that was still in operation. Some of its famous and infamous guest included: Buffalo Bill, Wyatt Earp,

Annie Oakley, Jessie James, Kit Carson, Billy the Kid and the notorious gunman Clay Allison, who once danced naked on the bar. No one was dancing naked on the bar when Stoney entered but he was sure if one had been, the crowd would not have noticed. Everyone seemed to be in a jovial, inebriated mood. Even the band sounded as if half were playing a two-step while the other half played a waltz.

Stoney took the one stool that happened to be empty at the bar and ordered his bourbon and coke. He was just about to have a taste of it when someone came up behind him and lifted his stool and himself, all 150 pounds of him, up, and easily set them on the bar, much to the delight of the other patrons, including the bartender. Stoney turned around; looking up at him with a big grin was Reno Bonomo.

Reno was an old college friend of Stoney's; both had been in ROTC while attending New Mexico State and had gone through basic training together. Stoney had hurt his back after being thrown from a bronc and flunked his last physical before receiving his commission. Reno went on to make a career out of the military; serving with distinction in Korea and later with Special Forces in Vietnam. He had recently retired as a light Colonel. The scuttle butt among some of their college friends was that he would have made full Colonel, or maybe even a General, if he could have settled down and not tried to visit every saloon in every country he was stationed in.

Although Stoney had not seen Reno since they graduated, he kept up with his career and knew he had returned to the little ranch in Mosquero, New Mexico where he was raised and which he had recently inherited. He was an imposing figure, six foot six, as flat bellied as the last time Stoney had seen him with, broad shoulders, and biceps almost as large as Stoney's thighs. Reno had a scar that ran from the corner of his eye to his chin, the result of a bayonet charge by a North Korean. It did nothing but enhance his rugged good looks.

He helped Stoney off the bar and guided him to a table where three cowboys and a beautiful, blond lady were sitting.

"Okay guys, *vamanos,*" Reno ordered and the three immediately were gone.

Reno introduced Stoney to Penny, his new wife. Reno married late, preferring the life of a bachelor rather than the responsibilities that comes with marriage. He had met her in Los Angeles the month he retired from the military, and despite the difference in age, they had fallen in love and were married within a week. She had been raised on a farm in Iowa and moved to California to pursue an acting or modeling career, neither which were successful. After 12 years of life in the fast lane she was ready to return to country living.

"But Mosquero, New Mexico? How much quieter can you get?" Stoney asked. Mosquero was the county seat of Harding County, which had a population of a little over nine hundred, and Mosquero's population barely reached a hundred.

Penny laughed and told Stoney she was crazy about it, and that they had been married over two years and wanted to spend the rest of her life on their little ranch. She went on telling him about her horses and about riding down in the Canadian River Canyon, which sliced through their ranch. Reno sat there smiling and nodding in agreement.

Stoney asked what, other than riding horses, they did for excitement. They told him that whenever they wanted to party and dance they would either come here to the St. James or Joe's Ringside in Las Vegas, New Mexico or down at Ute Lake where they had a trailer house and a dock for their boat.

They visited over several more drinks relating stories to Penny about their college days. Then they questioned Stoney how his life was running. The mood quickly changed as he ordered another round.

"Not good," he responded. And then he told them the whole story, even telling them of the strain it was putting on his marriage. By the time he was finished they were almost all to the point of tears. Due to a large extent, to too many drinks.

Reno told Stoney that they ran into Jim Bob two or three weeks ago at Joe's Ringside. He had mentioned the Goose Creek mine to them and told them that it was probably going to make him and Stoney rich. At that time they thought it was just one of Jim Bob's stories. He also told them that he was going to Alaska for six weeks as a cook for the outfitters that had the Moreno leased, and also a fishing camp on the Tikchik Lakes in Alaska.

At two o'clock the management began the task of moving everyone out. Reno bought a pint of brandy and the three of them sat on the curb outside the hotel. They passed the bottle between them until it was empty and the eastern sky had begun to lighten up. They said their good buys with hugs and a few tears. The Bonomo's made Stoney promise that he would call them and if he ever needed any help. Walking back to his room Stoney was thinking how fortunate he was to have so many true friends. He knew too, that many of his fair-weather friends would shun him after they found out he was broke and had lost his ranch. He thought how much he appreciated the Bonomo's offer, but knew there would be nothing they could ever do for him. Little did he realize how soon he would be calling on them for their help.

It was after nine in the morning when Pecos jumped up on the bed and awakened him. He groggily opened the door to let Pecos out; leaving it open, he slept for another hour. He showered and had steak and eggs at Hecks Restaurant. Before he had finished his breakfast, he ordered two steak sandwiches to go. One with all the trimmings the other just bread and meat. The waitress looked at him suspiciously but placed the order and it was ready when he left. On the way out of Cimarron he picked up a six-pack of Coors, a jug of water and a bag of ice; after throwing them in the battered cooler that he always carried in the bed of the pickup, he was on his way.

At Angle Fire he turned north toward Red River. After passing the road to the Moreno ranch ,where he had purchased the yearlings Jim Bob had scouted for him, he began watching for the little road that led to the Goose Creek Mine. He was almost to Red River when he knew he had missed it. Turning around he drove more slowly. He came to a highway sign that said "Trucks Turning" and a new gravel road that went west.

He passed it and went on another mile. Then it came to him. "Pecos, that has to be the road, maybe Jim Bob wasn't bragging to the Bonomos. We might be rich and nobody has got around to telling us."

They followed the well-used road that paralleled Goose Creek up the canyon. The creek was no longer a beautiful little pristine, mountain stream but now a silt-laden water way. They came to the feeder canyon that held the mine. The new road turned up the little canyon and continued pass a locked gate. A large sign read, 'No Trespassing, Danger, Property of Capitan Mining Co written in both in English and Spanish. Stoney and Pecos got out of the pickup and Stoney looked over the gate but could only see fifty 50 yards up the road before it made a turn and disappeared. He could hear no activity, that worried him until he remembered that today was Saturday.

"Guess miners don't work on weekends Pecos, us have a little picnic while we're here." He grabbed their sandwiches and the six-pack and walked back down to the confluence of Goose Creek and the little turbid stream that came from the feeder canyon. Walking on up Goose Creek, (it had changed back to its original state); a pristine, beautiful mountain stream. They found a small waterfall with a pool at the bottom. Looking closely he could see several small brook trout.

"Just what we're looking' for Pecos." They had their sandwiches, and afterward Stoney lay down, and the bubbling of an untouched Goose Creek quickly put him to sleep. Pecos investigated the forest before he lay down beside his beloved master. Much later that afternoon they left their little paradise and drove back to Angel Fire where Stoney rented a room for the next two nights.

Monday morning they were back to the locked gate where they waited for the activity to start. By 10:00 no one had shown up. Disgusted he climbed over the gate and headed toward his mine. Pecos easily cleared the gate and followed. A half mile up the road they rounded another bend and there was the Goose Creek Mine. Only one machine was at the site, a large front-end loader: no tucks, no large conveyors, just the one tractor. Stoney had a sinking feeling. They had destroyed the beautiful little wooded canyon that he remembered, but he was prepared for that. What he was expecting was lots of equipment, lots of trucks, lots activity. There were signs of a recent large operation. Many tons of rock and over material had been moved. He did find, what he assumed, was the mine itself, on the side of the canyon were two large metal doors that swung together. They were big enough to drive the large tractor through and were painted red with the words "Danger" and "Peligro" on them. Stoney stayed around the mine for an hour until he was sure no one was going to show up. Then he whistled for Pecos and they headed back to Clovis. It had been a disappointing day but he hoped it was just a temporary delay in the mining operation.

CHAPTER 19

On the way home Stoney stopped at Rigoni's Bar in Roy. He visited for a while with the owner, whom he had known for a number of years. He then used their phone so he could call Mickie, and tell her he would be home later that night, in case she wanted to go home. He was surprised when Betsy answered.

"Where in the world have you been?" she demanded.

When he told her he had been fishing up in the mountains she laid into him.

"Stoney, have you lost your mind? All we have to do, and you have been lazing off somewhere like you hadn't a care in the world. I have been here for the last four days, packing up everything. I've cleaned out the kitchen and moved my clothes and everything into my..., I mean our condo. You need to get home and go through things, and throw out a bunch of stuff you're not going to use anymore. I bet you have 10 pair of old boots you haven't had on in years. I called the moving and storage people and they will be here Thursday and...."

Stoney had heard enough.

"Betsy! I'm at Rigoni's and using their phone. I'll be home tonight."

"If you can tear yourself away from the bar, I'll be at the condo," she hung up the phone.

Thanking the Rigonis for their hospitality he headed home. Without any intention of spending the night in Betsy's condo and leaving Pecos locked in the pickup.

The next day he started going through his personal possessions, such as old bank statements that went back twenty years, receipts, and all kinds of anniversary, Christmas, and birthday cards. It was taking longer than he anticipated. Too many memories of many good times, of steps taken in their lives, of happy times and sad times. Passages. Finally he gave up trying to separate the things out. He loaded all the papers, all the cards, everything he didn't need to start a new life into the back of the pickup, then drove over to the pens where he had a large metal incinerator. He set a match to them and watched as the smoke curled up and disappeared into a beautiful fall sky. Stoney hoped that the memories would also fade as quickly. Next he gathered up the clothes he wanted to keep and took them to the bunkhouse; the rest he threw in the bed of the pickup and headed to town.

Dropping the clothes off at the Salvation Army, he drove to Betsy's office. He pulled into the parking lot just as she was getting into her car with some customers. She told them she would be just a minute and walked over to where Stoney was standing by the bed of his pickup, stroking Pecos's head. He was surprised when she came right up to him, and without saying anything gave him a big kiss.

"I am glad you're home sweetheart and I'm sorry I hung up on you last night. I was so tired and you left without giving anybody a clue as to where you were going. I was so worried, and what with all we needed to do. What were you doing and where did you go."

"I just needed to get away for awhile and to try to figure out what I am going to do with my life. I guess I should have told you."

"I know," she said, nodding her head. "I know this is hard on you Stoney, but it's hard on all of us. You're not by yourself in this. We all loved the ranch. All of us are under such a strain and we need to be more considerate of each other."

She paused and looked up at him with tears in her eyes. She looked over at Pecos who was trying to get her attention. Patting him she said, "It will all be over pretty soon and we can start getting on with our lives. Think about it Stoney. It will be exciting, you have a college degree and no one can take that away from you, and..."

"Betsy, I am also 55 and...," he caught himself. He didn't want to hurt her by going any further with his gloomy attitude. "I guess I better be getting back to the ranch. I think I'll just go ahead and stop by the bank and sign the 'deed in lieu of', over to him. Just as well get it over with. I am sure he'll call and want you to come in and sign 'em."

She gave him another peck on his cheek and asked him if he was coming in tonight. She wanted him to see how cute she had decorated the condo and that she had rented a big storage unit where the movers were to take all of their surplus furniture. She told him that there would be room enough for all his saddles and horse equipment that he gathered up over many years.

He told her that he had moved over to the bunkhouse and would just stay there until everything was done. He promised he would call her that night.

He walked into the bank vowing that it would be the last time he would ever open their doors. They could keep the forty cents remaining in his account. Doris was not sitting at her desk when he approached Bud's office but he could see him alone, with the door closed. He had swiveled his chair around and was looking out the window with the phone pressed against his ear.

Stoney opened the door and walked in unannounced. It startled Bud who swung around. Seeing who it was he told the person on the other end he would call them later.

"Well..., what can I do for Mister Stone today?" he asked with a smirk on his face.

Stoney looked over at the adjacent office that belonged to Alex. He was busy at his desk with pen in hand. Stoney watched him for few moments until he knew Bud was getting uncomfortable.

Turning back to Bud, he said, "Just give me the papers to sign and I'll be gone. Betsy will be in whenever you call her."

"All right Stone, I got 'em right here. I knew you would be back. Just sign on the bottom lines..., where I put a little x for you. One's the deed. I haven't got the legal; I'll put that in later. One's the assignment on your state lease and the other is the settlement contract."

"I think I'll just read this before I sign it."

He picked up the settlement contract which said in part that in lieu of foreclosure and for all money owed to Merchants and Ranchers Bank, Bill and Betsy Stone agree to deed the following real estate and land leases over to the bank.

Stoney started to reach for the pen that Bud was offering him, instead he took his own pen from his shirt pocket. He then added an addendum to the bottom of the contract. It said, "Possession by Merchants and Ranchers Bank will be two weeks from the day of the signing of this contract by both parties." He then initialized it, put the date on it and pushed the papers back toward Bud. Bud looked at what he had written, nodded his head and said, "Fair enough."

They both stood up and Bud offered his hand and said, "It's been a real pleasure doing business with you Mister Stone."

Stoney looked at him, "Fuck you..., you fat turd." He turned to walk away and saw Alex watching him. When Stoney looked at him Alex smiled and waved. Stoney threw the finger at him, then looked back at Bud. "Same goes for that son-of-a-bitch too. He headed toward the bank's entrance and just as he reached the door, Doris entered.

"Doris, I'm outa' here but thank you so much for everything you have done for me over the past 30 years and I'm going to miss pestering you." He then gave her a big hug and a kiss and walked out of the bank.

He drove out to the stockyards hoping to run into somebody that might be interested in buying his horses. Walking into the horse department's office he sat down across the desk from Jim Hargrove. Stoney had known Jimmy for many years and considered him to be one of the most honest and knowledgeable horseman in the country. He told him that he had to liquidate his horses and did he have anyone in mind that might be interested. Stoney had sold lots of horses in his sales and Jimmy was familiar with them, and the bloodlines as well. He told Stoney that he did not know of anyone interested in the mares and colts but that there might be someone interested in the broke two year olds. The drought had affected the horse market as well as the cattle market and, to be honest, he told Stoney he was betting on a very depressed sale. Stoney thanked him and they visited awhile about the markets. Jimmy told him he would be sure and call him if he found anyone in the market for the mares. As Stoney walked out he saw Luther Hartzog sitting in one of the lobby's cushioned chairs. Luther was watching him intently and waved when their eyes met. Stoney thought about throwing him the finger, but thought better of it and simply ignored him.

He decided it was time to go to the City Limits and tie one on, figuring he had about all the good news he could stand for one day. He sat in the pickup for a few minutes thinking and decided he didn't want to visit with anyone. He would just get drunk on his back deck one last time before the movers arrived in the morning and hauled everything away.

"Pals"
Kenneth and Leo never strayed over 50 yards from each other when turned out on pasture.

CHAPTER 20

Stoney had had just three drinks while sitting on the back deck with Pecos laying beside him before he climbed in bed mentally exhausted. The next morning, upon awakening, he felt a little better to have that part over with.

After feeding the horses he decided to work on the corrals that had taken a beating this past year and needing some patching up. Going to the tool shed he gathered up what equipment he needed and started toward the pens with Pecos happily at his heels. He had taken only a few paces when he stopped.

"What the hell am I doing!" he said out loud. "These are not my pens anymore. This is not my place anymore. In three weeks I'll probably never see these sandhills again." He walked over to the saddle house, opened the door and stood looking in for a moment or two. He sat down in a chair that he had sat in so many times before, mending saddles, bridles, and other tack.

He took a good deep whiff of the wonderful smell of worn leather, saddle soap, livestock medicine, ropes and all kinds of ranch paraphernalia. He then had a good cry.

A half-hour later he walked out of the saddle house. He had it out of his system now, he had had his cry, he had said goodbye to the things he loved, the things he worked and sweated for. Now it was scrambling time, possibly even time to get even. It brought to mind one of his favorite bible verses. The third CHAPTER of Ecclesiastes:

A time to be born and a time to die
A time to weep, and a time to laugh
A time to mourn, and a time to dance
A time to love and a time to hate.

"Yep," he said to Pecos. "It's a time to scramble and scramble we will."

He saw Leo, ever alert, lift his head from the hay trough and look toward the county road. A cloud of dust was being raised by a large truck.

"Here come the movers Pecos, us go see if we can get in their way."

He watched the packers and helped when he could for a couple hours. The telephone rang, it was Travis..

"Are you selling your horses?"

It caught Stoney by surprise. "Looks like I am going to have to, some of them anyway. Why?"

"To Luther Hartzog?

"And watch them go to the killers. Hell no! That son-of-bitch. Whatever gave you that idea?"

"Well…, It's kinda strange. He called me up a while ago, asked if I had seen your horses lately. I told him I had and he wanted to know how many colts and older horses you had, what condition they were in, and what I thought they would weigh. It pissed me off, so I said why don't you ask him. He stuttered around a minute and he said he didn't think you liked him."

"That bastard. He got that right. I can't figure out why he thought I would ever sell him my horses."

"You are going to sell those mares then," Travis asked.

"Yeah, I got nowhere to go with them. Travis, can you figure something out for me. I just now got a feeling I better do something quick. I'm going to make a phone call and then I'll know if my hunch is right."

"You remember Billy Kiehne," Travis asked.

"Your bear hunter friend over in the Gila Mountains?

"Yeah, that's him. Let me call him. He likes your bloodlines and I'll see if he might be interested."

They hung up and Stoney called Doris. He asked her if there was anything in the contract he signed with the bank that mentioned his horses. She told Stoney to give her five minutes and she would call him back.

Stoney paced the floor trying to come up with some sort of plan if his hunch was right. Fifteen minutes later Doris called. She told him she had to wait until Bud left. That the contract wasn't in her office files but in his.

"Stoney, it says ranch, all rolling stock, livestock, feed and improvements. That would include your horses. But Stoney that is not the contract that he had me type up for you to sign. But this is the one with your signature on it. I can't believe that son-of-bitch. He's….."

Stoney interrupted her and asked what she thought about suing him and the bank. Even, maybe turning him over to the District Attorney or even the State Attorney General.

"Stoney! Have you forgotten whom this bank belongs to? He owns this town and he has chips all over Santa Fe. All he would have to do is pick up the phone and call them in. You wouldn't stand a chance against him and his cronies. And as far as our esteemed District Attorney is concerned, his dad is on our Board of Directors and his insurance company handles all of the bank's business. You're screwed darling."

Stoney remembered the insurance policy that Sadler had, and that the lack of coverage cost him his ranch and his life.

"Those sorry sons-of-bitches," were the only thing Stoney could say.

"Stoney, let me tell you something. Yesterday when you left the bank and I went back to my desk, Alex was in Bud's office, and they were laughing and slapping each other on the back and I heard your name mentioned, so I know they were talking about you."

"Let me tell you something, about what I been doing," she continued."My husband doesn't even know so you have to promise me...."

Stoney interrupted her again, "Doris, I'll talk to you later. I have to do something real quick...and thanks a bunch." He hung up the phone.

He left for the City Limits, hoping and praying that maybe, just maybe he would find someone that would have some extra wheat pasture or grass that he could lease. He didn't hear the phone ringing as he started the pickup. Pecos jumped in the bed of the pickup as he was pulling out.

As soon as he turned out his driveway and headed toward the highway he saw a car coming toward him, going faster than it should on the dirt road. A couple hundred yards away its red and blue flashing lights came on and Stoney recognized it as one of Randy's units. Coming closer, it slowed down and the driver started waving his arm out the window. Stoney pulled up beside it and rolled his window down after the dust had settled.

"Mister Stone, I'm glad I caught you," the deputy said. "The sheriff has been trying to get hold of you all morning but the line has been busy."

He then explained to Stoney that the District Attorney had called him and wanted him to send one of his deputies here and park at your front gate for the next two weeks, or until the bank takes possession of your ranch.

"What the hell for," Stoney asked.

"They're afraid you will move some of you horses or equipment that belongs to them," the deputy looked down and Stoney knew he didn't enjoy delivering the message. "Or at least that's what they say." The sheriff argued with the District Attorney and I thought he was going to hit him. But he told Randy he would have him arrested for dereliction of duty. I am really sorry about this but Randy just had to do it and we gotta' do what they say."

"I understand, not your fault. It's mine for being so damn dumb. Where you gonna' park?"

"They said I can't go on your property so I guess I'll park down at the gate leading down to your pens."

"Ok, if you need any water or want to use the bathroom, just come over to the house, nobody will be there. I'll be staying in the bunkhouse over at the pens."

The deputy thanked him and Stoney drove off to the City Limits.

The happy hour crowd had just started coming in when Stoney arrived. He took a seat at the long table next to Ben Green and related his need for some pasture. Everyone was in sympathy with him and told him they would ask around to see if they could find something. Ben told him he didn't have any wheat pasture for the horses but he did have some grass at his ranch up on the Huerfana Mesa. However it was just a summer country and he didn't keep anybody up there in the winter to look after them. Stoney thanked him and told him he might have to take him up on it and move up there himself.

When the word got around the table that Stoney was losing his ranch everyone felt bad and the crowd lost their usual jovial mood. There was no way that he could buy the table a round and Janie, who heard what was going on, kept his glass full. After a couple drinks Stoney left the table to use the rest room. As he walked by the bar he saw Emmett setting at one of the stools with three more of the Taylor hands. Their eyes met and they just nodded at each other. Stoney was standing at one of the urinals when the door opened and someone came in and took the urinal next to him. He looked over and it was Emmett looking at him.

"Hello Emmett."

"Hello Stoney. I heard about the bank taking your place, I'm real sorry 'bout that."

Stoney nodded.

"I got something for you," Emmett said reaching in his pocket. "Eddie and Pete are mad as hell at someone shooting up their sign and they think it was you. And if they find out for sure, they're going to have you thrown in jail.."

He handed Stoney five spent 30.30. casings.

"Thanks Emmett," he said as he put them in his pocket.

"*Bueno,*" Emmet replied and walked out the door.

Stoney followed and before he could get back to the table Travis came in the side door. He motioned Stoney over to one of the vacant table. Janie brought Travis his beer and Stoney's drink off the long table.

"Were in luck," he said. He went on to tell Stoney that Billy Kiehne had sold all his cows some months ago and was going to retire, just raise a few horses and hunt bear and lions when he felt like it. He was leasing the hunting rights out on his ranch and had plenty of grass and was real interested in making a deal on Stoney's mares, but he couldn't pay very much because it took all his cash to pay the bank off and clear the ranch.

"How about my saddle horses and the old horses I've turned out. I just can't let them go to the killers."

"Oh..., I can't blame you Stoney, but I don't think I can talk him into into those."

Stoney nodded and was silent, looking down at his glass. Travis knew he was deep in thought and was quiet. Someone from the long table started to come over and join them and Travis shook his head, motioning them away.

Ten minutes later Stoney looked up at Travis.

"See if he will do this. This is what I got. You have a paper and pencil so you can write this down,?" he asked.

Travis nodded and brought out his pocket notebook and pen.

"Okay, I have five saddle horses; all with a little age, three, no make that four old geldings and mares that I have turned out to pasture; six brood mares, six two year olds, broke and ready to ride, six yearlings, six babies and one stud. He can have them all. For nothing, he won't owe me a dime, just pay for the trucking and the shipping papers."

"But this is what I want," he continued. He has to keep all of the saddle horses, all the old horses and the mares and let them live out their life on the ranch. He can sell any or all of the young horses; they're his horses. What do you think?

"He'd be a fool not to take that deal. Let me run out to the pickup and call him. I'll be right back."

Travis wasn't gone long before he returned smiling.

"You got a deal and he said anytime you want any of saddle horses back just come get them and when you get on your feet, you can have the pick of the colt crops."

"That's great," a much-relieved Stoney responded. "Now then, we got another problem. How in the hell are we going get those horses to him with those deputies sitting at my front gate? I don't want to cause Randy any problems."

They sat there running through ideas and rejecting them for a half hour.

"Okay, I got it," Stoney said. "This is what we'll do. In the morning I'll drive the mares and colts over to the pens and let them kinda get used to the other horses. You drive out tomorrow night. We'll stay in the bunkhouse, the next morning we'll drive the whole remuda out my west pasture. There's an old gate back there that goes into the LT ranch, we can cross them and go into the Rocking K and I know they will let me use their pens to load them on a truck and we can take them out the back way on that farm market highway that runs between Melrose and Portales. The deputy won't even know they're gone. What do you think?"

"How 'bout their travelling papers?" Travis asked. He looked over at the long table and saw Benny Fulgham who was just pulling up a stool. Benny was an old rodeo friend of Travis and Stoney's. Now a successful cattle trucker. Stoney used him whenever he needed any hauling.

"There's our trucker," Travis said. "Let's call him over and see if he's going to be busy day after tomorrow."

Benny said he would have a truck loose on that day and wanted to help drive the remuda to the pens. The three discussed what to do about the brand inspectors. If they tried to haul those horses without papers everyone was going to get in trouble, especially if the banker and Luther Hartzog were looking for them.

"None of your horses are carrying a brand are they," Travis asked.

Stoney shook his head no.

"So here's what we'll do. Bill Kiehne brands a 5- on his horses. My neighbor brands a 55 with one of those new freeze irons. We can borrow his irons and equipment, run the horses through Rocking K chute and brand the 5- on them. We won't need to brand the babies since they will be considered nursing foals. When we're through, we'll call the brand inspectors, show 'em the horses, he'll write up the papers and Benny will be on his way. With the freeze brand, the horses won't feel a thing."

It was agreed on. Benny would have his driver over at Rocking K chutes day after tomorrow. Benny and Travis would spend the night at the bunkhouse with Stoney. They would ride Stoney's saddle horses, which would be loaded on the trucks with the rest and then catch a ride back to the ranch. The main thing was to have the horses gone before the bank found out about it.

The next morning Stoney rode out his gate and told the new deputy, who had just arrived for his shift, that he would be coming out of the pasture south of the road and he would drive his horses through the gate and to his pens a half-mile to the north. He asked the deputy to back his car up and block the road so the horses would turn into the gate and down the lane.

Stoney and Pecos found the horses shaded up in the thickets. The stud had to show off to his mares and make one or two runs at Leo, even though they were old friends. A pop at the end of Stoney's lariat rope quickly had him in line and leading his family toward the water lot behind the house. Every so often, when one of the babies would get too close to Leo, they would turn and snap their jaws at him then quickly return to their mothers side.

They were soon in the water lot. Stoney dismounted, led Leo to the other side and opened the gate into the driveway. He whistled to Pecos to get out of the way as the horses streamed out and then hitting the county road turned west at a high lope. The deputy had no trouble turning them down the lane when they reached him. Stoney let Pecos finish the job of driving them down the lane and into the big corral while he stopped to visit with the deputy. He told him he was going to have a couple friends out for supper that night and to come down and join them. The deputy said he really appreciated it, but he better stay at his post. Stoney asked if he would mind shutting and padlocking the gate after Travis came through; the deputy said he would be glad to.

Just after dark Travis and Benny pulled up. Stoney asked them if they had any trouble getting past his sentinel.

"Stoney," Travis laughed. "You got no idea how many good friends you have."

Stoney told him he was finding that out and to unload and make themselves at home while he threw some steaks and potatoes on the fire. After eating, they sat on the bench in front of the bunkhouse enjoying their smokes and a fifth of Jim Beam that Benny had brought along. They had to put on their jackets as the fall night chilled off; when the whiskey was gone they turned in with Pecos sleeping at the end of Stoney's bunk.

Before daylight Stoney was up, had the coffee brewing and bacon and eggs frying. By the time they finished it was light enough so they had no trouble saddling their horses. Stoney took the lead with Pecos, with the two cowboys following the horses out the gate and across the pasture. Leo had to stretch it out in a hard run to stay in the front. The mares, not used to running that far, finally became winded and slowed the pace down considerably. It gave Stoney the time to reach the gate, opening it wide and remount. After the horses were through the gate they slowed down to a nice easy gait for the next three hours.

Once they reached the Rocking K pens, the sorting and branding began. Stoney had called their foreman before and told him what he would like to do. The foreman said they would be glad to help and would have the gate to the pens open and would even have three of his hands there to help with the freeze branding and loading.

The deputy at the gate had been awakened by Pecos's barking and the nickering and squealing of the horses. He had stood on the hood of his unit and watched through binoculars as the horses were let out of the pens and disappeared behind the sandhills. He nodded his head got back in his unit and finished his nap. An hour later he received a message from the dispatcher telling him he would not be relieved as there had been a car wreck north of town and all the other units were headed that way. He got out and was relieving himself when he saw a pickup coming down the county road.

A grubby faced cowboy got out the pickup walked to the gate and jostled the padlock. He then looked at all the horse tracks that had gone through the gate the day before.

"Hey you, come here," he said motioning to the deputy who had been watching from his car.

"What's this?" he asked, pointing to the horse tracks.

"Well..., those look like horses tracks to me. Yep, see over there, those are horse turds."

"God-damnit, I know those are horse tracks. I want to know what was going on here."

"Well..., Looks like to me someone drove horses through the gate and down to the pens."

"Shoot that damn lock off."

"Do what?" the deputy asked.

"I am Luther Hartzog and the bank sent me out here to count those horses. Now shoot the damn lock off."

"I know who you are Mister Hartzog and I am not going to shoot that lock off. And if you try it, without a warrant, I'll arrest you for trespassing. Now sir, I suggest you move on, you're blocking traffic."

"Blocking traffic! You know damn good an well that the Stones are the only ones that ever use this county road. And I'll be back with the District Attorney and you damn sure better not let one horse out of that gate till' I get back.

"Yes sir, that's my instructions and that's my job. Have a good day Mister Hartzog."

Three hours later Luther returned. Following him was the Assistant District Attorney and a New Mexico Brand Inspector. Luther reached into the bed of his pickup, lifting out a large set of bolt cutters and started toward the gate.

"I am sorry Mister Hartzog," said the deputy as he stepped in front of the gate. "Not until I see that search warrant."

The Assistant District Attorney, dressed like he was going to a dinner party, with freshly shined shoes, immaculate dark suit and a red tie stepped out of his car," I got the damn warrant. Now step aside," the attorney demanded.

"Could I see it please?" the deputy replied.

He mumbled something but handed it to the deputy who read it very carefully, and very slowly; he also noted that the recently appointed judge, whom just happened to be the son in law of the banks president, signed it. The assistant was fuming by the time the deputy handed it back to him. The three then climbed into Luther's pickup and drove to the pens.

An hour later the deputy could see someone walking back down the lane. Taking his binoculars, he focused them on the figure. He then started laughing so hard he had to put them down. It was the very important Assistant District Attorney walking with a limp, his beautiful coiffured hair now looking like a mop, neck tie off, shirt pulled out, and stopping ever so often to pour sand out of scuffed shoes. He was over a quarter mile away and waving at the deputy, motioning him to pick him up. The deputy decided to check the oil on his unit.

"Didn't you see me waving and yelling at you," a very mad attorney demanded.

"No sir. Man you don't look so good. What happened," the deputy asked, trying his best to act concerned and not break into laughter.

"The damn horses weren't in the corrals, we tracked them into the sandhills and that damn horse trader got us stuck. They're trying to dig it out and I want you to get on the radio and get a tractor or something to pull them out."

"Yes sir. Right away sir."

"Did you hear anything this morning or see anything suspicious down at those pens?" the attorney demanded.

"Well..., now that you mentioned it, I did hear a lot of commotion down there."

"Well why in the hell didn't you investigate it?"

"That wasn't what I was ordered to do..., sir. I was told to park here and not let any equipment or livestock out of it."

"Shit..., get on the radio and get some help for them. I'll tell you one thing, I am going to report you to the sheriff for disrespect to a superior. Now I am going to go home and clean up."

"Yes sir," replied the deputy. "You sure do need to clean up and you have a nice drive home."

"Get on that radio now" the attorney ordered and drove away kicking up a small dust storm.

"I'll sure do that," the deputy said waving good bye. "Just as soon as I have another cigarette," he said under his breath.

Just as he was finishing his smoke he heard a tractor start up at the pens. Looking through his binoculars he saw the brand inspector driving into the sandhills with Stoney's utility tractor. It had a front-end loader on it so the deputy figured they wouldn't have any trouble getting the pickup out. Another half hour proved him right as he could see Luther's truck speeding back down the lane.

Pointing down the county road he asked the deputy if the gate was locked at the end of it. The deputy told him that he was sure it was and if he tried to cut it open he would arrest him for trespassing. The brand inspector grinned and winked at the deputy.

"Damnit, whose side are you on anyway," an angry Luther asked.

"I am on the side of the law...and Mister Hartzog, you need to move your truck from the middle of the road, your blocking traffic again.

"You ass-hole," Luther said to a grinning deputy.

"You follow me," he said to the brand inspector. We'll go around to that Farm to Market road and catch them coming out the Rockin' K's main gate."

"Get on that radio and have the sheriff stop them when they get on that road," he ordered the deputy.

"I would sir but my radio has been on the blink all morning and I can't call in."

"Shit" Luther said.

"Yes sir, you're the second one this morning that told me to do that."

As they left, the brand inspector, following Luther, reached out the window and gave the deputy a thumbs up.

As soon as they were gone the deputy called in to the dispatcher and asked her to call Stewart Laney, the foreman of the Rocking K's and tell them that Luther and the brand inspector were headed that way.

The branding crew were just about finished when the foreman's wife drove up and delivered the message. After the last mare was branded the mares were turned out with their babies. All they lacked was the stud, but before they could run him in the chute the foreman stopped them and asked Stoney if he could buy him. Stoney said he belonged to Billy Kiehne and to ask Travis. The two went to the pickup to call Billy. Billy told them he had his own stud and the mares needed to be outcrossed anyway and that the Rockin K's would be doing him a favor by taking the aged stud off his hands. Just as they finished making the deal the brand inspector from Portales drove up.

"Right on time," Travis said. "We're just about to load them."

The inspector walked through the horses checking the brands and writing down the sex and color of each horse. When he finished, he looked up the brand to make sure it was registered to Billy Kiehne of Datil New Mexico; then handed the papers to Benny.

'"Everything is in order. Have a good trip. I gotta get back to the sale in Portales, see you hombres later," he waved at Stoney and drove off.

The young horses were loaded in the front compartment, mares and colts in the large middle compartment and the older horses in the back. Just before they loaded Leo and Kenneth, Stoney asked them to hold up just a minute. He walked to the two of them, who were always just a few feet from each other, this time was no exception. Stoney talked to them, played with their forelocks and then led them up the loading chute and into the truck. He stroked them one more time, said his goodbye to his old friends and closed the gate. The other cowboy just stood and watched and not one of them said a word as Stoney walked down the ramp making no attempt to hide the tears forming in his eyes.

He shook hands with Benny, Travis and the Rocking' K cowboys thanking them for their help. Benny had just started the truck when Luther pulled into the compound, and blocked the truck.

"You're not going anywhere with my horses," Luther yelled up to Benny.

"Luther I don't have your horses and if you don't move your pickup I'm going to run over it," Benny answered, looking down from the cab.

The brand inspector that had been following Luther drove in and pulled up beside Bennie's truck. Stoney started walking that way when Travis grabbed his arm.

"Let Benny work it out Stoney. He has the papers and everything is legal."

The inspector asked Benny for the papers. After checking them over he climbed up the side of the truck and counted the horses, moving some of them around so he could check the brands. Finished he climbed down and handed the papers back.

"Guess you were mistaken Mister Hartzog. All these horses belong to the Kiehnes, over on the west side of the state."

"Bull shit," fumed Luther. He saw Stoney and started his way' but didn't like the looks of the cowboys standing beside him and stopped. "Those are your horses aren't they Stone?"

"Guess not," replied Stoney. "They're carrying the Kiehne brand, so I suspect they belong to them."

"You son-of-a-bitch, I damn near burned my truck up on your God-damn sandhills to get those horses and I..."

Stoney made a lunge at him but wasn't quick enough. Travis had Luther knocked down and was standing over him. Two of the cowboys restrained Stoney.

"You better get your ass in your pickup and get outta' here while you're able," Travis said. Luther rolled over and was getting up when Travis kicked him in the rear and sent him sprawling in the sand.

Luther stumbled to his pickup and was on his way, but not before he stopped and, (holding a handkerchief to his bleeding nose), yelled out at Stoney that the bank was damn sure going to hear about this. He then gunned his truck out the compound gate. Benny, waving his goodbye to the cowboys, followed.

The foreman turned to Stoney and said he would have one of them take he and Travis back to his pens. Stoney told him he appreciated it and then asked him if he might have a horse he could borrow for a few days, and if so, he would just ride him home and would trailer him back later.

"You bet," the foreman responded. "Take mine, I'm going to the Cattle Growers Convention tomorrow and be there all week, so I won't be needing him... Stoney..., there's a lot of people that's going to be there and asking about you. You'll be missed."

Stoney thanked him and put his saddle on the horse while Travis threw the other two saddles in back of the Rockin K's pickup. Before he left Stoney asked him if he had room for the two saddles in his saddle house and if he did, would he mind keeping them for awhile. Travis agreed and he and the hand drove off.

Stoney had twelve lonesome miles of riding before he reached his corrals. He was in no hurry and took it slow so a very tired Pecos could keep up. Besides, he thought, there is no one waiting for me anyway, no one wondering where I am or what I am doing. He reached down and stroked the horse's neck as he had done many times before, forgetting for an instant that it wasn't Leo, nor was it Kenneth. It was someone else's horse. Then it came to him; for the first time since he was five years old, he didn't own a horse! Just the thought of it made him sick.

After entering his west pasture, he stopped at its windmill and tank to let a thirsty Pecos rest. It was getting dark by then and he dismounted. Putting on the Levi jacket that had been tied behind the cantle he sat on the edge of the concrete drinking tub. He watched the half-moon reflected in the water's surface and the strange shapes it took in the ripples made by the small stream coming out of the discharge pipe. He listened to the creaking of the fan as it swung around trying to catch each breath of the dying wind and the mournful lugging of the slender sucker rod as it brought the sweet clear water from the shallow depths of the sand.

Looking up at the wooden tower that he had built by hand when he was a young man; he remembered his young bride bringing him his lunch and watching him work in the hot sun, and helping when she could. At noon she would spread a blanket on the sand and they would have a picnic. The two of them, and the three dogs they had at that time that followed Stoney everywhere. They would laugh and she would excitedly tell of her plans for their ranch house that they were renovating. He sat there until the light jacket no longer kept out the coolness of the night. Reaching down and petting Pecos he said again to him, "but that was yesterday, old friend, and yesterday is gone."

Before he left he looked once again at the tower.

"How much longer old friend," he said to the windmill. "Will it be before the irrigation wells will have pumped you dry. Your fan will turn and turn, bringing up nothing but the memories of your sweet water. The water that once slacked the thirst of my quail, the antelope and my deer and the coyotes whose fresh tracks I would see whenever I would come by and taste your treasure. You will turn and turn and nobody will close you down or oil your insides, and then you will no longer be able to turn, and then you will get old and weak and someday fall into this dry sand that once you kept cool and moist."

He mounted and continued home, arriving late at night he unsaddled and was feeding the horse when a deputy drove up.

"I saw some lights go on and thought I better check, Mister Stone," the deputy said. "I hope everything went okay for you today."

"They did and thank you, and would you tell the rest of your guys thanks for being my friend?"

The deputy nodded and went back to his post. Stoney fried some ham and made a sandwich for Pecos and himself. Exhausted, once again, both mentally and physically, he climbed into bed.

CHAPTER 21

He slept late the next morning and was frying bacon and eggs when he heard a car coming down the lane. Stepping out on the porch he was surprised to see Betsy driving up. He opened the car door for her and they gave each other a small kiss.

"I'm just fixing Pecos and I something to eat. Can I fix you something," he asked.

"No, I ate some time ago but you go ahead."

They continued talking while Stoney ate. She shook her head when Stoney fixed Pecos a plate of bacon and eggs and set it on the floor beside the table.

"I'm surprised Pecos isn't sitting up at the table with you and having a cup of coffee".

Stoney looked at her, and couldn't tell if she was teasing or disgusted, so he just ignored her remark.

"Whose horse is that in the corral and where are all our horses," she asked.

"He belongs to friend of mine. And our horses are gone"

"I know they're gone. Did you get them sold?"

"More or less."

"Stoney! Don't play games with me. What did you get for them?"

He looked at her and then formed a 0 with his fingers.

"Nothing! You mean you gave them away?"

Stoney nodded.

"I can't believe you. Have you lost your mind completely? Here you are, mid-fifties, not a nickel to your name and giving away what little assets you have. You act like you're rich and haven't a care in the world."

Stoney looked at her. He started to tell her that he gave them away because Bud Thurman was going to send them to the slaughter house so they could satisfy some rich Frenchman's craving for horse meat. But, for some reason he didn't. Later he would wonder why. He knew if he had told her she would have agreed with him. He wondered if it might have been some sort of self-flagellation.

"Why didn't you call so we could discuss it? After all, they were part mine too.

"I'll tell you why. Somebody had our phone turned off in the house, along with all the rest of our utilities."

"I had them turned off. Somebody has to have some business sense around here. If we are ever going to get on our feet again we need to watch every damn nickel."

She knew she had hurt him, but at that point she didn't really care.

After a minute of silence she said, "I have to get back to work. Let me tell you why I drove all the way out here.

The Chamber Banquet is tonight and I wanted to see if you would to go with me. We haven't missed one in years and I am going to be installed as a director."

"Congratulations Betsy. I think that's great. Let me think about it for a minute."

Betsy reached over and placed her hand over his. "Stoney, I know you and Bud Thurman aren't getting along so well, but he isn't really as bad as you think he is and he was just trying to do his job; and I am sure he hated to close you down. Anyway the Chamber and Junior Chamber decided to have a joint banquet this year," she stopped to make sure he was listening.

"Go on," he said.

"Well the Junior Chamber voted Bud Thurman the *Young Entrepreneur of the Year* and Phillip and I are presenting the trophy to him from the Realtors Association."

Stoney was silent, looking out the window at the empty corrals.

"Do me a favor, when you present him the trophy would you tell the son-of-a- bitch..., oh, forget it. No..., thanks for the invitation but I am not going. If that's the kind of greedy bastards they reward they can take their fucking organization and go to hell."

"Stoney! I have never heard you talk like that before. What in the world is happening to you? You're losing it, and either you straighten out or...," she stopped. They looked at other. He was waiting for her to finish. Instead she just shook her head and walked out the door. He heard the car leave and travel down the lane and knew that would be the last time Betsy would ever see the pens that she had helped Stoney build. Board for board, pipe for pipe, everything on the ranch had felt the touch of her hand. He shook his head hoping to rid himself of memories that kept coming back.

After cleaning the dishes he went back to the saddle house and looked at a *'hundred years of gathering'*, cowboy things that had been handed down from his father and his grandfathers. He spun the rowels of his grandfather's gal-leg spurs with the small jingle-bobs. His grandfather, on his dad's side, had been breaking horses for the Vermejo Ranch in northern New Mexico. A bronc had started bucking with him on the side of a mountain above Costilla Lake, and continued toward the lake. One of the other cowboys started to head him off and his grandfather said, "Let him go, I'll drown the son-of-a-bitch."They went into the lake with his grandfather spurring him all the way. The horse came up and swam to shore, his grandfather didn't. When they recovered his body he was still wearing those spurs. That and his father's silver inlayed, gal-leg bits were Stoney's prize possessions. He found a canvass bag to put them in and carefully laid them under the seat of his pickup.

He moved his personal saddle and blanket in the bunkhouse and put the rest of the tack he couldn't bear to part with in back of the pickup. The last to go in was a Tex Tan kids saddle that his father ordered for him out of a Montgomery Ward catalog many years ago; it was his first saddle and then Mickie's. He had been looking forward to putting it on Bobbi's first horse. After finishing with the saddle house he pulled over to the boxcar to see which tools he wanted to keep. It was a '*another hundred years gathering*': Shaking his head he picked up some small tools, among them was his fencing tools, and put them in a large tool chest, barely finding room for it in the bed of the pickup.

Driving up to his gate he recognized the deputy as the same one that had delayed Luther the day before. After showing the deputy that it was all his personal gear he was taking out and remembering that the young deputy had just bought a small acreage north of Clovis he asked him what he was going to do with it. The deputy told him he and his wife had moved a double-wide on it and were now building some corrals for their horses. Stoney told him to drive on down to his saddle house, which still had lots of halters, bridles, and other tack and take everything he wanted. He didn't want to leave one piece of leather left for the bank. The deputy was elated and thanked him profusely.

By the time he dropped his '*gatherings*' off at Travis's saddle-house it was time for happy hour and he drove to the City Limits. After several drinks he decided Pecos probably needed a drink since it was an unusually, warm fall day. Janie filled up a large beer mug with water and Stoney took it out to the pickup. The Limit's parking lot and the Holiday Inn parking lot were separated by two large vacant lots and as Stoney was waiting for Pecos to finish lapping up his water he glanced up and saw that the chamber members were beginning to arrive for the banquet that was being held there. Something made him want to watch the gentlemen, dressed in their very best for the number one social event of year for this small town, escort their ladies, equally dressed, into the large Holiday Inn banquet room.

His feelings were mixed. He knew he should be escorting Betsy, as he had done for many years, to this event, but then again he knew he could not have carried off a pleasant attitude when in fact he was so bitter and boiling inside at the people he would be sitting with. He was also aware that to some extent he was envious of them and the good times they were having and would be having at the dance that followed the dinner and presentations.

He was about to put the binoculars down when he saw Phillip's Buick with his real estate company's logo on the side, pull into the parking lot. Stoney was curious as to which girlfriend he would be bringing to replace his fourth wife, whom he recently divorced. Phillip walked around to open the door and Betsy stepped out, handing him a package that Stoney assumed to be the plaque for the Young Entrepreneur of the Year. Stoney gripped the binoculars tightly and as he watched, a new, sky blue Corvette pulled up beside them. The Corvettes were relatively new and rare in Clovis and Stoney was curious to see who would be driving one. Bud Thurman exited the Corvette as gracefully as an over-weight six foot two oaf could exit from a low-slung automobile.

Bud shook hands with a smiling Phillip and gave Betsy a kiss on the cheek. They then proceeded to admire Bud's new car. Stoney thought he was going to lose it. He threw the binoculars in the seat and started back to the bar, intent on getting drunk and taking Janie to bed. Just before opening the door he stopped, looked back at Pecos sitting in the bed of the pickup..., watching Stoney with an abandoned look on his face. Stoney turned around, walked back to his truck and they drove back to the bunkhouse.

The next morning he saddled his borrowed horse to take one last ride around his place, his ranch, and his dream. While in town the day before he had called the foremen of the two neighboring ranches and told them to come over through the back way and take whatever equipment, horse trailers, tools, branding chutes and anything else they wanted. He didn't want one item left for the bank. He would tell the deputy that there would be some activity down at the pens and not to worry about it, so they shouldn't have any trouble. He also asked the Rockin' K's to pick up their horse that he would be through with by the next afternoon.

He had decided to ride his south pasture first and then the thickets. It wasn't long after entering the thickets that Pecos, as Stoney expected he would, disappeared. More out of curiosity and to make the ride one more time, he rode over to the Sadler place. Coming to their house he was surprised to see a pickup unloading furniture. Riding closer he recognized the truck, with the Taylor Farm logo on it, as the one Emmett had been using. Sure enough Emmett came out the door answering Stoney's halloo.

"Emmett, what's going on? Did you lease, or buy this place from the bank?" Stoney asked.

"I wish," he replied. "No the Taylor outfit bought it from some company in Texas and I'm just gonn'a live here."

"No shit."

"Yeah, and you know what Pete told me?"

"No tellin'"

"He said that they gave Bud Thurman a third interest in it for setting the deal up. He still has to pay his third of the expense of breaking it out and putting it in production."

Emmett paused, like maybe he was regretting running off at the mouth, "But Stoney, I wasn't supposed to tell anybody. It's supposed to be a secret or somethin'. So please don't tell anyone I told you. I shoulda' kept my mouth shut."

"Forget it Emmett I wouldn't say a word. Wonder what they gave for it."

"I don't know but somebody said it was over double what the bank had in it. I bet your wife knows. She's the one that sold it to the company in Texas and then sold it again to Taylor's."

"Well it's a nice place; you and your family will enjoy it. I'll see you down the road and you take care."

Stoney rode off trying to figure everything out. How did the two sales happen so fast. Urging his horse into a lope he decided to go into Clovis and find out from Betsy what and how it came about. After entering the thickets he whistled for Pecos who came darting out from under some salt cedars and followed Stoney to the corrals. On arriving there he was met by his neighbors gathering up what they wanted. He told them they had better take his tractor out the same way they had driven the horses so as not to get the deputy in trouble. He loaded the Rockin' K horse into one of the stock trailers they were taking and took his saddle into the bunkhouse. Opening the refrigerator he took a milk carton out that now contained sixty-five one hundred dollar bills. He took one of the bills out and returned the carton.

Betsy's car was not in the parking lot when he arrived in town. The secretary told him that she would probably be out all afternoon. Stoney told her that he needed to get some personal papers from her files. He had helped her set up her filing system so he knew he wouldn't have any trouble finding the contracts. He was just taking out the sales closing sheet on each one when Phillip walked into her office.

"What are you doing in here?" Phillip demanded.

"Phillip..., I don't think that's any of your damn business."

"Well I don't think you should be in here unless Betsy is here. So I would emphatically suggest you return whatever papers you got out of her files and set in the lobby until she returns. And take off those damn spurs before you ruin my furniture."

Stoney slammed the papers down on the desk, "You sorry son-of-a-bitch, why don't you try throwing me out?"

Stoney pushed his chair back and started toward him. Phillip quickly retreated yelling to the secretary to call the police. Stoney glanced through the papers making sure he had the ones he wanted and then walked out of her office. Phillip was standing in the doorway of his office.

"Stone, I don't want you ever to come in my building again. You do and you're going to jail."

The lobby was full of clients and the other agents were standing at their doors. Everyone was aghast at the ruckus taking place. Stoney stopped, turned around and started walking toward Phillip who hurriedly slammed the door and locked it.

Stoney was pulling into the banks parking lot when he saw Doris driving off. He followed her until she was out of site of the bank then pulled her over.

Getting into her car he told her he didn't want to get her in trouble but wanted to ask her some questions.

"Get me in trouble? That's a laugh, I just quit. Told them to cram it, grabbed my briefcase and walked out," she said, pointing to the briefcase lying beside her. "Stoney, they are nothing but a bunch of crooks and I have enough evidence in this valise to prove it. That's what I was trying to tell you the other day when you were in such a hurry."

"I'm sorry Doris. I hope I wasn't responsible for you leaving."

"Stoney…, I am sixty-four, I was planning to retire in a few months anyhow. Now, what did you want to know?"

Stoney showed her the closing statements. The first showed the grantor as the bank and Ochelle a Texas corporation in Austin, as the grantee. The next statement revealed Ochelle as the grantor and Taylor Farms, Et. Al. as the grantee. The dates of closing were just 24 hours apart.

"Did you know who signed their name as the chief executive officer of Ochelle?" Doris asked.

"I didn't pay any attention. Who?" Stoney asked.

"Jack Stovall!" Jack Stovall was a hired gun realtor for the bank. He lost his real estate licenses in New Mexico and Texas, for forgetting where he put some escrow money.

"You're kidding, Fabulous Jack Stovall," Stoney continued. "The last I heard from him he was in somewhere in Texas selling vacuum sweepers."

"Not kidding. Ochelle is just some kind of shell corporation where they place properties they have foreclosed on, then sell them later for a profit…, it's all in my briefcase along with plenty of other things. Like changing collateral on notes etcetera. You're not the only one those bastards have screwed; there are plenty of others."

"Thanks Doris, thanks a lot. What are you going to do with all that crap?"

"The bank examiners are due in the fifth of next month. I get along with them real good and know where they stay when they are in town.... I'm going to turn everything over to them."

"Doris, you're a sweetheart. You take care of yourself. I think I am going to have one more talk with your old boss. I can't believe anyone would pull something like that on Sadler's widow and kids. He just the same as stole a hundred thousand dollars from her. The son-of-bitch. And then he wins an award for it?"

"Stoney, please don't do anything rash. Promise me. These guys are mean, tough and powerful."

Stoney gave her the closing papers for safe-keeping and told her he would be in touch. He watched as she drove off, then headed for the Limits. He was steaming mad and the scene of Bud giving Betsy a kiss yesterday kept coming across his mind.

It was mid-afternoon and the only customers in the bar were a middle age couple quietly playing a game of pool.

"Hi, my favorite cowboy," Janie said as she poured him his coke and whiskey. "Where did you go yesterday? Everyone kept looking for you to come back in and you just disappeared..., with my beer mug, I might add."

"I'm sorry, Janie, I'll go get it."

"Naw, I was just kidding'. Pecos can have it," Janie paused and gave Stoney a compassionate look. "You're not having a good day, are you?"

"Janie, it's been so long since I had a good day I'm not sure I would recognize one if it did come along," he answered as he finished his drink. "Let me have another one please."

"Okay, but take it easy. It's still early in the day. You keep that up and you'll be passed out by the time your buddies get here."

Janie left to wait on the couple playing pool, giving Stoney time to think. He thought about the deal that Bud had pulled on Sadler, from not carrying insurance on Sadler's new truck, selling his horses to a killer buyer, and falsifying the collateral on his note, just as he had done on Stoney's mortgage. He thought about the kiss Bud had given Betsy on the cheek. He had had enough. Glancing at his watch he had just enough time to get in the bank before it closed. He downed his drink threw a ten dollar bill on the table and left with Janie calling after him.

Bud saw Stoney enter the bank and knew immediately that there was going to be trouble. He told his new secretary to call the security guard and then shut his door He had no more than stepped back behind his desk when Stoney burst in.

"Don't ever come into my office when that door is closed. You understand….," he said with a smirk.

The words had barely left his mouth. Stoney's fist drove into his nose knocking him backward into his credenza and down on the floor. The force of his heavy body knocked the stuffed rattlesnake and prairie dog off the credenza and onto Buds head.. Stoney wasn't able to enjoy the sight long. The security guard came in, grabbed him from the back, and threw him to the floor and in a split second had his wrist handcuffed behind his back.

The guard was about to lift him into a chair when Bud came around the desk and told the guard to leave him on the floor. He was about to kick him when the guard stopped him. Instead he stomped Stoney's new hat, which had gone sprawling across the floor. Bud then ground it into the floor, and told his secretary to call the police. He was throwing Mister Stone in jail.

Stoney, was still lying on the floor of the bank when he heard multiple sirens pulling up to the bank, front and back. The owner of the bank, Alex, and other bank officials were gathered in Buds office deciding what charges they were going to file against Stoney and giving their condolence's to Bud, who had finally stopped his nose bleed. Stoney was extremely uncomfortable laying on his stomach and the hand that he had hit Bud with was beginning to swell and hurt, especially with the handcuffs that were placed on too tight. He asked the guard to loosen them a little. When the guard started to, Bud stopped him.

Two police officers lifted Stoney, not too gently, off his feet and escorted him into the parking lot where their unit was parked. Pecos was watching and not too happy about it. Stoney turned to one of the officers that he was acquainted with and asked him to call his daughter, and ask her to come to the bank's parking lot, get his pickup and take care of Pecos. He was giving the officer her telephone number when Bud, who was walking behind them, overheard him.

"Forget it," he ordered the officer. "That pickup is ours now and that damn mongrel is going to the pound."

Stoney started to protest when he was placed in the patrol car and the door slammed shut.

While Stoney was being processed at the Clovis jail on charges of assault and battery, Pecos was having his own trouble. Shortly after he had watched his master being hauled off, Bud and the bank security officer started to open the door to Stoney's pickup. They were frightened away by Pecos, who snapped at them from the bed of the pickup. About that time the Clovis City Animal Control truck pulled up and a uniformed officer with a snare loop approached the truck. Pecos had watched as men in the same uniforms had taken his Stoney away under duress and he was not about to have the same done to him. Every time the pound personnel would try to place the loop over Pecos's head he would duck, grab the pole holding the loop between his powerful jaws and try to wrestle it away from the officer. After three of four tries Bud had had enough. Still holding a towel to his nose, which had started bleeding again' he yelled at the officer.

"Shoot the son-of-a-bitch."

The officer looked at Bud then reluctantly brought out his tranquilizer gun from his truck, loaded it and took aim at Pecos, who was well aware of what a gun could do. Just before the officer could pull the trigger Randy drove in the parking lot. He had heard the chatter over the police radio about trouble at the bank involving a Bill Stone. Although several miles in the country, he had rushed back.

"Don't shoot," he yelled at the officer, as he came running up.

The officer's attention was drawn away and Pecos saw his chance. He made a mighty leap landing on the officer's chest, knocking him backward. As the officer toppled backward, with his finger still on the trigger, the gun went off. Bud Thurman had been standing behind the shooter and had turned to run when he saw the vicious dog jump from the pickup. The dart struck Bud in the butt who went down screaming that he had been shot. Randy watched, heartsick, as Pecos ran down the alley and disappeared. He then turned his attention to Bud who was still rolling around on the ground holding his behind and crying.

"How much tranquillizer did you have in that dart?" he asked the officer.

"As big as he is, not enough to hurt him; probably put him to sleep for an hour or two, that's all," the officer responded.

Bud was already getting drowsy and asking for an ambulance. Randy shook his head, and then went to his unit and called for an ambulance to pick up a fat banker asleep in the bank's parking lot. He then went looking for Pecos, after telling the Animal Control officer to watch for the dog but do not to attempt to capture him. Just call him and he would pick the dog up.

Unable to find Pecos, Randy alerted his deputies to watch for him and then went to the city jail. Stoney had been processed and was sitting on a bench in the holding pen rubbing his wrist. His face was bruised where he had hit the desk when he had been thrown to the floor. Two drunks were asleep on the other two benches. The jailer took Randy's gun and then let him into the pen. He sat down next to Stoney and neither said a word for a couple moments.

"Were you drunk?"

"No, not really, I had a couple, but I wasn't drunk, Stoney said looking up at his friend. "I really blew it this time…,didn't I?"

"Yep, it certainly appears that way. You want me to call you an attorney?"

"You know one that the bank hasn't got under their thumb?"

"There's a few, not many, but a few."

"Do I really need one?"

"Depends on if the banker lives."

"What the hell you mean? If the banker lives."

Randy cuffed Stoney on the shoulder. "Aw hell Stoney, I was just kidding you. But you missed all the excitement."

Randy went on to explain what happened and told him the last time he saw Pecos he was running down the alley behind the bank headed south.

"Randy! You have to get me out of here. I have to find Pecos"

"I know, I know, the jailer is working on it right now. The bail for simple assault and battery is a thousand dollars. I paid that, and he's getting the papers together. I have told my people and they're keeping an eye out for Pecos."

One of the guards unlocked the door and told them the head jailer was waiting in his office for them. As Stoney and Randy entered his office he motioned them to be quiet and pointed to the radio. The announcer had just broken into the regular programming with a news flash.

"A prominent Clovis banker was rushed to Memorial Hospital suffering from an assault and a gunshot wound. Bud Thurman was brutally attacked by an irate, long-time customer of the bank, who is the husband of a well-known local realtor. No reason was given for the unprovoked attack and the attacker is now in the city jail under heavy guard. Mister Thurman is reported to be in critical condition. Alex Maynard, president of Merchants and Ranchers Bank was quoted as saying that only the heroic effort by Mister Thurman and the bank's security guard kept other employee's lives from being endangered. We now return you to our regular programming but we will continue monitoring the situation and will keep you informed on this fast breaking story. This is Keith…"

The jailer turned the radio off.

"Talk about bull shit, but…, before I let you go let me call the hospital and see how he is doing. I don't want to turn such a mean desperado loose on our citizens," he looked up at Stoney and grinned.

Stoney and Randy watched as he talked to the head nurse on that floor. In a minute he laughed, said thank you and hung up the phone.

"Okay, free to go. He is just fine and they're trying to get him to leave, but he's enjoying the attention so much he swears they need to keep him all night for observation."

He looked at Stoney's black and blue face, his swollen hand and wrist. "Looks to me you're the one that needs to be in the hospital.

Stoney and Randy thanked him and walked out to the parking lot where Randy's unit was parked. As they did so, they saw Betsy's Cadillac pulling in.

"Thanks a lot, Randy. Here comes Betsy. I'll get her to take me to my pickup."

"Stoney, I better wait. There are some things we need to go over, plus..., you don't have a pickup anymore."

"What do you mean I don't have a pickup?" Stoney asked incredulously.

"It's been impounded. The bank says it belongs to them."

"Oh bull shit. Let me talk to Betsy for a minute. I'll be right back..., if you don't mind waiting."

"I'll be right here. Take your time."

Stoney walked up to her as she was rolling the window down.

"What are you doing out of jail?" she asked, way too calmly.

"Randy bailed me out."

"That's too bad. Get in the car; we need to talk," she ordered.

Stoney walked around the car, opened the door and gently slid in with a grimace. Some of his ribs were beginning to throb where they had hit a metal chair when he was thrown to the floor.

"Stoney you have completely lost it. Your gone. If I thought I could have you committed until you sober up I would. But..., now listen carefully, I am going to file for divorce. If I don't, you're going to drive me completely insane."

Stoney felt that the blood draining from him and felt dizzy. "Ah... Betsy, I wasn't drunk and he wasn't hurt..., the son-of-bitch deserved to be shot..."

She held up her hand stopping him. "I know he wasn't hurt. I just came from the hospital."

It was Stoney's turn to interrupt her. "Well that was damn sure nice of you. Did you take him some flowers. I suppose he and Phillip and you will have a big party with all the money you made off of Sadler's widow and kids. Excuse me, but I have to find a lost dog."

He got out of her car and slammed the door, almost bending double with pain from moving so fast with broken ribs.

"Stoney, let me tell you something about that money," she yelled at him as he left. Stoney kept walking.

"Let's go find my dog Randy," Stoney said as he got back into the sheriffs car.

"I need to get back to the court house Stoney; if you remember I have an election next week," the sheriff responded. "And the first thing we need to do is find a way for you to get around. You can use my pickup. But let me tell you what the bank has done. They have been real busy."

Randy went on to tell Stoney that the bank had received permission to block the county road going to your place. They're putting a gate up just off the highway. They have a promise from the County Commissioners that the county would vacate the road at their next meeting since Taylor Farms and you were the only ones that really used it.

"My deputy," Randy continued. "Radioed in and said that the Taylor people are already building a gate across the road and the DA's office sent word he could leave as soon they get it locked."

"Shit! Randy, can they do that?"

"You know by now who we're dealing with. You could probably hire a lawyer and he could get it stopped, but that would take time..., and money."

"How about my personal stuff in the bunkhouse?"

"I don't know Stoney, I honestly don't know."

"The deputy is still out there then?"

"Yeah, Dallas, the same one that was out there when your horses mysteriously disappeared out the back way," he gave a Stoney a sly grin.

"You heard about that. Okay, can you get him on the radio for me? I want to ask him to do a favor. If it's okay with you."

Randy soon had the deputy on the radio and Stoney asked him if he would mind going to the bunkhouse and picking up his saddle, gear and what few clothes he had there. The deputy was only too glad to help.

"One more thing Dallas. There's a milk carton in the refrigerator, that's the most important thing. It's got what little money I have left, and I sure could use it now."

The deputy told him they were almost finished with the gate and he should be back at the courthouse in a couple hours.

Randy looked at him quizzically and Stoney explained where the money came from and asked him to take him to the Ford dealership. It looked like he was going to have to buy a pickup. He then asked him about his personal stuff that he had in the pickup.

"Your .30- 30 is under lock and key at the police station and there's no way in hell they're gonna' let you have it back. The rest of the stuff I am sure they will let you have. We'll drop by there on the way and pick it up."

Sure enough they did and Stoney was relieved to retrieve the canvas sack with the spurs and bit.

Stoney found what he was looking for: a clean, low mileage used 150 Ford with four wheel drive. He told the dealer, who he had done business with for years, that he would have the thirty nine hundred dollars for him in a couple hours and drove off in search of Pecos.

After three hours Stoney felt as if he had driven through almost all of Clovis's alleys that lay south of the bank. He was discouraged, and it was getting dark when he drove to the courthouse and retrieved his belongings and the milk carton. Next he went to the Ford house where the owner was waiting for him. Stoney apologized for being late, paid him and then rented a motel room. He was so sore and tired he could hardly carry his saddle into the room, getting his boots off only aggravated his throbbing ribs. He finally gave up and poured himself a half tumbler of whiskey, lay down on the bed and thought about the day. There had never been a worse day in his life: he lost his dog, got beat up, was thrown in jail, his wife filed for divorce, he was locked out of what was once his place.. Finishing his drink, he fell into a fitful sleep.

He was up early the next morning and headed toward the ranch hoping to find Pecos. He stopped at every farm and ranch asking about his dog. No one had seen him but all said they would call Mickie if they did. Stoney reached the new gate barring him from entering the road that he had travelled for over 30 years. Looking for Pecos' tracks, he climbed over the gate and was searching the road when Emmett drove up followed by a pickup bearing Cheeny Engineering logo on the side. As Emmett was unlocking the gate to let the surveyors out, Stoney asked him what was going on.

"I don't know for sure Stoney. I was just told to take these guys out so they could survey around your old place again, and see where to put some sprinklers. What happened to your hat, it looks like a bull been sitting on it?"

"Yeah I know," Stoney replied taking off his hat and looking at it. "I can't believe that bank worked that fast. Did they give it to Taylor Farms already?"

"Don't think so. But the rumor is they are going to lease it to us' until they go through the motion of selling it." The surveyors honked their horn interrupting Emmett. "The son-of-bitches, wait till I tell you what they told me." He gave them a finger and then opened the gate for them. They sped through throwing a wad of dust on Stoney and Emmett.

"Anyhow," he continued. "Those guys said your house is going to be in the way of one of the sprinklers. They looked at it real good and decided the cheapest way to go would be to bulldoze it, the corrals and all those old trees into a pile and set fire to 'em. Aint that the shit's. All that work you and your wife put into that old place."

Stoney shook his head and felt like he could almost cry. "Emmett, look, I lost Pecos in town yesterday and am sure he will try to try to come back home. Could you do me a favor and let me go in and look for him. I'll lock the gate when I leave."

Emmett took off his Taylor Farms cap and scratched his head. After a moment he replied. "Stoney I would really like to, but if Pete or any of the rest of them caught you out here they would fire me in minute. I just can't do it. I am sorry."

Stoney told him he understood and asked him to keep watch for Pecos and to call his daughter if he should happen to see him. A dejected Stoney drove back to town.

His first stop was the Limits, where Janie told him that Travis was looking for him. He had given her his mobile number. Stoney used the phone in the package store to return the call.

"I hope you have some good news for me," Stoney said when Travis finally answered.

"Don't know about good news but Jim Bob called the house yesterday. I wasn't there but he talked to Joann. Said he just called to see how everyone was and that he was back in Eagle Nest getting ready for hunting season. I thought you might like to know."

"Thanks Travis. I sure need to talk to him. Don't guess he left a number where he could be reached?"

"He never does Stoney."

"Yeah, I figured. *Bueno.*"

Stoney hung up the phone and looked around. Janie had come into the package store and had been watching him.

"It doesn't take long for news to get around this little town," she said.

"What are you talking about?" Stoney asked.

"That your wife has filed for divorce."

"I guess it's true, Janie. Look, I have to leave town for a few days. Do me a favor and check that pound ever so often for Pecos. I would really appreciate it."

Janie nodded her head, walked up to him and put her arms around his neck. "Stoney I have always been in love with you and I don't mind being second choice. I want you to know that I'll be here for you…, if you want me."

Stoney was embarrassed by her honesty. He gave her a short kiss then backed away.

"Thanks Janie, maybe someday. Everything has happened so fast I don't really know who I am any more. Or what I'm going to do. I know what I want to do. I want to hurt someone. I know that sounds silly but I really do. I want to hurt that damn bank. I want to hurt Bud Thurman and that damn Taylor Farms outfit. Somehow I'm going to figure out how."

"It looks like you are the only one that's getting hurt," she said, putting her hand softly on his bruised face.

He gave her a hug and went to his pickup. Reaching under the seat he opened up the milk carton and counted the money he had left. Including what he carried in his money clip it came to $2400. Enough to get him by for several months. His next stop was to an RV center where he purchased a camper shell and then to an outdoor store where he picked up a bedroll, portable mattress, and other camping material including a used Winchester .30-30. He was determined to stretch what money he had as long as possible, and motel rooms were a luxury he could do without. Picking his saddle and clothes up at the motel, he then went to Mickie's house to tell her and Bobbi goodbye and to watch for Pecos; he then headed north.

As he was driving it occurred to him that he was missing Pecos more than he was Betsy. He would have never believed a person's life could change so dramatically in such a short period of time. How a person could lose so many things he loved? How could a marriage that lasted over twenty-five years end so quickly? He was on a guilt trip most of the way, blaming himself for the hole he had dug for himself and his family, and then he started thinking about Eddie, Phillip and Betsy coming down the hall of the real estate office laughing and the look on their faces when they saw him. The innocent kiss on the cheek that Bud gave Betsy. He could visualize Sadler's children as their horses were dragged away to the killers. He could visualize the people he had come to hate shooting the quail he loved and then the tractors plowing up the grass that he had carefully managed and nurtured for so many years.

His mind began to play, the *Might Have Been, Could Have Been, Should Have Been,* game. If he had just done it another way…, if that son-of-bitch hadn't done so and so, this is the way it would be instead of driving by himself to the mountains alone…, no wife, no ranch, no horses, and no dog. By the time he had reached a camping area on the Cimarron River, between Eagle Nest and Cimarron, he was sipping on a coke and whiskey he had picked up in Springer, and had absolved him of the blame and placed it all, unfairly, on the others.

The next morning he started his search for Jim Bob. Some said he had gone to Albuquerque; others that he had taken his horse and pack mule and was somewhere in the Pecos Wilderness locating elk for the coming hunting season. Stoney figured this to be a credible story since he had found no animals at Jim Bob's camp next to the mine. Stoney shot the lock off the gate and decided to camp out at the site until Jim Bob returned.

On the afternoon of the third day he went into Eagle Nest to get some supplies and was sitting in the bar having a beer when the sheriff of Colfax county walked through the swinging doors. He surveyed the few patrons then walked over to Stoney.

"I guess you're Bill Stone," he said with a thick New Mexican accent.

"Yes sir..., I am. Am I under arrest or something?"

"Not at this minute, but if you don't call my friend Randy, like *muy pronto,* you could be in a lot of trouble. And one more thing Mister Stone, if I was you I'd stay out these bars for awhile."

"Yes sir sheriff," Stoney replied, wondering what was so urgent. "Uh, by the way you don't happened to know how Randy's election came out do you?"

"He won it. It was close but he did win it. I gotta' be going but if I was you I'd get to phone right away," he touched the brim of his hat, said adios and walked out.

Stoney paid for his beer and found a pay phone. After a wait, Randy came on the phone and Stoney could immediately tell he was none too happy.

"Stoney! Did you happen to look at that release order I gave you when I got you out of jail."

"No Randy, I meant too, but forgot about it. I think it's still on my dash board. You want me to go get it."

'No! I'll just read one to you. It says right here. Number one. You will not possess a firearm. I know you pretty well and I bet you got a Winchester lever action out in pickup. Am I right?"

"Yes sir," Stoney replied weakly.

"Number two. You will not possess or consume alcohol or enter liquor establishment. Is that somebody playing pool, in a bar, that I hear in the background?"

"Yes sir."

"Number three. You will not leave the county without permission. You're up in Colfax, Mora or San Miguel county aren't you??

"Yes sir…, I guess I should have looked at that paper."

"You get your ass down here right now, don't stop to have a drink, don't stop to pee, don't stop for anything. You understand me…, and one more thing. You hide that Winchester and that fifth of Jim Beam that I know you got in your truck, better yet throw that damn whiskey away. And Stoney…don't dare go over the speed limit. If the state police would pick you up, you are going to jail and there won't be one thing I can do to help you. You got that."

Yes sir…, I'm leaving right now…and Randy, congratulations on your election.

Randy slammed the phone down and Stoney started back to Clovis.

Stoney arrived in Clovis after dark and went to Mickie's house, to make his call. Randy told him to be in his office at nine the next morning. Sitting down to his first home cooked meal in weeks he realized how much he missed his family and how alone he was. After dinner he played with Bobbi until it was her bedtime. After tucking her in bed, he spent most of the night visiting with Mickie and Scotty about his problems and mostly about the divorce. He told them how sorry he was and how he wished it had not turned out the way it had, but not to blame Betsy. It was his fault and his alone.

Mickie told him not to put all the blame on himself, that she had never known of a more perfect marriage and how two people could love each other any more than he and her mother did. But that it was as if a number of circumstances, which neither one of you had any control of, forced you all to a fork in the road. And that you had taken one and her mother had taken the other. She also told him that as much as she hated it she could not see their paths ever joining together again. Stoney, as much as it hurt, had to agree.

The next morning Stoney was in the sheriff's office and Randy was in a much better mood.

"Okay, this is what's coming out of the chute," Randy announced. "I got the hearing in front of a magistrate changed to this morning at ten o'clock in Tuck Bodie's court."

"Tuck Bodie's! He's in the banks pocket bigger than shit," Stoney exclaimed.

"Hold on," Randy held up his hand. "He ain't gonna be there. You remember Martha Proctor, she used to run barrels when you and I were going down the road."

"Yeah," Stoney answered. "She and her husband had a nice little ranch over in the Gerhardt Valley. I think I heard they lost that ranch a couple years ago.

"That's right, a horse fell with her husband coming off the caprock and killed him. They didn't find him for a week. There wasn't a way she could hold onto that place together, what with the drought and all and without the extra pay check he was making day-working for some big neighboring ranches. Anyhow, she ran for magistrate in DeBaca county a couple years ago and won it. Tuck is out of town and there's not much going on in Fort Sumner so she is filling in for him for a few days. I think we might have a chance of getting it thrown out. They tell me the bank examiners are in town and the rumor is that the Merchants and Ranchers Bank is scared shitless. So, with any luck maybe they won't show up. What do you think?"

"It's damn sure worth a chance, and Randy I really appreciate you taking care of business for me. Don't know how I will ever pay you back."

Randy stood up, put on his hat and said, "Let's go, we don't want to be late for the pretty lady."

The hearing could not have gone better. As Randy figured, Judge Proctor remembered Stoney, and was naturally sympathetic to anyone losing his or her ranch. The bank didn't show up and the judge dismissed the charges and even waived the court cost. Stoney thanked her as he walked out the Martha called him aside and told him that she knew how he felt, she had wanted to punch her banker in the nose a couple of times but for him to play it cool.

Stoney drove out to the locked gate keeping him from the road to his ranch. The road that he had driven so many times, the road that led to his place, his home and the many things he loved and cherished. He got out of the pickup and whistled for Pecos, knowing full well that it was in vain. He returned to his pickup just as a car drove by, slowed down and then backed up. It was the minister from the little church he had been attending.

"Hello Bill," the minister said as they shook hands. "I been looking for you; in fact I was on the way to your wife's office to give her this letter. Sadler's wife sent it to me. She had mailed it to your ranch address and it was returned so she wanted me to deliver it."

He handed Stoney the letter and asked him if he was all right and if there is anything he could do for him.

Stoney thanked him and said there was only one thing he could do, and that would be to pray for him, and that he wasn't sure what was going to happen to him or which way he was headed.

"Bill," the preacher said. "Let me share something with you. If you have just a minute."

Stoney nodded a yes.

"I know what you are going through and you're not the only one of my beloved congregation that's passing through this tribulation and losing their places. I have counseled and prayed with several of them and I think this verse out of Psalms seems to be the most appropriate."

"For man is like grass. For the wind passes over it, and it is gone. And its place knows it no more."

"What it means Bill is that you never really owned this place, these sandhills and the grass that grows on it. Not anymore than that antelope that I see on that knoll over there or the coyotes, badgers and other wildlife that live and raise their young here. Or that hunter that left his spear head in that mamouth 13,000 thousand years ago," he said pointing in the direction of the Blackwater Draw Site. "He thought that this was his place, but all of you were and are mere travelers, who stops, uses these sandhills, and then proceeds on to your next great adventure. And one more thing Bill. Only God will be the final judge of the stewards of his land, not the banker, not your neighbors nor the business man in town. And Bill you have been a good steward, you do not need to apologize to anyone. Okay?"

"Okay," Stoney nodded in agreement. "I never thought about it that way, but you know..., I think you're right."

The minister assured him that he would pray for him, and for Betsy. They shook hands and the preacher laid his hand on Stoney's shoulder, said a short prayer, and drove off. Stoney leaned against his pickup and read the letter.

Dear Betsy and Bill,

I want to thank you for all your prayers and concerns for my family and myself. Betsy, I especially want to thank you for your letter of encouragement and thank you so much for giving us all the commissions you earned when you sold and resold our ranch.

I bought a small house next to my parents with that money and the kids have met new friends. They are enjoying school and I know that we will all survive this.

I love you both,
Brandi Yates

Stoney checked the dates on the letter and was embarrassed when he discovered that Betsy had given her the money before he had even found out about the sales and worse, before he had berated her for making the commissions. He hated himself to even think that Betsy would have been so greedy as to make and keep a commission off a sale that destroyed a family. He thought about it all the way to town. He had to apologize and searched for the right words to express it.

Driving into the parking lot he was almost relieved when he didn't see her car. Barely nodding at the secretary he went into her office, shut the door and sat at her desk to compose a note.

Dear Betsy,

I am so sorry that I ever thought you would keep that Yates commission. I know now what you were trying to tell me that day at the jail. I guess I forgot how kind and sweet you have always been. I am so sorry for the way things have turned out. I know I have hurt you deeply through all this. Please forgive me, I will always cherish the memories of all the good times we have had over so many years.

I love and will always love you,

Stoney

He had just finished signing it when the door opened and Phillip stuck his head in.

"How come you're not in jail," he demanded. I told you never to set foot in this building again. I'm calling the police right now."

Stoney sat looking at him, then laid the pen on the letter, slowly got to his feet and started toward Phillip. Phillip, again, ran to his office, locking his door and shouting for someone to call the police. Stoney told the secretary never mind that he was leaving anyhow. He leaned across the desk gave her a kiss on the cheek and walked out.

Ranch Corrals in a state of despair a few years after Stoney lost his ranch.

CHAPTER 22

Stoney arrived at the Goose Creek camp after dark. Jim Bob wasn't there but there was an empty bottle of Jim Beam by his old campfire, next to it was a note tied to the neck of an unopened bottle of Jim Beam, .

The note read ***Stoney, I found your calling card so replaced it with a full one. Going to Las Vegas for a poker game. Will be there for a couple of days. If you get back, come on down to Joe's Ringside. He'll know where you can reach me. JB***

Noon the next day Stoney arrived in Las Vegas. The winding eighty mile drive through the changing colors of a late fall in northern New Mexico was enough to soothe anyone's troubled spirits and Stoney was no exception. By the time he drove into the the small, historic town of Las Vegas he was feeling better.

Pulling into the parking lot of Joe's Ringside, Stoney didn't see any pickups that might resemble one that Jim Bob would be driving. Joe's was one of Stoney's favorite watering holes when he used to be on the road trading cattle. As he opened the door he was welcomed by the smell of long-spilled booze, that had soaked into the wooden floor for close to a hundred years and permeated the air. He walked into the large room with its small stage where an occasional stripper passing through town would practice her profession, stay a few days, and move on. It was rumored that Joe actually auditioned strippers for the big joints in Las Vegas, Nevada. The room also had a few pool tables and a medium size dance floor. With the exception of a couple young men playing pool the place was empty of patrons.

Coming out of the bright sunlight and into the darkened interior Stoney could hardly see. After his eyes adjusted to the dark interior he could discern an old man of Mexican descent setting behind the bar reading the Albuquerque Journal. He never looked up as Stoney sat down on a stool across from him.

"What's your pleasure cowboy?" he asked.

"Give me a draw and I was wondering if you'd seen Jim Bob Nuckols around here?"

For the first time the old man looked up at him. "Coors or Bud?"

"Coors please," Stoney responded.

The old man reluctantly folded the paper, placed it on the bar, and drew Stoney a beer.

"I said I was wondering if you had seen Jim Bob Nuckols around here."

"I heard you the first time. You a friend of his?"

"Yes sir, and a partner too."

He looked Stoney over real good before he answered. "They're in a business conference over at the El Fidel."

He pointed in the general direction of the hotel that was the gathering place for ranchers, politicians, and sportsmen.

"I guess they're discussin' fifty two items," Stoney said smiling at the bartender.

He smiled back and was warming up to Stoney. "Yeah, I spect' so, those and a couple jokers." He looked up at the large Hamm's clock hanging behind the bar. "They outa' be in here in about an hour." The bartender sat back down in his chair, ready for some conversation.

Just as the old man said, in about an hour Jim Bob and three or four others came in. Jim Bob saw Stoney, he said something to the others, shook their hand and told the bartender to bring them a drink on him.

"Let's get us a table," he told Stoney and motioned to one on the back side of the bar, away from the others. When they were seated Jim Bob pulled out a roll of bills showing them to Stoney.

"Been a good afternoon," Jim Bob said smiling. He put the roll back in his shirt pocket and got serious. "I visited with Travis on the phone last night. We talked for an hour or more. He told me all about your troubles. Stoney, I'm real sorry. I just wished the mine had paid out like it looked like it would, for awhile."

"Yeah, you and me both, friend," Stoney replied. "So..., what are we going to do with it? They sure tore up a pretty canyon. Wouldn't make much of a cabin site now."

"Not much and anyhow it goes back to Forest Service if someone doesn't work it a little every year."

"Would it pay someone to work it?"

"Ah..., there will always be a little silver in there. Enough that it would make a pretty cheap cabin site and all a fella would have to do is work it just a few days every year to keep his lease. I guess we could shove it onto somebody for a little money. We would have to clean it up though."

They sat there for awhile discussing how they could turn a dollar on it when the door opened and a figure stepped in. They looked up, but could not make him it out silhouetted against the fading light outside. They were about to turn back to their conversation when the figure, still standing in the doorway spoke in a loud English accent.

"Good evening gentlemen. And oh, what a beautiful evening it is," he said addressing everyone in the bar. He strolled in and addressed the bartender in the most beautiful Spanish language that one could imagine.

The bartender, who had immediately jumped to his feet when the man entered, said, "My honor, how gracious of you to patronize my humble establishment. And what would please your royal taste this evening?"

"Well I'll be damn," Stoney exclaimed. "That could be just one man. The one and only Milnor de Santos, the Duke of Mora County."

"Who in the hell is the Duke of Mora County?" Jim Bob responded.

"An old friend of mine who was my mentor when I was involved in politics. Just a minute and I'll introduce you.

The Duke was in deep conversation with the bartender when Stoney tapped him on the shoulder and was immediately rewarded with a kiss on each cheek.

After a prolonged greeting Stoney escorted Milnor through the tables and introduced him to Jim Bob.

"Jim Bob it is my pleasure to introduce you to the Duke of Mora County. Considered by many to be one of the finest 'flimflam' artist west of the Mississippi."

"Oh, you're much too gracious my good friend," Milnor injected.

Stoney went on to explain that he had met Milnor when both were serving as commissioners in their respective counties. They had instantly become friends and the Duke had sent his son to Stoney's ranch for several summers to learn the cowboy way.

Milnor and his son were the last descendants of the de Santos land grant that, at one time, encompassed many thousands of acres in Mora and Colfax county. Through bad luck and inattentive management, the land grant had dwindled to a few hundred acres with an old, large house and outbuildings…, all in disrepair. Minor now lived by his wits and while trying to give his son the same extensive education and travels that his parents had lavished on him. Milnor could converse fluently in English, Spanish, French and German. Although Milnor had travelled extensively, he loved Mora County and its inhabitants, and was treated as royalty by them.

After the introduction Stoney inquired about Milnor's son Zack and was told that he was attending an exclusive college in Ecully, France and doing well, although he was somewhat homesick for the mountains of New Mexico. It was then Milnor's time to ask how Stoney and Betsy were doing and what brought him to northern New Mexico.

Stoney looked down at his drink and Jim Bob shook his head and took a long swallow of his.

"I am sorry," Milnor said, noting the immediate response of both. "I didn't mean to upset you."

"No, no," replied Stoney. "You have every right to ask. It's just that things have not been going my way…, not for some time. I am not sure you want to hear all about it; nor have the time and patience for a long sad story."

"Of course I have time…, I promised to meet our mutual friends the Bonomos here this afternoon for a couple days of partying…please proceed."

And proceed Stoney did. He had just started his narration when Reno and Penny arrived and drew up chairs with the three of them. After they received their drinks, and at the Bonomo's insistence, Stoney reiterated to Milnor how his life had changed since they had last seen each other and then brought everyone up to his current status.

After he had finished the five of them sat in silence for a brief time and then Milnor slapped the table. The noise startled the bartender who looked their way as Milnor motioned him to bring the table a round.

"*Mi companeros,*" he exclaimed. "Life is too short to be so sad. Let us put our heads together and think of a way to help our *triste amigo.* Bill, do I understand that the villain, the banker, has an abnormal amount of avariciousness and tends to be narcissistic."

"If you mean, is he greedy and thinks a lot of himself; the answer is yes, and a double helping of both, more so than anyone I have ever met."

"Ah ha." Milnor said with a devilish grin on his face. "The two personality traits that can lead to one's downfall, and the ones most easy for us to take advantage of, and hasten him to his deserved destiny."

"And," Milnor continued, looking at Jim Bob. "You say this mine still looks like a mine and a person could still find some of its treasurer; all-be-it, a very small quantity."

The rest of them looked at him, their curiosity showing.

"That's right. And I think I know where you might be going with this," Jim Bob replied.

By the time drinks were delivered they were all in agreement that something could be salvaged, if nothing more than the satisfaction of giving the banker and his friends their just rewards. Four hours later a plan was in place The more rounds that were consumed, the more elaborate the arrangement became.

CHAPTER 23

Pecos wasn't sure what had happened at the banks parking lot. Something was terribly wrong and he had to get back to his ranch. Stoney would surely be there, or Betsy, or Mickie. It was his home and everything would be all right as soon as he returned.

Jumping on the man with the gun, and hearing the shot, had completely unnerved Pecos, so much that he didn't recognize his friend, Randy. He raced down the alley heading south. He knew the route by heart, after so many trips into town in the pickup. The second time he crossed a street there was screeching of brakes and a horn blaring. The car was on him before he was aware of it and he lunged to the side as the tire clipped his back foot barely breaking the skin. He rolled over and headed to the next alley where he found a place to hide beneath an old abandoned trailer house.

He lay there quivering. After he finally quit shaking he began to lick his injured foot and tried to reason things out. Something bad had happened in town. Something had been changing for the last few months. Betsy no longer came home to the ranch. The horses were gone as well as the cattle. He and Stoney were living in the bunkhouse - not the home where he was raised. He could also feel the stress that Stoney had been going through.

After he had rested and gotten a drink from a leaky outdoor faucet he started home. He had little difficulty figuring out which direction to take. The many times he had ridden with Stoney had given him a good sense of direction and the landmarks had become familiar to him. It took some courage to run across the overpass but he managed using the pedestrian walk. Next was the stockyards and then across the tracks where he had faithfully guarded their pickup until Stoney returned from his train ride. After crossing the tracks he was in the country where there was very little traffic.

He was travelling on the edge of the highway and not paying a lot of attention to the few pickups and cars that whizzed by until one that was headed in the opposite direction slammed on its brakes after passing him. Pecos looked back over his shoulder. It was Pete and he was getting out of the pickup with a rifle. Pecos jumped into an irrigated field of corn as the bullet cut through the stalks. He continued running through the corn until he was tired and his injured foot started hurting. He rested for awhile and then continued on, only this time keeping off the highway and traveling in the borrow ditch where he could quickly run into a field or pasture for cover. He also became more watchful; and when he heard or saw an automobile he would hide until it passed. In so doing he missed Stoney in the new pickup, neither recognizing it or the sound.

It was just before daylight when Pecos finally reached the ranch. The first place he went to was their house. Still deserted. On to the corrals and bunkhouse. Stoney was not there, neither were Kenneth and Leo, the rest of the horses nor the cows and their calves. A very tired, sad and lonely Pecos crawled into his hole under the saddle house and sank into a deep sleep.

Pecos had excavated the hole beneath the saddle house when he was just a pup. It was a place to hide when Stoney scolded him, and a place to rest during breaks of working cattle.

It was mid-morning when Pecos awoke and came out of his hole. Thirsty and famished he went first to the stock pond; walking into the water until it was up to his neck, he drank his fill. Next, he tried to find something to eat but finding none' he returned to the hole and slept sporadically. He would lick his foot briefly and then listen for Stoney's pickup, then drift back to sleep.

At mid-afternoon he was laying on the bank of the stock pond when he saw dust rising from the county road. His tail started wagging knowing it had to be Stoney. When the vehicle stopped to open the gate at their lane, he realized it was two automobiles, a pickup followed by a suburban. When they started down the lane to the corrals Pecos could tell by the sound that it wasn't their pickup, and he hurriedly ran to his hiding place. Normally he loved for visitors to visit the ranch, and would greet them with a couple love barks and his wagging tail. Not this time; things had changed and every vehicle was a potential enemy.

He was well hidden in his dark sanctuary and could watch the activities without being seen. The pickup came to a stop in front of the bunkhouse followed by a suburban. Two men stepped out of the pickup and five from the suburban. A quiet growl escaped from Pecos and the hair on his back arose when he recognized Pete. The group proceeded to the bunkhouse after walking around the corrals and looking for any kind of equipment. Pecos could hear them slamming doors and opening drawers. Exiting the bunkhouse, they went into the saddle house and he could hear them stomping around above him. Every so often one would say something and the others would laugh.

"I don't know what the damn little thief did with all the fuckin' rolling stock and all the damn tack that shoulda' been in here. I would like to get my hands on the son of a bitch. I shot his fuckin' dog yesterday and he crawled off in Merricks corn field and died." Pecos recognized Pete's voice.

The group filed out of the saddle house and took another look around.

"Nothing here but a bunch of crap. Hell, he even took his portable loading chute and that Green River cattle squeeze chute," one of the other men said. With that they got in their cars and left, ignoring the doors and gates they had left open. Pecos listened till he could no longer hear their vehicles and then warily climbed out of his hole. He went to the pond, drank and then headed south, south to the thickets. All of a sudden he had this overwhelming urge to see the coyote, the one that he often felt torn between his loyalties to her and to Stoney.

It wasn't long till he caught her scent and followed it into the deepest part of the thickets. There the thickets gave way to a field of waist high love grass and on the side of a small blow-ou, he found her den. A strange new smell mingled with hers as he carefully sniffed the opening. Putting his head deeper into the den, his nose was suddenly bitten by small canine teeth. He jumped back realizing that he had just been bitten by one of her pups. He sat down on his haunches, tilted his head to the side, and stared at the den.

Pecos was startled by a soft whine behind him; turning quickly he looked into the beautiful yellow eyes of his mate. While he was investigating the den she had silently come up... not over four feet from him. She immediately rolled on her back in submission and they nuzzled and licked each other joyously. Abruptly she quit their play, laid down on her stomach, her paws extended out, and emitted a soft yip. Three balls of light tan fur emerged from the mouth of the den and ran over to their mother who turned over to let her young suckle. Pecos watched the pups nurse. Then he carefully approached them, smelling each one, lifting up their bottom with his nose as they nursed and softly licking their protruding bellies. He knew they were his. They were coydogs.

Pecos, although hoping and waiting for Stoney to show, easily fell into the father mode. He quickly learned, from her, how to forage for food. The two of them, hunting together, became adept at bringing down rabbits and other small prey for their young brood who were quickly weaned from their mother's milk to a more solid diet. Those were happy days for the two who enjoyed their hunts together. But, as more and more of the grassland was being destroyed by the huge machines of Taylor Farms, the food that Pecos relied on to feed his family became more and more scarce.

A month had gone by. It was afternoon and Pecos and his mate had split up, hoping that one of them might be able to catch their evening meal for their fast growing pups. Pecos had been lucky and caught a cotton tail near their old ranch headquarters. He was returning home when he saw the hated diesel smoke coming from the sand hills that hid their den. He could hear the roar of the motor the closer he got. Finally, coming over a small dune, he witnessed the large plow digging into a badgers den not far from their den. They were neighbors and respected each other..., each going their own way and tending to their own business.

The plow tossed the badger to one side breaking its back. The badger laid there, unable to move, biting the air, with blood streaming from the exposed wound. He finally quit, rolled over, quivered and died. The huge tractor was headed toward their den and Pecos dropped his rabbit and ran as hard as he could to get there first.

He was too late. The plow tore into their just as it had the badgers. His mate, and two of his pups, were killed immediately. Pecos licked the three of them and got no response. He then realized that one was missing and he dug frantically trying to find it. After five minutes of digging he was exhausted and lay down beside the bodies of his family.

Five minutes passed then he heard something behind him. Jumping to the side and turning around in one quick movement, his teeth were bared and he was growling. It was his other pup crawling on his belly in submission toward him. The pup had ventured from the den while his mother and siblings were napping, and was exploring some distance away, when he heard the tractor coming. The frightened pup crawled under a dead soap weed and hid until he saw Pecos.The tractor had made it's round and was returning. Pecos grabbed the pup by the back of his neck and ran into the thicket.

Pecos took on the raising of his pup, hiding him during the day while he looked for food. At night he would let the pup follow him on hunting expeditions. It was on one of these early evening hunts that he heard the sound of Stoney's pickup and bounded up a sandhill to greet him.

CHAPTER 24

Three months after the meeting in Las Vegas ,the plan, now called the "Arrangement" at Milnor's insistence, began to unfold. Stoney had wanted immediate action, but Milnor, who by now was the acknowledged leader, mainly because of his expertise in the flim-flam business, convinced the group that in the game of deception, "patience is bitter but its fruit is sweet". At the meeting at Joe's Ringside he gave each of them their orders.

"Stoney, this is what you must do," Milnor directed. "Disappear. Go someplace and let no know one know except for our little group, which will now be known as the Coven Five because there are five of us and we will be the most terrifying nightmare that this banker can ever imagine. We must also swear never to reveal any of our secrets or disclose the identities of any of its members."

"Agreed?"

"Agreed!" the other members of the Coven responded enthusiastically.

"Jim Bob we need to have that mine looking like it is has just been worked. Do you think you can have it ready by, say.. the middle of July? Some machinery around it would help a lot."

"Won't take me a week to have it ready," Jim Bob responded.

"Good. And now, Penny and Reno, I have something in mind for you too, but it just hasn't come together yet." Milnor carefully watching their reaction asked. "Reno and Penny, be honest with me. Would either of you mind if Penny does some flirting with our target, for the sake of the Arrangement and the coven?

"Absolutely not!" They responded at the same time.

"Stoney, where are you planning to hide out?" Jim Bob asked.

Stoney told him he really didn't have any idea. Jim Bob settled it for him by telling him he had a good friend that had a dude ranch over at Show Low, Arizona and his dude wrangler got kicked by one of the pack mules and would be laid up most of the summer. He had called Jim Bob and wanted to hire him for a couple months, but Jim Bob turned him down. Stoney said he would take it and Jim Bob went to the phone to see if the job was still open.

Milnor had borrowed a yellow legal pad from the bartender and told Stoney to write down the names of the banker, sheriff, secretaries and everything he could think of that might be helpful to the Arrangement. By the time Jim Bob had come back and told him that he had the job, Stoney had finished writing down everything he thought would be useful and shoved the legal pad back to Milnor.

Milnor glanced through it and looked at his fellow conspirators.

"Okay fellow members, we have to talk about money. I want to keep some checks going into that bank from some mining company, whose name I'll think of later. We know that villain will immediately confiscate the checks and, it will whet his curiosity and greed even more."

The group nodded in agreement.

Milnor continued. "I believe we can all be rewarded handsomely for our time and effort. Not to mention the fun of it. But I think we all need to ante up."

"No way!" Stoney said emphatically. "No one puts a dime in but me. Milnor, I have complete faith in you but... I also know, oh too well, that the best laid plans of mice and men are oft," he stopped for moment trying to think of the rest of the quotation and couldn't. "Turn to shit...,excuse my language Penny," an embarrassed Stoney said.

He continued, "I am the one that made the mistakes, not you guys. I really appreciate all of you, and the time and effort you will be putting in this, but if there is any cash that will be lost it will be mine. That's final. Okay, Milnor how much money are we talking about to keep that son-of-bitch nibbling at the hook?"

Milnor thought for a minute. "I don't think it will take much if he is as greedy as you say he is. Around three thousand..., two thousand the first month and twelve hundred the second month."

"I think I can cover that, it's in the pickup. I'll go get it."

"Wait a minute Stoney." Milnor said. "Are you going to Show Low now? If you are I will follow you to Santa Fe and we will open an account under… Let me think."

"We'll just go ahead and use the same name that was on the first check." Milnor looked at the legal pad. "Capitan Precious Metals. And we will have some checks made up with that name."

"Stoney, one more thing. The banker's secretary, your friend." Milnor was looking at the legal pad while he was talking. "There it is, Doris. Do you think you can call her and find out how she is coming with the bank examiners?"

"I'll call right now. But I'll have to call information first and get her number.

Twenty minutes later he returned to the table.

"Those son's-of-bitches. They broke into her house ransacked and stole her brief case with all the papers."

The group had one more round, toasted the Coven Five and the Arrangement, and went their separate ways.

Things were not going well at the Merchants and Farmers Bank that early summer. Doris had already contacted the bank examiners before her briefcase was stolen. When the bank examiners arrived in Clovis, Doris told them what was in the briefcase; but she could prove nothing. The examiners were very much interested in her story and told her that the bank could not have hidden everything. With her help, they would eventually find any proof of miss-dealings or if indeed they were involved in any illegal or unethical activity. Instead of their usual five day examination, it had extended into two weeks and more accountants from the main office had been called in . As the officers and board of directors became more concerned,they became more short tempered with their employees, who were also beginning to wear down under the stress. The examiners were everywhere in the bank, emptying out filling cabinets, going through them and then leaving them scattered for the employees to put back in order.

The second week in May, Bud Thurman was informed by one of employees that a twenty-two hundred dollar check had come into the bank to be deposited to the Bill Stone account. The check was from Capitan Precious Metals and marked Goose Creek Mine royalties. Bud told the girl to deposit the check and then draft that account for that amount. A week later another much smaller check arrived. The examiners had left by that time, taking a van full of documents they had copied from the bank files. Everyone in the bank breathed a sigh of relief with the exception of the head officers who felt somewhat better but still apprehensive.

The last week of June brought another check for a thousand and Bud's curiosity was running away with itself. He was sitting behind his desk trying to figure out what was generating these checks and how maybe he could profit from the information when he looked up and saw an impeccably dressed, dignified gentleman cross the lobby and go to the information desk. The girl pointed toward Bud's office and many of the employees watched as the man walked over to Bud's office and was escorted in by his secretary. This in itself was unusual. The secretary would generally just point the way, but this gentleman was so atypical of the usual bank customers, who were generally clothed in levis, brogans or boots, or business people whose attire was everyday informal. The handsome stranger was mid-sixties, with median height and weight, rather dark complexion, with beautiful dark hair greying around the temples. The way he carried himself, with confidence and authority, demanded respect.

Bud was standing with his hand extended when his secretary ushered him in.

"I am Raymond du Maurier with Rare Metals of France," he announced in a very French accent.

A very impressed Bud introduced himself, asked him to sit down and motioned his secretary to close the door.

"I will get right to the point. I know you are a busy man and my driver must have me in, how do you pronounce it, Lubbock, you will have to pardon my English. Our company plane will be awaiting my arrival in just a few hours."

He continued, "One of your patrons has a piece of property in the northern part of your state that we are most interested in, and our very best investigators have been unable to locate him. It seems he has just vanished. His name is Bill Stone. Are you familiar with him?"

"Yes I am, but it has been some time since we have heard from him," Bud answered. "I am curious. What made you think that we might know?"

"Mister Thurman," Maurier took a gamble. "We have some of the best international investigators in the world. We know that you endorsed two of the checks.

Bud stammered, "Oh... okay. Just checking. You understand my concern I am sure."

"Of course."

"If it is really important to you, I think I could possibly find out and maybe even contact him," Bud continued, thinking about maybe tricking Betsy into finding out... if, even she knew.

"It is of the most utmost importance."

Bud was feeling more confident in his ability to match wits with the Frenchman, "First I need some more information about this property. What exactly is it, or on it that you are so interested in?"

Maurier looked surprised that Bud would even ask him such a thing. He looked a Bud for a moment and Bud began to wonder if maybe he had pushed a little faster and a little further than he should.

Maurier looked around cautiously, then leaned forward and lowered his voice as two conspirators would. Bud instinctively did the same.

"Can I talk to you in all confidence?" Maurier asked.

"Of course, you have my word," Bud answered almost beside himself in excitement.

"There is a mine on it that can maybe produce something that would fit nicely into our business."

"Can you tell me what it is?" Bud asked.

"Of course not," Maurier sat back abruptly.

"I understand and forgive me for getting so inquisitive." The wheels were spinning fast in Buds head, "Let me tell you something about Bill. He has been a good customer, and a good friend of mine, for a long time. He and wife have had a falling out, and he kinda lost it, just disappeared. I know him well and l will tell you this. He is very greedy and money would bring him out of the woods in a hurry, especially money that he might not have to share with his wife."

"Proceed, this is very interesting."

"I could possibly negotiate a deal for your company. You see he is drinking a great deal, and with bad management, lost all he had. We hated to foreclose on him and, in lieu of that, he agreed to surrender all of his property held as collateral, which was everything he owned. Lock, stock and barrel, as we Americans would say." Bud hesitated and let the Frenchman absorb that.

"That is," he continued, "everything but this piece of property, which we knew nothing about.

Maurier nodded.

"I tried to help Bill all I could, but he was in too deep and too far gone. He knows that I am about the only friend he has in town and he trusts me. Are you following me?"

"Go on," Maurier responded.

"I would do anything to help my buddy get back on his feet. But, I am a business man too, and I respect the fact that you might hesitate in giving me any kind of exact figure. But if I could tell him, you know, just a ball park figure and if it was enough I think I could talk him into a deal for you. Of course, as I said, I am a businessman and would expect some sort of compensation for my time and effort."

"Of course, I understand." Maurier thought for a minute. "I am going to trust you also, because I think you are sincere. And additionally… I can assure you that our investigators delight in making sure that people we do business with can be trusted and sincere, and I cannot emphazie that point enough. Now, do you understand what I am saying."

Somewhat taken aback and knowing that the Frenchman was very, very serious Bud said, "I understand you completely."

"We have covertly taken samples from the mine. One million dollars on the top, three quarters on the bottom. Your ten per cent will be added on."

Bud almost peed in his pants.

"Have we reached an agreement?" Maurier asked sternly.

"Yes, yes of course," Bud stammered, his mind already planning what he was going to do with his hundred thousand.

"Good, here is my card." He handed Bud a beautiful embossed card with his name, company name and the phone number and address of the head office which was in Ecully, France. "You will call this number when you have convinced Mister Stone to sell. Now then, let me tell you a little about our company. We do business all over the world, and we have operations in three different continents. This will be our first in North America. Feel free to research our company, but I can tell you now, you will find out very little. We are a very private company, privately owned and private in nature. Our business demands it; our headquarters is housed in a non-descript building without a sign of what transpires inside. Phone calls will be answered by a recording that will ask your name, where you can be reached, and to whom you wish to talk. After the call is screened by our investigators I will be contacted and then I will return your call. Do not be alarmed if I do not hear from me for a day or two. My position in the company takes me many places in the world..., some places that I am sure you have never heard of. Do you have any questions? If not, I must be on my way."

Bud shook his head. He was almost in a dream world and still thinking of what he was going to buy with the hundred thousand.

"Good," Maurier continued. "I want to remind you, and impress upon you, that I insist upon strict confidentiality. There are entities all over this world that are very interested in what we do. And…it irritates our investigators very much when someone betrays the confidence we have placed with them. Once again, you do understand what I am saying, don't you?"

"Of course," Bud responded.

"Then our meeting is concluded. I will expect to hear from you in the next few weeks."

They stood up, shook hands and Bud escorted the gentleman out of the bank where a black Ford Expedition was parked. The driver immediately stepped out and opened the back. He was tall, and broad shouldered with a military man's posture. A deep scar ran from the corner of on one eye to his chin. He was wearing dark glasses and a chauffeurs uniform and cap. Bud was even more impressed; and when he returned to his office, Alex Maynard immediately motioned him into his office to question him about the impressive visitor.

Bud, remembering what Maurier had cautioned him about, told him he was some foreigner that was trying to open up a mortgage company in New Mexico and wanted Bud to go to work for them. Bud then told Alex that he indicated he wasn't interested. Alex looked at him suspiciously and dismissed him with a wave of his hand. Bud knew Alex didn't believe him.

As the large suburban drove off, the driver adjusted the rear view mirror where he could see the passenger in the back seat.

Milnor smiled back at Reno and said, "Hook, line and sinker. The cheese has been placed in the trap. Now then, if Jim Bob can fulfill his part, the trap will be set and if I have judged our dear, fat friend correctly, his greedy little world is about to collapse. Now then, let's get this big monster back to Santa Fe in one piece. My rich lady friend will never know we borrowed it, if we can return it to her garage in the next three hours."

Reno took off his cap and threw it in the seat. "Congratulations my Duke of Mora County." They both laughed and headed west.

CHAPTER 25

Bud spent the next two days trying to find Stoney. When he wasn't working on that part of it, he was figuring out what he was going to do with his commission. His list of 'want things' was outgrowing the hundred thousand by a large margin.

"Let see," he thought. "I could probably coax another two hundred and fifty thousand or maybe even a half a million more out of my French friend, but that's just going to give me twenty-five or fifty thousand more for my commission." That was still short of his want's.

By Wednesday morning Bud could feel his dreams slipping away. He had been unable to find Stoney, his family had no idea where he was or when he would return. He was sitting at his desk tapping his ring on the top in frustration when the solution to his dilemma, in the form of a tall, broad shouldered cowboy in his late forties or early fifties strolled into the bank and went to the information desk.

Bud had glanced up and saw the cowboy arguing with the lady at the information desk. He watched as he became more and more agitated. Bud picked up the phone and asked the employee what the trouble was. She informed him that the man was claiming he and Bill Stone had an account at the bank, and that it was half his, and he wanted his share of the royalties. She said she could not convince him that an account with both their names does not exist.

Bud practically ran to the information desk. He tapped the man on the shoulder and the big cowboy turned around so fast Bud jumped back, afraid he was going to hit him.

His face flushed, Bud said, "I think I can help you Mister …."

"Alhizer. Do you know something about this?

"Well Mister Stone was a customer of mine and I knew quite a bit about his business. Why don't you come into my office and we will try to figure this out."

On the way to his office Bud was quickly trying to figure out the best way to approach the big man.

"Okay." Bud commenced after they were seated. "Now then, Mister Alhizer, that is what you said your name was, wasn't it?"

"That's right, Bob Alhizer.

"Well 'er, did anyone ever call you Smokey?

"They did at one time. What difference does that make to you?"

"Oh, none Mister Alhizer. I just recall Mister Stone talking about you."

"Where is the little bastard and what about my money?" Alhizer asked.

"That's exactly what we would like to know. He ran off owing us a bunch of money and emptied out his account."

"I'll kill the son-of-bitch," Alhizer said as he got up leave.

"Wait, wait," Bud almost screamed when he saw all of his 'want's' almost walk out the door.

"There might be a chance I can get some money for you."

Alhizer turned around, looked at Bud then sat back down.

"You all were partners on a mine up North. Isn't that correct?"

"Partners hell, that was <u>my</u> mine, <u>my</u> diggings. I just didn't have any cash at that time. I had made some bad decisions in the past and he was supposed to just hold things for me until…well, till things settled down."

Bud felt better. He knew now that he could outsmart this over-grown cowboy anytime, anyplace.

"What kind of mine was it, if you don't mind telling me?

Alhizer seemed to relax a little.

"It was gold. I got a pretty good showing of,… I mean a real good showing… of gold, and this big company was supposed to be sending the checks here."

"That's real interesting, you know my grandfather was a gold miner and used to tell me stories about it," Bud lied. "And, I guess I got his gold bug running in my veins." He could tell he had Alhizer's interest.

"Tell me something about it. Is it in the mountains? And I know you don't want to tell me where exactly, but someplace near it that I might be familiar with?"

"Hell, I'll draw you a map if you want. It's about halfway between Eagle Nest and Red River on the west side of the road."

"Really, that's pretty country, I have always wanted a place up there."

"Look Thurman," Alhizer said looking down at Bud's name plate. "If you're serious about wanting a place up there and interested in having a gold mine. My diggings are for sale."

Bud leaned back thinking "this red neck is playing right into my hand. All I have to do is play it slow and cagey."

"Oh I couldn't afford to buy something that big,"

"Well you might be surprised what it might take. I have just scratched the surface but it's got real potential to be a rich vein of gold. I just haven't had time to work it like it should be worked. You seen the checks, so you know it's got the potential, and besides all you got to do is just work it a little every year and you can keep the lease from the feds, and have a great place to hang out in the summer."

"Let me tell you something Thurman," Alhizer continued. "I'll be honest with you. I owe some people some money…, real money. Like these are not the kinda guys that like to wait very long, they get real impatient. In other words it's what you bankers would call a distress sale."

"How much of a distress sale are we talking about?" Bud couldn't hardly contain his excitement.

Alhizer thought a minute. "A hundred and seventy five thousand. You would damn near pay that much for a cabin site up there with your own little private trout stream in your front yard."

"Whew!" Bud said. "That's a hell of a lot of money."

Alhizer again acted like he was ready to leave.

"I might give you a hundred thousand… After I look at it."

"Are you a gambler? Alhizer asked. "If you are, I'll flip you if you owe me a hundred and fifty or a hundred and twenty five. And it has to be cash, no money order, no checks, no fancy little banker tricks. Just the old green bills."

Bud was thinking how could he come up with that much cash. But he wasn't going to let this get away. He would figure that out later.

Bud won the toss and was pleased to see the sour expression on Alhizer's face.

"Okay banker you won this one. When do I get my money?"

Bud was already looking at his calendar and doing some fast figuring and a plan was already developing. This was Wednesday and the following Monday was July the Fourth. Alex always took off for a long weekend on the Fourth and he would be leaving on Thursday with most of the other officers, leaving the bank in the hands of his recently appointed senior vice president. It would be no problem to take out a loan for ninety thousand and with the thirty five thousand he had in his account; it would work.. He would then have the Frenchman wire the million plus Monday and by Tuesday the ninety would have been replaced. He would make up some kind of inheritance story to satisfy Alex, who would be sure to come with questions on how Bud became a millionaire over the weekend.

Bud explained to the cowboy, "I want to see the mine Saturday, and if I like the looks, I'll pay you then. But.., I want you to have a notarized deed and transfers from the feds and everything that I need to claim the mine. All nice and legal. Except on the grantee's line just leave it blank. I want to put it a sheltered corporation. Can you get it done and notarized with it blank, and without me being there?

"My girlfriend is a notary so that won't be a problem," replied the cowboy. "You know where the Vietnam Memorial is in Eagle Nest?

"Never been there, but I am sure I won't have any trouble finding it. I can be there by nine o'clock Saturday morning. Ok?"

Bud continued, "Take one my cards in case something happens and you need to get a hold of me. And how do I get in touch with you?

"Call Joe's Ringside in Las Vegas..., Las Vegas New Mexico. They'll know how to reach me. And make damn sure it's cash. Don't try to play games with me banker cause if you do – I'll guarantee you, you won't like it," the big cowboy said, getting up to leave.

"What's the number?" Bud hurriedly asked.

"Look it up," Jim Bob Nuckols, a.k.a. Alhizer, said over his shoulder, trying his best to contain a big grin.

Seventy two hours; thought Bud. Not much time to make a million plus. He started to pick up the phone and call the number in France, but thought better of it. He might have a hard time explaining to others why he was calling France on the bank's telephone. He left the bank telling his secretary he had some errands to run and drove to his new condo on a recently developed golf course subdivision.

His fat fingers dialed the number in France. After three short rings a recorded woman's voice came on the line. He didn't understand her first sentence and assumed she was speaking in French, her next sentence was in English.

"If you wish to speak in English please press two." Bud was so fascinated with the beautiful voice that he listened while she spoke four other languages before he pressed two.

"Please state your name, who you represent, with whom you wish to communicate, and the number where you can be reached. The party will return your call as soon as possible. *Passe une bonne journée.*"

Bud was disappointed but impressed, and followed the instructions at the indicated signal.

As soon as Jim Bob left the bank he drove to Travis's home to use the phone and report his success to Milnor.

Travis had lots of questions, which Jim Bob evaded. Then he decided to really arouse Travis's curiosity.

"Hello, is this the Duke of Mora?" Jim Bob asked when Milnor answered the phone.

"Things went well your highness," Jim Bob continued, raising his voice so Travis would be sure to hear. The spring is set and ready to snap. The day of judgment will begin Friday."

Jim Bob nodded as Milnor congratulated him.

He continued, "I'll return to your kingdom this afternoon and await your commands."

Jim Bob hung up the phone.

"What in the hell was that all about," Travis demanded.

Jim Bob grinned shyly. "I gotta' go Trav.., I'll tell you all about it maybe sometime next week..., if all goes as planned. But, I will tell you one thing. I have never had so much fun."

He put on his big Stetson and left for Goose Creek, thinking it's all up to Milnor now.

When Milnor's son and girlfriend returned to their apartment, after classes at Ecully University, they checked their messages and immediately called his father. They had followed his instructions well and were happy to get the expensive answering machine Milnor had bought for them.

They played Bud's message to Milnor in which said he had not been able to contact Stoney, but had found the real owner of the mine and he was willing to sell at a price. He asked for Mister du Maurier to call him as soon as possible because they just had a very short time to consummate a deal or lose it.

Milnor asked the kids how late they stayed up. Milnor wanted to return Bud's call but first wanted him to sweat it for a few hours and the time difference would make it quite late for them. Zack assured his dad that it was unusual for them to go to bed before midnight. Milnor told them he would call them shortly before midnight to return Buds call. He also gave them instructions on how it would be handled..

By mid-afternoon Bud was fit to be tied. He called the bank telling them he wasn't feeling well and unless he got to feeling better he wouldn't be in until tomorrow.

Shortly before five pm his phone rang.

The same French accent was on the phone, "Mister Thurman, I am returning the call for Monsieur du Maurier. I am sorry but he is in a very remote location in Angola where there are no telephones."

Bud's heart sank and he had to sit down.

The lady continued, "However, we do have him on the radio and if you will consent to do so, you can state your business to me, and I will relate it to him via the radio. Would you agree to do that?"

"Of course. Tell him I have been authorized to broker the sale of the mine. If the sale can be closed by this coming weekend."

He heard the lady talking in French and could barely make out a man's voice, whom he assumed was du Maurier, also in French, on what sounded like a radio in the distance. The voice he heard was actually Milnor's son talking through a rolled up magazine and listening to his dad on another phone..

The lady came back on the line, "Monsieur du Maurier congratulates you on your success and wishes to know how many US dollars you were able to purchase it for."

Milnor hesitated a minute. "One million and four hundred and fifty thousand. He wanted two million but we traded for an hour and finally got him down to that amount. That's the best I could do."

Bud held his breath when he heard the radio voice talking fast and loud. "Oh crap, I blew it," he thought.

"Monsieur du Maurier will call you back in less than an hour." Click, the phone went dead.

Bud went to the kitchen and poured himself a straight shot of Crown Royal. I can't believe I did that, why in the hell didn't I just say a million and let it go like that. He gulped down the drink and made himself another. Twenty minutes later he had just finished that drink when the phone rang.

"Mister Thurman, Monsieur du Maurier has decided to proceed with the purchase. How do you wish to effectuate the deal?"

Bud was elated and went into detail on how it would happen. He would meet with the owner, inspect the mine, and receive all the papers for clear ownership of it. His bank would then pay the owner in cash which he would carry with him and which is the only way the mine owner would do business. He would expect the money from the French company to be wired to the bank into his personal account as soon as possible. Preferably by Friday. He gave the account number that it would be deposited in.

The lady repeated the details to the Frenchman. There was a long discussion and she came back on the line.

"Monsieur du Maurier wishes me to inform you that this is the way it will be done. He is sending our company attorney that represents us in your country. She will meet you at a place of your choosing on Saturday. She will go over the papers to make sure they are in order. If they are, she will inform our company and the funds will immediately be wired to your account. She will fly into Santa Fe aboard our company jet and be driven to the place of rendezvous."

Bud wanted to have his hands on the money first, but letting greed take priority over caution, just as Milnor predicted he would, agreed to the meeting. The only place he could think of to meet the attorney was the name the cowboy had given him: Joe's Ringside in Las Vegas.

After setting a time of six o'clock in the evening for the meeting the conversation was ended.

Bud was overjoyed. He could not believe how easy he had made a million-four hundred thousand, plus ten per cent of that amount, for a measly hundred and twenty five thousand. "You shrewd, young, entrepreneur," he thought. "You deserve another drink. you just pulled a hell of a deal on a big cowboy and a high-fluting Frenchman."

CHAPTER 26

Milnor called the Bonomos to meet with Jim Bob and him in Eagle Nest. There, they would go over the up-coming transaction. The next day over lunch at Texas Reds Steakhouse, it was decided that they should call Stoney and have him come over for the great farce; even though he would have to remain hidden. After all, the money was just added compensation for their time and effort. The main objective was to teach the banker a lesson he would never, ever forget, and have fun doing it.

When all the details were worked out, and everyone had their instructions, Milnor rose and offered a toast with his goblet of wine and the rest with their mugs of beer.

"To the Coven Five. Let the games begin."

Bud Thurman was walking on a cloud Thursday and Friday. The bank employees could not believe how happy and amicable he was, which was certainly a change to his usual egotistical personality. Getting the cash was no problem. He made out a loan to himself for ninety thousand, (which was highly illegal without going through the loan committee), and deposited the money in his account. Friday afternoon he went to one of the cashiers that he knew to be especially intimidated by him and withdrew one hundred and twenty five thousand, and another five hundred for walking around money. This withdrawal almost emptied his account.

After a fitful night, Bud arose before daybreak and left for Eagle Nest. Arriving early he drove into the practically deserted parking lot of the Vietnam Memorial. The doors did not open until ten so Bud parked his Corvette where he could watch the road coming up to the Memorial. Shortly before nine he watched as a pickup turned off highway 64 and into the parking lot. The muddy, well-used truck pulled up beside him and the passenger's window rolled down.

"You got the money?" Jim Bob asked.

Bud nodded and pulled a large brief case out of the front seat holding it up for Jim Bob to see.

"Get in, and us get this damn thing over."

Bud did as he was told and they headed for Goose Creek.

By the time they reached the canyon Jim Bob's demeanor had softened considerably and they were joking with each other like old buddies. Jim Bob had done a good job cleaning up the area around the mine. He had borrowed a tractor, a gasoline operated generator and other mining equipment, and picked up the whiskey bottles and beer cans. He and Bud ventured a little way into the cavern until Bud said he had seen enough.

"Let's go over to my camp and get you the documents and a beer would sure taste good," a grinning Jim Bob said.

Bud agreed, so they went into a small cabin with a sign that said, 'Goose Creek Mining Company'. Underneath it, in smaller letters it read, 'If Your Close Enough to Read This -Your in Range. Get the Hell Out!' The interior was rustic to say this least. Jim Bob went to a refrigerator, opened the door, and pulled out two manila envelopes. Bud was taken aback.

"You have electricity clear up here?"

"Hell no," replied Jim Bob. "I just put my beer in there in the winter to keep it from freezing. And use it for a filing cabinet. Keeps the pack rats from chewing up my papers."

He handed the envelopes to Bud. One had,"USDA Forest Division, Colfax County, New Mexico" stamped on it. The other "Superior Title Company, Las Vegas, New Mexico". While Bud was examining those Jim Bob went to the creek and, from a hidden hole, pulled out two bottles of Coors. He handed one to Bud and motioned to a log that Jim Bob had fashioned into a bench. Bud started going through the papers..., acting like he knew what he was reading when it came to USDA papers.

"They look alright to me."

"Good," Jim Bob said. "Let's take a look at what's in that brief case of yours."

"Uh...," Bud stammered. "There just one more thing Jim Bob..., I know these are all right, but my attorney is in Las Vegas and she wants to look at them first. I told her that I would meet her at that place you told me about, Joe's Ringside at six this afternoon...That's okay with you isn't it."

Jim Bob placed a big hand on Bud's shoulder and squeezed.

"I warned you about any little tricks didn't I?" he squeezed a little harder.

"No Bob, honest to God , I am not pulling anything on you. I'll show you the money," a panicked banker said, wincing under the cowboy's strong grip.

"Okay, I am going to trust you. Let's have another beer and go to Las Vegas," Jim Bob said releasing his grip.

A relaxed Bud breathed a sigh of relief and agreed.

By the time they had picked up Bud's Corvette, stopped for lunch at a couple of bars on the way, (with an expansive Bud buying), it was a little after six when they pulled into Joe's.

There were just a couple of pickups and a few cars in the parking lot, but one garnered Bud's immediate attention. It was a black Ford Expedition with a chauffeur leaning up against it. Jim Bob started to get out of his truck when Bud grabbed his arm. By this time, with the drinks they had nurturing it, they had become buddies again.

"Look..., Bob. That's her car over there with the chauffer but, this is kinda of a touchy thing. My attorney is a really a strange kind of woman, and she won't talk in front of anyone that's not one of her clients."

Lame as it was, it was the only thing Bud could think of to keep Bob from hearing their conversation and finding out that Bud was making way over a million dollars off of him. He was surprised that Jim Bob accepted it so easily.

"Okay, I'll just stand up at the bar and keep that brief case in my sight. Let's go."

They entered the bar with Jim Bob leading the way. There was only one woman in the establishment and she was sitting by herself, completely relaxed at one of the tables sipping a mixed drink. Jim Bob walked over to the end of the bar where the bartender was sitting. Milnor had instructed the bartender well and he winked at Jim Bob as he handed him his beer.

Bud had made his way to the table and was promptly captivated by the attorneys beauty. She introduced herself as Lana and he apologized for being somewhat late. She passed it off saying she was enjoying herself. The bartender arrived at the table, Bud offered to buy her another drink. She accepted and ordered a Fuzzy Navel. Bud had never heard of the drink and ordered himself one. After the bartender left, Bud pulled out the envelopes. She carefully scanned through them.

"I have looked at hundreds of these, perhaps thousands, and these are all authentic and legal. I have one question however. Why is the space for the grantee blank and why have they already been notarized without a grantee's name placed there?"

Bud explained that he didn't know what name they wanted there, and he just pulled a few strings to get the notary to stamp it.

Jim Bob watched the bartender mix the drinks. Orange juice and a little peach schnapps in Penny's drink a triple shot of vodka in Buds. He looked up and gave a sly grin to Jim Bob.

When the drinks were delivered Penny asked Bud to go to the parking lot and summon her chauffer. Bud did so and recognized the huge fellow as the Frenchman's driver. Reno followed Bud to the table.

"Rebaldo, radio our office and have them wire the funds immediately to Mister Thurman's bank. They have all the information they need to do so."

Reno acknowledged the order but returned a few moments later.

"I am sorry mam, but our radio is not reaching out and has not been able to ever since we left Santa Fe."

Penny wrinkled her forehead. "Telephone will do no good. Everyone will be out till Monday, but our comptroller has his radio on all the time. Drive to Santa Fe at once and reach him. You can spend the night there. I will have to stay here until Monday or Tuesday in order to file the papers at the court house."

"We saw a Holiday Inn coming into town. I will be there there tonight if.., Mister Thurman, will take me there after dinner." She looked coyly at Bud.

Bud hastily agreed and left with Reno to retrieve Penny's travel bags and place them in his Corvette. He was so excited over Penny that he had forgotten who was waiting for him at the bar. Just as he sat down at the table Jim Bob walked up, a scowl on his face. He nodded at Penny, touching the brim of his hat, then looking down at Bud he said, "I think you have something for me." Buds face turned red. He apologized and handed the brief case to Jim Bob.

"I think you'll find all the papers you need in there, Mister Alhizer" he said, forcing himself to smile. He had tried to think of some way he could con the cowboy out of the money, but couldn't come up with one.

"Bueno," Jim Bob said and walked out, got into his truck, drove around to the back of the building, parking his truck where it could not be seen from the highway. He knocked on the back door which was opened by a smiling Milnor and Stoney. They were in a medium size room with two poker tables and a handmade crap table. Two illegal slot machines stood to one side. On the other side was a one way window that looked out on the bar. It purpose was to protect the gamblers from inside the room in case of a raid on their activities. They had watched the whole proceedings happening inside the bar and marveled at Penny's acting skills. Jim Bob placed the brief case on one of the tables and they commenced to count. It was all there, and they turned their attention back to the window. Reno had joined them after taking the Expedition to a hiding place and retrieving his car. The fun was about to begin.

Two hours later Penny and Bud were still at Joe's Ringside. Bud had, in a very short time, become the world's greatest lover. He was, after all, a millionaire, and not yet forty years old. A beautiful blonde at his table was obviously impressed with him and showing an interest in maybe even sharing a bed with him. An hour later Bud was sure of it. They drove up to the motel and were registered in two adjoining rooms. Milnor had prearranged the accommodations and they were located at the back of the compound.

Shortly after entering their respective room Penny had opened the adjoining door and invited Bud into her room. She had stripped down to her panties and bra. Bud had never felt so impassioned in his life and quickly discarded all of his clothes. She had started to slip her panties off when she smiled at Bud and suppressed a giggle at the small size of his full erection. She asked him if he would like to pull them off for her. Bud was almost delirious at this point and started to do so just as there was a loud knock on the door.

"Lana! Open the door now, you damned two-timing bitch!"

"Oh my God, it's Rebaldo!" Penny exclaimed and started sobbing.

"You mean your chauffeur?" an incredulous Bud asked.

"No, my husband. I mean yes. He's my chauffeur too. Oh God, he will kill you. You have to get out of here."

Bud thought he was going to faint. His erection had shrunk and was hiding in the folds of his overlapping stomach.

"Quick, out the bathroom window," she said pushing him that way. He started to get his clothes and she jerked them away from him.

"You don't have time," she said sliding the window open. He put one foot on the commode and started squeezing himself through the small opening with her pushing him.

"I don't think I can make it," he whined.

There was more pounding on the door.

"Yes you can. You have to, or we will both be dead."

She gave him one more push and he fell to the ground scraped and bruised. Just as he hit the ground there was a blinding flash.

Then a huge hand grabbed him by his fleshy arm.

Goose Creek Mine today.

"You and I gonna have a little prayer meeting." It was Rebaldo holding a camera in his other hand. He half-drug Bud around the corner of the building and back into the room, shoving him down into a chair.

Bud looked around for the attorney. She had disappeared, as well as her suitcase. There was not a trace of her. The chauffeur sat down on the edge of the bed and was doing something with the camera. It was a Polaroid, and he was developing a photo.

When he peeled it off he laughed.

"The jury is gonna love this if I kill you and have to go to trial. It will prove you cuckolded my wife and they ain't gonna like you. You wanta' see."

He held it up for Bud to see. Bud couldn't believe how bad he looked completely naked.

Rebaldo took something out of his pocket and pressed a button on it. A six inch blade sprung out and he tested its sharpness with his thumb. He then went into the bathroom and grabbed all the towels and laid them on floor. Bud was shaking uncontrollably.

"Come over and lay down on the towels and spread your legs," Reno said.

His voice shaking, Bud asked what he was going to do.

"I am going to castrate you. Don't worry, it will be real quick and when I finish just grab those towels real quick and shove them where your balls used to be. The bleeding will stop in a little while. Trust me, I done this before."

Bud got down on his knees. "What do you want. I am a rich man. I'll give you anything you want. Please don't do this to me."

Reno looked down on him. Bud was hanging his head and crying. Reno began to feel sorry for him. He walked to the door and looked outside and spying Bud's Corvette he had an inspiration.

"You said, anything?

"Anything," Bud sobbed.

"I want your car and you can keep your nuts."

"You can have it, you can have it," Bud said with a glimmer of hope in his voice.

"Okay, go take a shower. You pissed all over yourself. Then get dressed and I'll take you to the bus station and you can go back to whatever hole you came out of."

On the way to the bus station Reno explained to Bud what he had to do.

"The first thing I want you to do, the minute you get home, is destroy the title to your car. You're to forget you ever owned it, and if you screw up I want to remind you of that beautiful photo of you and how you would like to see it posted on every light post in Clovis. You understand me don't you?"

Bud nodded.

"And you know I damn sure mean it. And you do want to keep your nuts. Right?

"Yes sir," Bud replied.

Reno tossed him his billfold that Bud had dropped in his haste to take his clothes off. Reno let him off at the station and drove off laughing and slapping the steering wheel of his almost new Corvette.

Bud was fortunate enough to catch a bus to Clovis shortly after arriving at the station. By the time it had stopped at every little village and town it didn't arrive in Clovis until 10:30 on Sunday morning. Bud had recuperated by Tuesday morning and was at the bank early. He felt much better knowing he had a fortune coming across the wire. By mid-afternoon he was getting worried. By closing time his account still had only a few dollars in it, and he got a terrible sinking feeling. Leaving the bank just as they locked the door he rushed home in the car he had borrowed from the dealership, until his new Corvette came in. He had ordered it that morning before coming to work. He dialed the number in France his fingers shaking. When an operator came on that could speak English he was informed that number had been disconnected. When he asked for the name of the person or company that had the number the operator said they could not divulge that and he asked to be transferred to the police station. When he finally got someone on the phone that could speak English he was told that the there was no address in Ecully that matches the number on Maurier's card.

Bud did not sleep well that night. In the morning he called in sick and said he would be in the bank sometime that afternoon. He then got busy on the phone and shortly before noon finally located the number of the Forest Service that had jurisdiction over that part of the Carson National Forest. He finally was able to talk to the lady who handled the mining leases and asked her about the Goose Creek Mine. She asked him to hold the phone while she checked, but she did remember that something had come across her desk earlier that day concerning that lease.

Bud felt better, surely that was the change in ownership and he had been worried for no reason. The wire just had not had time to reach the bank.

Moments later she was back on the phone.

"Yes sir, I have it in front of me now. It appears that the lease expired two years ago and has not been renewed."

"There must be some mistake I was up there last Saturday and there were all kinds of machinery around and everything," Bud was almost screaming into the phone.

"Just a minute sir and I'll let you talk to the ranger that was up there yesterday", she replied.

A man's deep voice was on the phone, "Sir, we were up there yesterday and there were some fresh tracks but there was not any machinery on the premises and only one small, vacant cabin with nothing in it except an old refrigerator, so we burned it down. Our regulations entitle us to return a mining lease back to its original state when a claim has been inactive for over twenty four months. Is there anything else we can help you with."

Bud hung up the phone and sat there in a daze.

His phone rang. It was Alex. "Bud I want you down at the bank right now. We have a problem, a real problem. Let me put it another way, you have a problem, like a ninety thousand dollar problem. If you're not here in fifteen minutes I am sending the police for you."

Bobbi and the Coydog

CHAPTER 27

The money was evenly divided between Milnor, Jim Bob and Stoney. The Bonomos had refused to take any, saying they had so much fun they would have paid to be members of the Coven, and besides that, they came out with a great sports car that would be the only Corvette in Harding county.

Stoney had driven in the day before and spent the night with Mickie. He told her he was going to leave town but not before he did everything he could possibly do to find Pecos. He spent the rest of the day playing with Bobbi. On Friday afternoon he had called Travis who told him Jim Bob had called and was coming over and for him to drop by..

Travis got a big kick out of the parody the Coven had pulled on the bank and the three decided they ought to celebrate a little and headed toward the Limits.. The long table was full, so Travis and Jim Bob secured a small table toward the back while Stoney went over to greet and visited his old drinking buddies. He had been gone all summer and they were glad to see him. Stoney looked around for Janie and not able to see her he asked Ben Green if she was still working there. Ben was surprised at the inquiry.

"Oh, I guess you didn't hear. That big son-of-bitch over there," Ben said, pointing to Pete sitting at the bar with Emmett and several other Taylor Farm hands. "Got drunk one night, and after everyone had left the bar, and she was cleaning up, he came in and raped her. She pressed charges but Taylor Farms asked the bank to help Pete get out of it, and they did. They also put the pressure on Spence and he had to fire her."

"She went to someplace in Texas and nobody can find her. We took up a collection to help her out, but she vanished before we could get it to her. I am sorry about that Stoney, I know you thought a lot of her."

Stoney just shook his head and started for the table where Jim Bob and Travis were sitting. A cowboy sitting at the end of the long table grabbed his arm.

"Stoney, I think you need to know. Pete has been in here for an hour bragging about shooting your dog this afternoon out at your old ranch."

The blood rushed to Stoney's head and he headed for Pete. Coming up behind him he grabbed him by the shoulders and catching him off guard he pulled the big man over backwards. Pete tumbled to the floor still holding his beer bottle.

"You little son-of-bitch, I'll kill you," Pete busted the bottle over the brass foot rail as he was getting up. Holding it by the neck with the jagged end pointed toward Stoney he started for him when a hand, with an iron grip, grabbed his wrist. In a split second Jim Bob had his arm twisted behind his back with Pete screaming that he was breaking his shoulder.

Spence, who had been looking for a way to run Pete out of his bar, heard the commotion, and came charging out of the package store. He sized up the situation quickly.

"All right, that's enough," Spence yelled. "Turn him lose Jim Bob. Pete get your ass out my bar and don't ever come back. You're nothing but trouble and if you ever stick you head in here again I'll have you arrested for trespassing."

"You can't do that," Pete said picking up his Taylor Farms cap from the floor.

"The hell I can't. This my place and I'll serve whoever in the hell I want to. Now get. The rest of you Taylor boys are welcome to stay." He looked at Stoney and shook his head, "Good to see you again Stoney, but I got a hunch you might be mixed up in this. Try to behave will you?"

Things quieted down and Jim Bob and Travis were trying to console Stoney about his dog. After awhile Stoney got up to go to the rest room. Emmett had been watching him and followed him in.

"Stoney," Emmett said, after he locked the door behind him, something which few people ever did. "I was with Pete when he shot your dog."

"Go on Emmett," Stoney replied.

"I wanta' tell you. I think the reason why your dog just stood there is he thought it was you. Bud Thurman got it fixed so Taylor Farms ended up with your old pickup and I been driving it. Bud didn't want to get his new pickup dirty this afternoon so we were in it when we spotted your dog . But let me tell you, I don't think he killed him. I was watching through my binoculars and it looked like to me like he just grazed him.

"Are you sure Emmett? Can you tell me exactly where it was and how I can get there.?

"Yeah I can, but that gate is locked."

"I'll take care of that."

"Yeah, I'll bet you will," Emmett smiled and then went on to explain where they had parked when they saw Pecos, and about where he was standing.

Stoney placed a hand on Emmett's shoulder, thanked him and went back to the table, telling Jim Bob and Travis he had to go. When they asked where, he told them to find a dog. They wanted to go but Stoney turned them down and left.

It was a full moon and, after he left the Clovis haze, it was almost as bright as day; so much, that one could actually drive without headlights. Stoney pulled up to the gate and fired three shots before the lock was broken. He drove in, closing the gate behind him. It wasn't just the coyotes that heard the shots this night. One of the Taylor hands, who was baling alfalfa, had just shut his machine off to clear a jam in it when he heard the shots. He radioed Pete, his boss, and told him that he thought someone was shooting at the sign again. Pete told him he would be right down.

His country, his ranch, had changed so much that Stoney hardly recognized it driving down his old road in the moonlight with the lights off. He passed where their house once stood. The beautiful elm trees were gone. In their place stood a field of corn, just beginning to tassel out. Everywhere he looked he could see the red clearance lights on the circular sprinklers blinking, letting the irrigators know they were still working.

He soon passed a field of peanuts. The plants lush and green.

Driving slow with the windows down, he could hear the soft click, click, of the sprinkler heads and the water hitting the thirsty plants. It made him think of his windmills. They were probably dry by now as the big wells sucked the water out from under them and sent it through the sprinklers and on to the plants to feed their unquenchable thirst. He counted the sprinklers as he drove and, when he passed the sixth one, he turned south as Emmett had instructed. Another mile and he was on the edge of the thickets that had been deemed too rough to be turned into crop land.

He stepped out of his truck taking his flashlight just in case the clouds that were floating around obliterated the bright moon. Unbeknownst to him he was not the only one driving in the sandhills that night. Pete had stopped, looked at the shattered lock, turned his lights off, and started down the same route.

Stoney began picking his way through the salt cedars, cottonwoods, and dead locust trees, softly whistling and calling Pecos's name. An hour later he was about to give up and started for his truck. Rounding the corner of one the old barns, with it's roof caved in and only two walls still standing, he stopped short. In front of him was Pete, holding his Sako rifle.

"You lookin' for something cowboy," he said in a quiet voice.

"My dog…, ass hole," Stoney responded.

"I imagine the coyotes are makin' a good feast of him right now. You know, as soon as I saw that lock shot off I figured it might be you. And I figured that damn Emmett been talking to you. I'll take care of him later."

"Maybe so and maybe not. Now if you'll pardon me, I have enjoyed this little conversation all I want to, and I'll be on my way."

Pete bolted a .243 into the chamber. "Not so fast little man. You're trespassing on Taylor lands and I got ever right to blow your head off. Now get down on your knees," Pete raised the rifle to his shoulder and took aim. Just as he was squeezing the trigger something fierce and heavy hit him from the side and a set of large canine teeth sunk into his flesh so deep they scraped his ribs. He screamed in pain and rage as he slung the rifle away from him. Reaching around, he grabbed Pecos by the throat and began choking him. Stoney, his adrenalin surging, had not even felt the bullet grazing his head. Picking up the rifle and grabbing it by the muzzle and with all the strength he could muster and with three years of frustration, bitterness, and vengeance behind it, he swung it against Pete's leg, shattering his left knee and breaking off the stock of his rifle. Pete, screaming in pain, heaved Pecos away and fell to the ground holding his knee.

They were not the only ones that had been out hunting on that beautiful moonlit night. This one, whose species had been inhabiting these sandhills for thousands of years, had also been after it's quarry, and was hunting for mice or rats in his favorite hunting ground among the crumbling buildings. The three and a half foot prairie rattler, large for his sub-species, had been interrupted from his hunt by all the commotion. When the large, strange, screaming body had fallen almost on top of him the rattlesnake struck blindly, striking the body in the neck, and injecting him with all the venom he had been storing up since his last meal a week before. He then slithered off into the darkness, irritated that he had to waste his venom on something too big to swallow.

Stoney had seen something darting out of the shadows, and heard the short warning rattle just before the snake had struck. He knew what had happened. Pete too had heard it and also knew what had happened... and was going to happen.

"Stone, you got to help me, get me to a doctor, I'm gonna die, please, please," Pete was crying and holding his throat. He tried to stand but couldn't control his broken knee and fell back to the ground.

Stoney put his hand to his head and felt blood and a stinging sensation; only then did he realize how close he had been to losing his life.

Stoney looked down at Pete. "I am sorry Pete, you're too fat to carry, besides where that snake struck I don't think it'll do you any good."

Pecos came wagging his tail to him and Stoney fell to his knees hugging his dog around the neck, the dog, licking and whining, was returning the loving. A small figure came out of the shadows and joined them. Stoney picked him up and recognized him as a coydog.

"Pecos, you rascal, this is yours isn't it?" he stood up carrying the pup. Pete was crying and curled up in a fetal position.

Stoney walked over to him and shook his head, "Pete, don't you think it's kind of ironic that as many

Ten years later Stoney returns to the windmill in his west pasture…It's water gone and never to return.

of these snakes as you have killed, one of 'em finally got revenge. That's probably his uncle that's holding up your pants…I'll see you down the road."

Stoney turned, picked up his hat, now with a bullet hole in the brim, and carrying the pup started walking to his pickup, "Pecos if you got any relatives around here you better gather them up cause we are saying goodbye to these sandhills."

The moon had almost disappeared by the time they reached the pickup. Stoney let the tailgate down. Pecos jumped in and Stoney knew that there were no more. He placed the pup in the cab beside him, turned on the lights, and headed to town.. On reaching Clovis he stopped at a pay phone and called the sheriff's office. He reported an accident with injuries and gave the dispatcher the location of Pete as best he could, telling them they needed to get out there as soon as possible. When the dispatcher began to question him on what happened, and who he was, he hung up the phone and drove to Mickie's.

He woke Mickie and Scotty and they helped bathe Pecos and his pup. They found dry blood on Pecos's chest where Pete's bullet had cut through the fleshy part but not doing any permanent damage. They also doctored Stoney's wound remarking how lucky they both where. After much urging Stoney told them what had happened. After Mickie had fed her three guests she and her husband ushered them to the spare bedroom where they fell into a deep sleep.

Mid-morning and Stoney was awakened by Pecos putting one paw up on the bed. Stoney arose and let the dogs out in the front yard, knowing they would not venture far.

He was finishing the late breakfast that Mickie had made him when the doorbell rang.

Mickie answered it and after a hug invited Randy in for coffee. She took Bobbi off of Stoney's knee, interrupting the story she was telling her grandfather, and left the sheriff and her dad in private.

"I see you found your dog."

"Yeah I did… and dang if doesn't have a pup," Stoney replied.

"I saw that, looks as ugly as Pecos."

"Thanks, I'll tell Pecos your compliment. You look like you had a hard night Randy. Something bothering you."

"Yeah…something is bothering me and I thought maybe you could help. And right, I have been up all night."

"I'll help you if I can," replied Stoney.

"Well…I got a real strange case. You know a big fella that worked for that Taylor outfit named Pete Benson?"

"I've heard of him; he still works for them doesn't he?"

"Not any more. He's dead."

Stoney felt the blood drain from his face. "Really, I guess I am sorry to hear that. What happened?"

"Snake bite. Don't know for sure till' we get the toxicology report back from Albuquerque, but I've seen enough of them to think that's what it was. There were two little fang marks on his throat."

Stoney, not knowing what to say, just shook his head.

"But what we can't figure out," the sheriff continued "His knee looks like it was broken…really bad. Not only that we found his rifle and the stock was broken off of it. But it had been fired once…Real recently."

"No shit," Stoney replied.

Randy looked at the side of Stoney's head. "That's a pretty nasty lookin' cut on the side of your head. How did you did that?"

"Oh that, I was climbing through a barb-wire fence looking at some of Travis's horse's yesterday and cut it on barb."

"There was a set of boot tracks around there. Justin's soles. But they don't tells us nothing. Half the cowboys in the county got a set of Justins."

"Yeah, your right on that," Stoney said taking a sip of his coffee. Even though it had grown cold by then.

"And some dog tracks too. A set of big ones and a set of what looked like a pup's.

"That is strange Randy. I wish I could help you out, but that buffaloes me."

"Okay." Randy rose from the chair and put his hat on. He thanked Mickie on the way out and Stoney walked him to his car.

On the way Randy stopped and looked at the dogs that were following Stoney.

"Yes sir, those dog tracks were about the size these two dogs would make."

He turned and looked at the hat Stoney had put on. "You're damn sure hard on hats Stoney. That almost looks like a bullet hole in the brim." He put both hands on Stoney's shoulders. "Look old friend. I know the son-of-a-bitch deserved to be killed. That lady out at the City Limits, your old friend, wasn't the only lady he did that to; she's just the only one that had guts enough to turn him in. But..., that Taylor outfit thinks you had something to do with it and they got the bank behind them, and with the District Attorney in their pocket. He's really burning my ass to make an arrest. I want you out of this town... now. Not next week, not tomorrow.. today. And don't come back for a long, long time. It's an outa sight, outa mind sort of thing. You know what I mean."

"I do Randy, and the sun won't set on me in Clovis tonight. I guarantee it."

The sheriff got into his unit and rolled down the window, "You know, I used to know a fella' that engraved every tool and piece of equipment he had with his brand. Well...I happened to pick this up where Pete had his little confrontation with the snake," he reached under his seat and pulled out a flashlight handing it to Stoney.

"It kinda looks like your brand on it. Hard to tell, you could of lost it a long time ago."

"Yeah," Stoney replied. "Yeah...a long time ago. Thanks Randy."

"See you down the road partner," Randy said, driving off and giving his siren a couple of tweets.

Stoney could hardly bear to leave Bobbi and Mickie, knowing it would be a long time, if ever, that he would see them again. Late that afternoon he loaded up Pecos and the pup and headed west. Just outside of Portales he glanced at the rear-view mirror and saw a white Cadillac coming up fast behind him. It was Betsy, she pulled beside him and motioned him to pull over. He came to a stop alongside the highway and she parked behind him. She walked up to his window.

Stoney didn't say anything as he lowered the window.

She reached through the window and past Stoney to pet Pecos, who was standing in the seat wagging his tail.

"Hi Pecos, I missed you. What's that funny little guy you have with you," she said looking at the little pup trying to escape Pecos's large wagging tail.

She paused and, looking at Stoney said, "I am so glad you found him Stoney. I know how important he was to you, believe me. Mickie told me everything. I wanted to see you, I just had to see you before you left." A tear rolled down her cheek.

"I love you and always will, but I know it could never be the same. We are too far apart now."

Stoney reached out, pulled her to him and kissed her on the forehead, "I know you're right, and I am sorry for all the heartaches I caused you. I just keep thinking of all the fun we had and wished like everything it would have worked out."

She pulled her head back and wiped her tears away, "What are you going to do now. Forty thousand isn't going to last you a lifetime."

Stoney looked at her, "My forty thousand?"

"I told you that Mickie told me everything. Stoney I am sorry you did that to Bud, he really isn't a bad kid. Just a little mixed up."

Stoney started to defend himself then decided this was not the time to start an argument. He ignored the remark.

"Tell me... Where are you going and what are you going to do," she continued.

"I don't know Betsy. I just want to get away, maybe for a year. Maybe longer. Just someplace where nobody knows me and I don't know them. Maybe get a job tending bar someplace."

"Well you have had plenty of experience at that," she bit her tongue wishing she hadn't said that.

Stoney looked at her, shook his head, then pulled her close to him and kissed her again on the forehead.

"Goodbye Betsy, I love you."

"Goodbye Stoney, I love you too."

Stoney pulled back on the highway and drove off.

Betsy stood there watching his taillights fade away, then walked slowly and tearfully back to her car.

As he drove down the highway Pecos laid down in the seat and put his head on Stoney's lap, the pup curled up beside him. Pecos had his eyes fastened on his master, they slowly closed and he fell asleep. Stoney reached over and turned the radio on and a Bob Dylan song came across.

Oh I have stayed around and played around this old town too long
Summer almost gone, winters coming on
*And I gotta' be moving on.**

"BUENO"

*Lyrics from 'Gotta Travel On' by Billy Grammer.+

*Stoney's ranch today. No water – a wasteland.
For man is like grass. For the wind passes over
it, and it is gone. And its place knows it no more.
Psalms 103; 15-18*

EPILOGUE

TEN YEARS LATER

Bud Thurman was convicted of embezzlement for the ninety thousand dollar he illegally borrowed from the bank. He had to sell all his assets to make restitution and pay his attorneys. Served five years of a ten year sentence. Present whereabouts unknown.

Merchants and Ranchers Bank was found guilty by the FDIC of gross mismanagement and ordered to cease and desist business. They were taken over and became a branch of a large bank in Albuquerque. All top executives and owners were fired and left the area. Present whereabouts unknown.

Milnor married the rich widow in Santa Fe and is enjoying life. It is said he quit the flimflam business but, *quien sabe?*

Reno and Penny thoroughly enjoyed their Corvette for a year or two and then traded it in for a large party houseboat on Ute Lake. They are still enjoying life..

Jim Bob took his money, went to Las Vegas, Nevada and parlayed it into enough to buy his own little ranch in the Sangre de Cristo mountains. He owns and operates a super successful outfitting company.

Betsy married a retiring base commander from the Air Force Base in Clovis and moved to Florida where they bought a charter fishing boat. She is also very successful in real estate in that state, and is very happy and very rich. She and Stoney exchange Christmas and birthday cards every year. Other than that they never communicate.

Stoney worked on dude ranches on the Mogollon Rim in Arizona and New Mexico for a couple of years. Then Billy Kiehne sold his ranch to some Georgia bankers who are using it strictly for a hunting ranch. They put it into a conservation easement, a government program that allows the owner of the land to retain ownership but the land will forever remain in its natural state, they then hired Stoney as caretaker and manager. They built a large hunting lodge and let Stoney move into Billy's house. They kept all of Billy's horses including Kenneth and Leo, who were glad to be under the care again of their old friend. Bobbi spends every summer with her grandfather and is turning into as good a horsewoman as her mother.

Pecos spends most of his time just hanging out on the front deck of Stoney's house, watching over his territory, horses, Stoney and his pup, who is fully grown and taking his dad's place riding in back of Stoney's pickup.

Stoney is happy. The entire forty thousand is in a bank drawing interest. A bank that Stoney trusts.

The Coven Five has a reunion every Fourth of July on the Bonomo's party boat on Ute Lake. They have a good time.

Made in the USA
Charleston, SC
09 October 2013